BY THE AUTHOR

STARK SECURITY
shattered with you
shadows of you-short story
broken with you
ruined with you

THE STARK SAGA
novels
release me
claim me
complete me
anchor me
lost with me

novellas
take me
have me

play my game

seduce me

unwrap me

deepest kiss

entice me

hold me

please me

indulge me

Praise for J. Kenner's Novels

"*Shattered With You* is a sultry little page turner that comes brimming with scorching passion, edge of your seat action, and heart-wrenching emotion." *Reds Romance Reviews*

"J. Kenner is an exceptional storyteller. The drama, tension, and heat were perfect." *About That Story*

"PERFECT for fans of *Fifty Shades of Grey* and *Bared to You. Release Me* is a powerful and erotic romance novel." *Reading, Eating & Dreaming Blog*

"I will admit, I am in the 'I loved *Fifty Shades*' camp, but after reading *Release Me*, Mr. Grey only scratches the surface compared to Damien Stark." *Cocktails and Books Blog*

"It is not often when a book is so amazingly well-written that I find it hard to even begin to accurately describe it . . . " *Romancebookworm's Reviews*

"With her sophisticated prose, Kenner created a love story that had the perfect blend of lust, passion, sexual tension, raw emotions and love." - Michelle, Four Chicks Flipping Pages

BROKEN
WITH YOU
J. KENNER

M&O

Broken With You Copyright © 2019 by Julie Kenner

Excerpt from *Tame Me* © Copyright 2014 by Julie Kenner (used with permission from Evil Eye Concepts, Inc.)

Cover design by Michele Catalano, Catalano Creative

Cover image by Annie Ray/Passion Pages

ISBN: 978-1-940673-90-5

Published by Martini & Olive Books

v. 2019-6-9P

M&O

A NOTE FROM J. KENNER

Dear Reader,

Denny first appeared in *Shadows of You*, a short story that became a prologue to *Broken With You*.

While you don't have to read *Shadows* in order to enjoy *Broken*, I've included it at the end of this print edition as a bonus for you.

You can find it after the epilogue. Enjoy!

XXOO
JK

Faith is a tricky thing. Faith in people. In the universe.

Faith that at the end of the day, the power of good will overcome the power of evil.

I've managed to keep that faith through my entire life, even when the world was battering me like a raft on a stormy sea. Loss, pain, heartache—through it all, I somehow managed to hold tight to my unflappable optimism.

But that was before.

Now ... well, now is harder.

Now, I stare down loss and loneliness on a daily basis. Now, I look back over the last two years and wonder how I've managed to survive without him.

Now, I fear that he's never coming home. The man I love. The husband I need.

I know I must stay positive. I understand that I should keep hoping.

"Have faith," they all say, and I try. I really do.

But the truth is that my faith in the universe disappeared along with my husband.

And I'm terrified that I've lost both forever.

1

———

DARKNESS.

For an eternity, that's all there was. Just darkness. A void. An empty hole where nothing existed. Not even him, whoever the hell he was.

There was comfort in the dark. As if he was wrapped in a womb. Safe now. Not like before.

Before?

Strands of emotion, the precursors of thought, twisted inside him. There'd been pain in the before time. So much pain. Like fire in his gut. Like glass in his eyes.

How long had he suffered, his mind screaming, his body so exhausted that death would have been a welcome relief?

He didn't know. For that matter, maybe death *had* come to release him. Or maybe none of it had happened yet, and his pain wasn't a memory but a forewarning.

He didn't know. He was simply *there*—no longer attached to time, to space, to anything. He was free. Not hot or cold. Neither happy nor sad. He was secure in the comfort of simply being, and it seemed as though he could stay that way, safe and warm and content—for all eternity.

Except...

Except there was something hidden beneath the calm acceptance of this new reality.

Something important. Something urgent.

A secret? A task?

It was right there, at the edge of his memory, but every time he grasped for it, it slipped away. He shouldn't—couldn't—let it go. But how could he follow? How could he leave this safe, warm place?

He longed to stay forever. Secure and comfortable and free.

And yet at the same time he didn't. He wanted more. He wanted...

He didn't know what.

He just knew that something was nagging at him. Something he missed. Something he craved.

Her.

A shock of awareness cut through him, along with a jolt of something he recognized as fear. And loss. And regret.

Mischievous green eyes flashed in his mind's

eye. Warm laughter teased him even as soft strands of golden-blond hair brushed against his skin.

She was his—and he yearned for her with a longing so intense it bordered on pain. Urgency roiled within him. Danger. Terror. Those dark secrets that he needed to—

No!

Oh God oh God oh God, please no.

His body—his *being*—lurched, trying to reach her. Trying to battle back the horror that was looming, coming faster and faster. But he couldn't see it. He couldn't fight it. All he could do was sink into the whirlpool of disconnected, incomprehensible voices and images that were suddenly swirling around him, thick and fast and hot.

Where is it?

You might as well tell us?

Nothing to go home to. Nothing at all.

But there was. *She* was there. His life. His woman.

He had to get back to her.

Back? There's nothing for you back there. She's dead. I fucked her, then I killed her.

His body burst apart from the force of his scream, but the relentless, horrible words wouldn't stop.

Do you know why she's dead? Because you went to her. You told some useless cunt our secrets.

Beep-beep!

We had to punish you. Had to show you that we can always get to you.

His mind was spinning, trying to remember. To see her. To feel her.

To save her.

Remember, dammit. Remember the roadrunner. They can't kill the roadrunner.

But he couldn't move. Couldn't think. Couldn't do anything but exist in this cold, dark limbo as more voices assaulted him.

It's all your fault.

Your friend? I was never your friend.

It's not a tunnel. Just a black hole painted on rock.

32355 5-null 717

That won't help you anymore. Not anymore, you wily sonofabitch.

You think he's the only one? Damn naive considering your reputation.

Guess you're not made of brick or stone after all, are you fucker?

Beep-beep.

Wily? Maybe once, but you're not wily anymore.

Again and again, the flat, emotionless voices pounded against him as he struggled to find himself. To understand. But there was nothing. Only the words and the nonsensical images of numbers floating against a black background as a variety of tones beeped in his head.

32355 5-null 717

Beep-beep!

Most of all, there was fear. A cold, harsh terror that ran through him like ice, freezing his blood, making his skin prickle.

His blood? His skin?

Slowly, realization came. He was returning. Heading back from wherever he'd gone. Going back to the pain. The hell.

Mostly, though, he was going back to her...

———

The first thing he noticed when he woke was the cold. An icy blast from a wall mounted air-conditioner. An ancient unit with white plastic strings streaming from it, flapping in the frigid air.

He sat up, realized he was naked, and pulled the dingy, gray sheet up to his hips. There was no blanket, and the thin sheet did little to relieve the chill. His palms stung as he clutched the sheet, and when he looked down at them, he saw that the heels of both hands were abraded, as if he'd fallen onto something rough, like asphalt or gravel.

Maybe he'd been in an accident? Thrown from a car? A motorcycle?

He didn't know.

Squinting against a violent headache, he let his gaze sweep over the rest of the room, looking for —what?

Something, anything, that would tell him where he was and what had happened to him.

And, most of all, who in God's name *he* was.

Because right then, he didn't have a clue.

A cold shaft of panic impaled him, and he fought against it, determined not to lose his shit. Not when control, reason, and observation were all he had going for him.

Observation first.

He cast his gaze around the room. A pair of threadbare jeans hung over the back of a straight-back desk chair. He stood, planning to walk toward them, but was forced to clutch the bedside table as his head dipped and swam.

What the hell was wrong with him? Had he gone on a bender? Been involved in a drunk driving incident?

He didn't remember, but he didn't think so. He didn't think he was a man who'd drink to excess.

Was he?

Christ, what the hell was going on?

He drew in a breath and ordered himself to be calm, not actually believing he'd get anywhere with such nonsense. But to his surprise, it worked. As if something in him was programmed to focus. As if this was just one more problem he could tackle.

Hell, yeah, he could.

He took another step, relieved when the room seemed to spin a bit less this time. He hadn't passed out drunk—he was certain of it. Considering his vertigo and queasiness, that would actually be a reasonable guess, but the evidence suggested otherwise. There was no smell to his breath. No fuzzy sensation on his tongue. He hadn't vomited that he could tell, and he didn't need to. He didn't need to piss, either.

Without any evidence that he was lost in the mother of all hangovers, he moved methodically on to the next option. But after running his fingers through his short hair and over his scalp, he found no bumps or abrasions.

So not a head injury. *Strike two.*

He thought of his red, raw hands. Something more sinister, then?

He shivered a bit, certain he was right. He didn't know why he was so sure, but at the moment he didn't know much of anything. If intuition was knocking, then he'd damn well open the door.

He continued to the chair, but didn't stop. He just ran the tips of his fingers over the filthy denim. He glanced at the dust that attached to his fingertips, but since he had no explanation, he pushed the questions away. His head was clearing, and he needed to focus on what he did know. Solid facts based on his surroundings, not to mention any memories those facts might provoke.

He'd start with himself.

The bathroom door was ajar and he stepped over the threshold into a small but surprisingly clean bathroom with a porcelain basin on four thin chrome legs, a fiberglass bathtub with a clear plastic shower curtain, and a toilet with a dingy brown mineral stain at the waterline.

The only mirror hung above the sink. A fogged-up piece of shit glass with a long crack marking off one corner. But it was large and mounted in a way that tilted down, so that he could see his head and his hips at the same time. And if he backed up, he could see even more.

He looked, his dark brown eyes taking in the image reflected back at him. His left brow was broken by a scar—probably a knife wound—but a quick check confirmed that his vision was fine in both eyes. The question of why someone had come at his face with a knife was one that would have to wait.

He focused next on his body as a whole. His chest and abs were rock hard, but laced with scars, most white, but some still slightly pink. None tender, though, and he assumed that even the newest was several months old.

The same couldn't be said of his neck, where five fresh, circular scars rose from his skin in a

jagged line down from under his jaw to his collar-
bone. Cigar burns, maybe?

He filed the possibility away to contemplate
later. This was a time for inspection, not for
opining about why someone would hold a lit cigar
against his flesh.

Still, he had to acknowledge that the wounds
didn't hurt, despite two of them clearly bordering
on infection. Which meant that he was in shock or
someone had drugged him and the effects still
lingered.

He didn't know, but he assumed the latter.
Especially considering the odd, frenetic quality of
those dreams he couldn't quite recapture.

Once again, he mentally filed the question and
returned to his assessment.

He guessed himself to be about thirty-seven
years old, and since he had the kind of body a man
only got by working out regularly, that gave him a
solid bit of information about himself. From his
position facing the mirror, he could see that he had
a tribal band tattooed on his left arm and something
else inked on his right, though he was at the wrong
angle to make out the design. He didn't bother
turning for a better view. All in good time, and right
then he needed to be as methodical as possible.
Anything detail could be a clue to his identity. Any
wound or bruise might bring back a flood of
memories.

His dark hair was short, but still long enough to be sleep-tousled. An ungroomed beard suggested he hadn't picked up a razor in ages, and that lined up with his sense that he'd been passed out for days.

He turned his attention to his hands. Notwithstanding the scrapes, they were strong, and his fingers were calloused. He wore no wedding ring and had no tan line suggesting that a ring had once been there. That thought made him pause, as a glint of green eyes and golden hair flashed in his mind. *His dream.*

Was she real? A girlfriend? Sister?

Was she in danger?

In the dream, someone had been speaking to him, saying vile things about a woman. But who?

Try as he might, he couldn't recall the dream. Damn frustrating, but it would come back eventually. And he had more than enough to worry about at the moment.

Drawing in a breath, he continued his self-inventory. His teeth were white and mostly even, so he'd probably had money for braces as a kid. But his nose was crooked, and he guessed it had been broken more than once. Possibly sports, possibly fights.

Considering the scars that decorated his chest, abs, and eyebrow, his money was on fights.

He turned sideways, and once the tattoo came

into view, the crisscross of scars over his body made more sense. It was a skull wearing a green beret on what looked like a coat of arms. The words *de oppresso liber* filled the space at the bottom. He recognized it, though he didn't remember the circumstances around him getting it.

The Special Forces motto.

So he was a soldier. Or he had been. And though he didn't remember one minute of combat, knowing that he was part of that brotherhood gave him some comfort. And it proved what he already felt in his gut—that he could take care of himself, no matter what the world threw at him next.

Based on the man he saw in the mirror, it seemed that the world abused him regularly.

Christ. What had he been into? And who the fuck was he?

A wave of panic crested over him and for a moment he let it sweep him away. He let himself wallow in fear and self-pity, losing himself in the black hole of his mind.

And then he turned that shit off. He had more pressing things to do than wallow. He didn't have a memory? Fine. That was his starting point.

So, first question: what did his lack of memory tell him?

That something had happened to him.

Okay, but what?

Best guess—trauma. Either physical or emotional.

As for which, he didn't care. For the moment, the question was academic. Either way, he was dealing with the same blank slate.

The situation stank, but God knew it could be a hell of a lot worse. He'd once watched a movie about a guy with no short term memory at all. He'd had to tattoo himself to hold on to facts. Great flick —*Memento*, it was called.

And goddamned if he didn't remember *that*. He had some memories, at least. He remembered the names of the planets and the months of the year. He knew how to read. And he remembered that Luke Skywalker was Darth Vader's son.

He didn't have a fucking clue what the names of the elements on the Periodic Table were, but at least he remembered there *was* a Periodic Table. And he had a feeling he'd never known the elements, anyway.

So his mind worked. To a point.

His name, his age, his background? As for *those* facts, he was completely at a loss. But he'd get it back, damn right he would.

And if he didn't ... well, he'd coped with shit situations before. Not that he could remember any of them, but there was a certainty in his gut and the evidence was on his body. He might not know who he was, but he damn well knew *what* he was. And he wasn't the kind of man who curled up into a fucking ball and whimpered.

A sharp rap sounded on the door, and he spun around, his right hand crossing over to his left side as he reached for a holstered weapon.

For a moment, he froze in that position. Then he slowly pulled his hand back and repeated the motion, a smile breaking across his face.

Muscle memory. Three cheers for muscle memory.

A key rattled in the lock, and he sprinted across the room and practically threw himself against the door before whoever was rattling that key could enter.

"Who is it?" His voice came out raspy, as if he hadn't spoken in months. He coughed, then tried again. "Who's there?"

"Housekeeping. I clean room, yes?"

He shifted, then peered through the peephole at the wisp of a woman standing next to a rolling cart. Behind her, a battered Toyota was parked in front of the door. His?

He didn't know.

All he knew was that she wasn't coming in. "It's fine," he said. "I've got everything I need."

Not the truth, but not exactly a lie, either. He had air in his lungs and a beating heart, didn't he?

"Okey-dokey, mister," she said, then pushed on toward the next room. He stayed at the peephole, his attention now on the Toyota's plates. California.

Frowning, he returned to the desk, then grabbed the jeans and shook them, sending dust flurries into the air and a pair of navy blue boxer briefs tumbling to the floor. He scooped them up, sniffed them, then shrugged and put them on, following the underwear with the jeans.

In addition to being filthy, the jeans were a mess. Ripped at the knees and not in a way that was fashionable. More like he'd taken a nasty fall.

He looked at his palms, looked at his knees, and as he did, he remembered. Not everything. Not his life. Not even his name.

But it was something.

Darkness. And motion.

He was blindfolded in some sort of moving vehicle, probably a cargo truck, his ankles tied together and his hands tight behind his back. He was listening, trying to gather as much information as possible, but there was nothing. Just heat and motion. And that was all he knew. Literally, all. It was as if he had been born into that moment, fully adult, and into that truck. There were things he remembered, yes. But not him. Whoever he was, he'd just popped into existence. A blank slate. An empty jar.

But he was aware now...

The truck bumped and rattled—and then it screeched to a stop.

A door rumbled up, and light seeped in around the edges of his blindfold. Strong hands grabbed him, pulling him to his feet and making him stumble forward. He was standing—he must have been right about it being a cargo truck—and then he heard the sound of a blade slicing through cord. His ankles were freed first, then his wrists. And before he could react, the truck started to move.

At the same time, someone shoved him from behind, and he fell onto the rough, hot asphalt, his hands thrust out to break his fall.

He turned, yanking off the blindfold and squinting into the sun, as someone in a black T-shirt and jeans rolled the truck door down from the inside as the vehicle peeled away, careening down the deserted highway toward the horizon.

In the motel room, his memories flooded back. Nothing before the truck, but now he recalled the feel of the road beneath his hands, the sun beating down on him as he walked for miles, the relief of finally coming across this shitty little godsend of a motel.

He'd stumbled into the office, found a hundred and fifty dollars in his pocket, and bought six bottles of water, five cans of mixed nuts, and three Hershey's bars. Then he'd booked a room for two nights.

That left him with just over thirty dollars, which he remembered shoving back into his jeans.

He'd had no identification, but the woman behind the counter hadn't seemed to care. He'd registered as Jack Sawyer. He couldn't remember his name—or anything about his own life from before the ride in the truck—but he did remember the television show, *Lost*, and he'd claimed those two characters' names for his own.

Now here he was, Jack Sawyer, in a shitty motel with no memory at all. His whole goddamn world was this tiny room and these filthy clothes. And wasn't that a happy notion?

He shook his head, tamping down on the fear and frustration that was returning. Yes, it sucked, but at least he was alive. And he was going to stay that way.

Resolved, he tugged on the T-shirt. Originally white, the shirt was now a dingy gray with sweat stains under the arms and at the back of the collar.

A pair of dark brown loafers peeked out from under the desk, and he shoved his feet into them, unable to find any socks. At the same time, he patted himself down, his hands searching the pockets of the jeans and the seams, just in case there was something sewn in. But he found nothing except the thirty-three dollars he'd received in change and a room key with 107 etched on it.

Finding no help on his own person, he searched the desk and bureau drawers, but the drawers were empty except for a Bible, a Book of Mormon, a black pen, and a takeout menu for a pizza place in Victorville, California.

His stomach growled, and he started to reach for the phone to order something, then decided against it. Thirty dollars wouldn't last long. Better to stick with what was in the room.

He popped nuts as he paced, analyzing his next steps. His fevered dreams still lingered, but the words had no more clarity than they'd had while he was sleeping. Less, even. In his dreams, he'd felt trapped, but not confused. Now, the strange words and threats and cartoon references were just nonsense, the numbers even more so.

Without anything else to write on, he pulled out the menu, then scribbled what he remembered: 32355 5-*null* 717

Presumably, the word "null" meant zero, so he crossed out what he wrote and started over: 32355 50 717

Still nonsense, and he scowled at the numbers and their refusal to provide him any information whatsoever.

But, fine. The numbers meant nothing to him? Then he'd start somewhere else. He knew that something had happened to him, and after that mysterious interlude, he'd been blindfolded and bound, pushed from a truck in the desert heat, and abandoned.

Not a scenario he wished to repeat, and since

he had no idea whether his captors had truly abandoned him, he intended to be ready if they returned.

In other words, he needed a weapon.

He could splinter a drawer and use a length of wood, but he had a feeling the nice lady in the office would frown on that. Instead, he returned to the bathroom, then tugged the key out of his pocket. He shoved the end between the mirror's frame and the glass in the lower right corner, then gently pried. As he'd hoped, the crack was both long and deep, and as he increased the gap between the frame and the mirror, he was able to pop it out, an icicle-shaped piece of the mirror, about five inches long.

Just what he needed. Because he sure as hell didn't know what to expect when he walked out the door.

He wrapped one raw edge in toilet paper, forming a makeshift handle, then shoved the whole thing deep in the pocket of his jeans as he crossed to the door. He opened it slowly, then stepped hard into a wall of heat.

The sidewalk was clear on both sides, and only a few empty cars dotted the parking area as heat shimmers rose off the asphalt. The world was a fucking inferno, but all things considered, that seemed apropos. Hadn't he been tossed right out of the frying pan and into the fire?

A sign that looked like it hadn't been updated since the fifties sat perched atop vertical steel poles and identified the rundown little motel as the Stay-A-While Motor Inn. Hopefully that was only a suggestion, because he wanted to get out of there sooner rather than later.

He walked down the sidewalk toward the sign, passing the pastel colored doors along the way. Green, room 106. Blue, room 105. Yellow, room 104.

This path was familiar, and there was some comfort in that.

At the same time, having the full extent of his remembered life marked by the Easter egg colors of a half dozen doors wasn't exactly enough to have him jumping for joy.

The same woman was in the office. About sixty with Lucille Ball hair—he remembered *I Love Lucy!*

She smiled at him from behind a counter. "Well, you're looking much better today. Got yourself some sleep, I guess?"

"I did," he said, then cleared his throat as he glanced around the room. "You got a bus schedule?"

She shook her head. "Sorry, no. Where you heading?"

"Just meandering," he said, as if he was Jack

Reacher, and it was perfectly normal to wander aimlessly around the country.

"Well, let me see if I can find a schedule online for you." She inched toward a computer that looked to be older than he was, but stopped midway down the counter to answer the phone as she rummaged through a drawer.

He cocked his head, his hand sliding into his pocket as his senses went on high alert.

The phone.

He relaxed.

Of course. He should have realized immediately. The numbers. They were a phone number. 323-555-0717.

"Oh, good, I found it," she said after ending the call. She pulled a crumpled brochure from a drawer. "So the Greyhound station's not too far away. That what you're looking for? Or did you want local routes?"

"Greyhound," he said, thinking of the 323 area code. "I need to make a phone call. And then I think I'll head to Los Angeles."

"Friends there?"

"I guess I'll find out."

2

BACK IN HIS ROOM, Jack sat at the edge of the bed, the old-fashioned keypad phone in his lap as he held onto the handset, which was tethered to the base by the curlicue cord.

He didn't know who, if anyone, would be at the other end of that number. The only thing he knew for certain was that he knew nothing else. He was a blank slate with this one, scribbled note on it.

So dial the fucking phone, Jack.

He lifted his hand, then hesitated. What if it was a trap? A memory deliberately put into his mind.

But to what end?

Refuse to call, and he denied them the satisfaction of seeing their plan succeed.

But what if there was no plan? What if they were done with him, and they'd tossed him out onto the highway with no memories and no resources, fully expecting that was the last they'd see of Jack Sawyer, or of the man who'd come before?

Then again, if they'd wanted him dead, why not just kill him? Why stuff cash in his pocket and leave him alive?

If he refused to dial, he might be screwing them, but he'd definitely be screwing himself.

And, goddammit, right then the possibility of finding even the smallest clue about the man he was before outweighed every other consideration. A trap? Maybe. But he'd survived worse. Or, at least, he'd probably survived worse. He was a scarred-up, badass member of the Special Forces. Or so he assumed. At a minimum, he should be able to make a phone call without triggering Armageddon.

In his hand, the dial tone changed to a squawking wail. He tapped the switch hook, tucked the handset between his ear and his shoulder, and dialed the number that had been running through his head.

On the other end, the phone rang twice before an efficient male voice came on the line. "Monrovia Travel Adventures. Are you a client?"

"Ah, yeah."

"Your user name, please."

He hung up. Wrong fucking number. Either that or he'd misremembered the number.

Frustrated, he stood and paced and re-ran the nonsensical dream through his mind again. Nonsensical being the operative word. Cartoons and disembodied voices and random phrases and numbers that wouldn't make sense to anyone.

Except...

With a frown, he turned and looked at the phone. Maybe they did make sense. In the world of Ethan Hunt and Jason Bourne, those nonsense phrases might make a lot of sense.

Not that he was Bourne, but maybe ... just maybe...

He dialed again, and this time the call was answered by a woman. When she asked for his username, he took a shot in the dark, having parsed through all the nonsense in his head to find the most likely handle.

"Road Runner," he said, hoping to hell he was right.

For a moment, there was only silence. Then her voice returned, curt and crisp. "Hold, please."

He held, his gut churning. He wasn't sure what he'd just done, but he was certain that he'd set wheels in motion. But whether that was a good thing or a bad thing, he really didn't know.

The line clicked, and this time the speaker was male. "Pass phrase?"

He started to speak, his posture straightening as if he was reporting for duty. As if this was a familiar routine. At one time, he assumed, it had been.

Today, he didn't have a clue.

"Pass phrase?"

"I'm sorry, I—"

"Please state your name, your location."

"Victorville," he said. "I need to speak to someone in charge. It's urgent."

For a moment, there was silence. "This office utilizes certain protocols. This call will be terminated in five, four—"

"*Wait.* Something's happened. I can't tell you the pass phrase because I can't remember it. I've been drugged or brainwashed, or I don't know. Just let me speak to your superior."

Silence.

Mountains and mountains of silence.

Then, "I'm sorry, sir. Protocol requires that—"

"Wile E. Coyote! Looney Tunes! Beep-beep!" He sounded like an idiot. "Shit, I don't know. Who is this? Who am I calling?"

"Hold, please."

The dispassionate voice disappeared, replaced by a rhythmic ticking in lieu of hold music. For what felt like an eternity, he simply held the line.

He was about to give up and start the process all over again when he heard a series of clicks followed by a gravelly voice saying, "Good God,

Road Runner. Where are you? What's your status?"

He started to answer. He actually started to open his mouth and spill everything to the man with concern in his voice. Then rational thought returned, and he said, "Why don't we start with who you are."

Silence. Just long enough to be noticeable. He'd surprised the guy. Good. Jack was getting tired of being the only one behind the curve.

"I'm Colonel Anderson Seagrave. And right now, I'm the only one willing to trust you." The words were stern, but not hostile.

"Because I didn't know the pass phrase."

"Didn't you?"

Good point. He must have rattled off the correct one—or at least come close enough to pique this colonel's curiosity.

"No," he said, figuring it was better to be all in or all out. "I took an educated guess."

"I see." The voice had tightened, and when he spoke again, Jack heard a dangerous edge. "And how exactly did you manage to get so well-educated?"

"You mean did I beat the shit out of someone to learn the secret handshake?" He knew he was being ballsy, but this guy was a colonel. That meant military, the government, some sort of heavy shit. And no way was Jack strolling into that environment like some meek little lost puppy. He'd lost ninety-nine percent of himself; he was damn well going to cling to that final one percent like grim, fucking death.

"Something like that," Seagrave said. "So you tell me—are you the Road Runner? Or have you just poked around in his mind?"

Jack closed his eyes, then pinched the bridge of his nose between his thumb and forefinger. Moment of truth time. Hopefully, this wouldn't prove to be the biggest mistake of his life.

The good news, at least, was that he couldn't recall any bigger mistakes to compare it with.

"Truth?"

"In this business, that would be nice for a change."

"Fine, then maybe you can tell me who and what I am. Because I haven't got a goddamn clue."

He waited, anticipating an explosive response. A series of verbal slaps to put him in his place for playing such stupid games with someone who was obviously well positioned in the intelligence community. Jack may not know his pass phrase, but he knew the hallmarks of a covert intelligence operation that managed agents in the field.

Whether he was still a soldier or not, he was certain that he was some sort of intelligence officer. What he didn't know was if this guy was a friend or someone who'd screw him over six ways from Sunday.

"Can you?" he demanded, as the silence lingered—and this time he was certain it was a tactic. "Can you tell me who the hell I am?"

"I think so," Seagrave said. "I may even know what happened to you. Some of it, anyway."

"I'm all ears."

"Hmm. Have you been calling yourself something?"

"Not for long," he admitted. "As far as I can tell, my world began when I woke up a few hours ago. With a little bit of a prologue before that. The exciting kind with a mystery thrown in."

"A mystery?"

"I've been calling myself Jack," he said, ignoring Seagrave's unstated request for the details of Jack's ignominious dive from the back of the truck. "Jack Sawyer."

Seagrave burst out laughing, and the sound was so real—and so damn familiar—that Jack found himself chuckling, too.

"Why doesn't that surprise me?" Seagrave asked.

"Under the circumstances, I'm the wrong one to ask." He was getting pretty quick with amnesia-laced repartee.

"You were a huge fan of *Lost* back in the day. Used to watch it with—"

"With?"

"Me," Seagrave said, though Jack was certain he heard a lie in the man's voice. "We'd drink beer and watch the absurdity."

"So we were friends."

"I hope we still are."

"Then tell me who I am."

"I can't do that. Not right now."

Jack tensed. "Why not."

"Because you might not be my friend anymore. And if that's the case, I don't want to give you anything more to work with."

"Fuck." At some point he'd stood without realizing it and started pacing. Now, he sat. "We need to meet. Face to face. I need to see you to know if I trust you. And apparently you need the same thing."

"Where are you?"

"Doesn't matter. Just tell me where to go in LA and I'll meet you."

"Better if we extract you and bring you in."

"Not going to happen," Jack said.

"Why not?"

"Because right now, I'm a man with no friends. I don't know who I am or who did this to me. So you tell me straight—do you really think that I would trust you with my location?"

"I'm sorry, Jack. And you're right. I never thought you'd give me your address."

As Seagrave spoke, a steady *thump-thump* filled the air, and the cardboard walls of the tiny motel room started to shake.

"Christ," Jack whispered. "What have you done?"

"I swear no one will harm you. Just let them take you in."

He didn't bother answering. Just ended the call, his mind whirring. His hand went to the swathed end of the mirror shard, and he clutched it tight, ready to slice or stab.

But that was a pipe dream. He could already tell from the increasing volume that this wasn't one lone helicopter. These were military choppers, and his best guess was at least five of them. Probably two in the parking lot, one in the air, and two behind his room.

One bit of a broken mirror and his scathing wit were hardly going to hold them at bay. Which meant he had a choice. He could cower in the room and try to fight them off, or he could open the door, walk out onto the sidewalk, and accept the next step of what was turning into a most unusual adventure.

3

So HERE's the salient fact of the day: I, Denise
Ellen Marshall Walker, am a horrible person.

Or at least a very screwed up one.

I must be, right? Because here I am soaking up
the sunshine in one of the most posh backyards in
all of California, and instead of thinking, *wow,
lucky me to have such amazing friends and
colleagues,* I'm seething with envy.

Not about the house, although no one could
blame me for that. After all, this is Damien Stark's
Malibu property, and that man does nothing half-
assed. I can't prove it, but I'm ninety percent sure
he imported the sunshine along with the patio's
gorgeous Italian flagstones.

But no, it's not real estate that's turning me the
color of Elphaba. Instead, it's my partner, Quince,
and his girlfriend, Eliza, who are holding hands and

looking like they could eat each other up. And why not? They've finally gotten back together after an interlude long enough for dinosaurs to evolve all the way to extinction. But am I happy for them?

Oh, please. Of course, I am. I'm screwed up, but I'm not a bitch.

I *am* happy for them.

I'm also sick with jealousy, and hating myself because of it. But the simple truth is that I don't have the patience to wait for another era to pass. I want my husband back. I haven't seen Mason in over two years. Not since he left on a deep-cover assignment, and I miss him so much that sometimes I'm afraid I'm going to curl up and die just from the pain of my loneliness.

I'm pushing through, though. My friends help. My work helps. And my certainty that he's out there—that he still wants and misses me —helps, too.

But none of that helps enough to dull the knife-edge of jealousy when I witness a happy reunion.

And today, I'm pretty much drowning in a sea of happy.

If it were just Quince and Eliza, maybe I wouldn't be such a basket case. But the point of this day is to celebrate the successful wrap-up of a Stark Security case, along with the impending reunion of a European princess with her extremely relieved royal father.

The Stark Security Agency is a relatively new division of Stark International, a huge conglomerate owned by former tennis player turned entrepreneurial billionaire Damien Stark and operated by Ryan Hunter, who used to head up Stark International's corporate security.

Formed after Stark's youngest daughter was kidnapped, the SSA is staffed by some serious badasses, most of whom left other law enforcement or intelligence jobs because they believe in Stark's mandate of providing help where it's needed, no matter how big or small the job.

I'm one of those badasses now, having left my covert government job a while back. I'm not feeling particularly tough right now, though. Instead, I'm moody and lonely and jealous. Because everyone else is celebrating, and I just feel lost.

Really not one of my finer moments, and I force myself to look away in case either Eliza or Quince notices my melancholy expression and it puts a damper on their happiness.

Frankly, it's a good decision, because once I shift my attention to the pool, it becomes much harder to remain melancholy. Not when dark-haired little Lara Stark is splashing water on her giggling younger sister, all while the recently rescued princess tries half-heartedly to interest both Stark girls in the colorful pool noodles.

From the opposite side of the pool, Eliza's

sister, Emma, is watching the girls as well, a smile crinkling the corners of her eyes. She's in a tank top and shorts, her thigh tightly bandaged after yesterday's battle.

Only yesterday.

Honestly, it already seems so far away, and the despicable truth is that I want another case. And soon. Even though that means that there's someone in trouble. I want it, because without it, I don't know how I can keep my thoughts from wandering back to Mason, or my heart from breaking into pieces all over again.

Damn. I wipe my damp eyes and hope no one notices. I really should have worn my sunglasses...

The thought still lingers when I realize that Quince is coming my way. I'm desperately in love with my husband, but that doesn't mean I don't appreciate a good-looking man, and Quince definitely qualifies. He's British, which is really neither here nor there, but that awesome accent definitely adds to the appeal of his dark, lean looks. He has an edgy, dangerous air, but at his core, he's one of the kindest men I know. And the most loyal.

Most of all, he's completely smitten with Eliza. Honestly, it's kind of adorable.

As he approaches, I look past him for her, then realize that she's disappeared. Probably inside the house where Nikki, Damien, and the rest of this morning's crew have gone for coffee and a buffet-style breakfast.

"So, we did it," he says as he sits on the edge of my chaise.

"You and Eliza?" I quip as I scoot over to make room for him. "I should hope so, the way you two have been making puppy dog eyes at each other for the last few days."

"Funny girl," he retorts, but he's grinning so I know that he doesn't mind me teasing him. He knows perfectly well that I adore Eliza and think they make a terrific couple. "I want to hear it straight from you."

"Hear what?" I'm genuinely confused.

"That you and I make a great team, and you're going to stay in the field and not decide this was a one-off and go back to riding a computer."

I make a scoffing noise, as if he's saying the most ridiculous thing. But he's not. After all, that's what I'd done right before we met. I'd been so morose at Mason's long absence that I'd left my government assignment and taken Ryan up on his offer to recruit me over to his security team. But I'd refused field assignments.

Quince is the one who convinced me to get back in the field. We worked a bit together during the Stark kidnapping investigation and hit it off, probably because both of us were walking around under the same dark cloud. Whatever the reason, we ended up as friends, and the assignment that we just wrapped marked our first official job as partners.

"No way you're getting rid of me now," I tell him honestly.

His brows rise. "Now?"

"Sure." I flash a mischievous smile. "Now that you're with Eliza. That means I have someone I can gossip to about all your annoying habits."

"Ah, well, then I guess it's lucky that there's not a single bloody thing about me that's annoying."

"Yeah," I say, deadpan. "Lucky."

We share a grin, and then I reach out and put my hand over his, which is resting on the chaise cushion. "I'm so glad you two are together," I tell him sincerely. "You were meant to be, you know."

"I do," he said. "And I'm determined not to blow it. We're even doing counseling. First session next Thursday."

"Good for you," I say, wondering if maybe I should try that, too. Maybe I could learn how to fill this cavern that's growing in my soul. I shake the thought away; this moment isn't about me.

He shifts his hand so that he can close his fingers around mine and gives them a gentle squeeze. "Can you tell me what's wrong?"

Such a simple question, but it's said with so much genuine concern that my eyes water, and I have to blink away tears. "Just melancholy. I love you, and you're one of my best friends, so don't take this the wrong way, but I'm so goddamn jealous I can't see straight."

"I'm sorry, Denny. I wish I could give him back to you."

"I know," I say with a nod, and even though Quince has always called me by the nickname that Mason tagged me with, this morning, that name makes me want to burst into tears.

Over Quince's shoulder, I see Eliza step through the open doorway, a tray full of coffee cups in her hands. I point toward her, suddenly desperate for a few moments alone. "Looks like she brought coffee for everyone. You should give her a hand."

"I'll bring you a cup."

I shake my head as he stands, and his brows rise in surprise because he knows damn well I'm addicted to the stuff. "I think I caught a bug. My stomach's been rebelling when I have coffee on an empty stomach. I'll grab some food soon," I say before he can offer to bring me that as well.

"Fair enough," he says, obviously hearing my underlying plea that he leave. Most of the time I'm doing just fine—truly. But today, with the celebration and the love and—

I sniff and blink and will myself not to cry as I watch him stride toward Eliza, and my breath hitches at the way she lights up upon seeing him.

I swallow. Must. Stop. This.

Seriously, I have got to stop feeling sorry for myself. But, dammit, I don't know what's happened to him. I don't know if he's safe. I don't even know if he's alive, although surely I'd feel the pain in my heart if he'd already left this world.

The only thing I know—or think I know—is that four months ago, I thought—

"Born in the USA..."

My phone's ringtone is both loud and totally unexpected—because that particular Springsteen song is assigned to my former boss, Colonel Anderson Seagrave. I snatch my phone up eagerly, then answer with a mix of hope and trepidation. Because Seagrave is still Mason's boss.

"Have you heard anything?" I ask without preamble. I know it's not his assistant making the call. Anderson's a busy man, but he wouldn't do that to me; he knows too well that I'm desperate for news about my husband.

"Denise." He clears his throat. "We need to talk."

———

"Where is he?" I see no sign of my husband as I peer into what looks like a nice studio apartment, but is really a secure, government hospital room. The walls are painted a soothing beige, made even calmer by framed landscape paintings that are artfully arranged on the walls.

"He'll be back soon," Seagrave assures me, but all I can do is shake my head. Mason might come back into the room, but he won't really be back. Not if what Seagrave told me on the phone is true.

"This will be hard for you to hear," he'd said, and my body had turned to ice.

"He's dead." I was sure of it. Seagrave's the commander of the Western Division of the ultra-secret Sensitive Operations Command. He's a good man, but highly placed. And he doesn't have time to call about routine matters.

"No, no," Seagrave's rebuttal spilled out, breaking through the rising hum in my ears. "He's alive. But he's lost his memory."

I made a strangled sound, then immediately looked down at the flagstone patio, not wanting Quince or anyone else at the party to notice my expression. "His—what? What exactly do you mean?"

"He doesn't know who he is. He doesn't know who I am."

"And me?" My heart was pounding so hard I could barely hear his response.

"I'm sorry, Agent Marshall," he'd said, the reference to my professional title obviously intended to shore me up emotionally. "But he doesn't know you, either."

I don't remember ending the call. I don't remember talking to anyone, but I must have, because Quince and Eliza drove me into downtown Los Angeles.

I'd managed to gather myself during the drive, but I'm still in shock. Slightly queasy. Cold, despite Quince loaning me an oversized sweat jacket that he'd found in the back of his immaculate black Range Rover.

Most of all, I'm in denial.

Because despite what Seagrave told me about Mason remembering nothing about his life or me, I'm absolutely, one hundred percent certain that the moment he sees me, it will all flood back. Maybe not work. But me. Him. *Us.*

Considering what he and I share—the intensity of our relationship, the strength of our bond—how could any other result be possible?

And yet doubt still niggles at my soul...

Now, I draw a deep breath and focus on the room that has been my husband's home for almost a week. I'm still angry that Seagrave didn't contact me right away, but those emotions will get me nowhere, and I've pushed them out of sight, hidden them in the trash can of my mind where I store all useless facts.

Instead, I let my gaze play hopscotch around the room, wishing that he were in there at this moment. But all I see are the furnishings. A dresser, a small writing desk, a kitchenette, a bed. The IV rack and monitors mark the only clue that this room is anything out of the ordinary.

That, and this window made of one-way glass. From Mason's perspective, it's a full-length mirror next to the bathroom. I wonder if Mason remembers enough about his past life and career to realize that's total bullshit.

The thought makes me frown, and I glance at Seagrave. He's looking into the room, too, but he must feel my eyes on him because he tilts his head up, then wheels himself slightly backward so that we can face each other more directly.

He's in his mid-forties with an easy smile and dark hair that's already graying at the temples. I don't know how he lost the use of his legs, but I heard through the grapevine that it wasn't in battle, though he's seen more than his share of action.

He's efficient, fair, and a natural leader. I would have happily worked under him forever had it not been for Mason's disappearance. I'd wanted to head up an extraction team. Seagrave not only flatly refused to authorize the mission, but also denied me any lead or clue as to Mason's where-abouts. Continent. Country. City. I had no clue where to start, which meant that even a vigilante-style extraction would have been impossible.

I respected his decision—truly. But I resented it, too. And as the months dragged on, I couldn't

stay with the SOC. Not with my fears and memories beating down on me every damn day.

"How are you doing?" he asks me now.

"Stupid question," I mutter.

"Is it?"

I shrug, wishing that Quince and Eliza were
still with me. But this is an authorized personnel
only situation, and they have no connection with
my former government job.

"You were one of my best agents, Denise. And
you handled everything I threw at you. You'll get
through this, too."

I look away from him, because I think we may
have just found my limit. Because I'm not handling
this well at all. Instead of facing reality, I'm clinging
to the scenario I've been playing out in my head.
Me walking into that room. Mason standing
politely, his head cocked in that way he has when
he's trying to work out a puzzle. For a terrifying
moment, his expression will be blank. Then a smile
will spread across his face and sunshine will fill
those chestnut eyes. "Denny," he'll say, as I slide
into his arms. "Christ, Denny, I thought I'd lost
both of us." "Never," I'll whisper. "I'll always see
you home."

That's what I want. That's what I'm imagining.

But I know it's not real.

I spent too many years working the tough cases.
I've seen too many horrors, and over the years my

skin has gotten too thick. The optimism I clung to as a child has been chipped away, replaced by a dark reality where every happily ever after comes with a price.

And now I'm terrified that this is the price Mason and I are paying for our years of bliss.

From the speakers mounted above us, I hear a click as the bathroom door inside the room opens. Mason steps out, absolutely and completely nude. Seagrave immediately spins his chair around, as if to give Mason privacy, but I stay as I am, looking over Seagrave's head at my husband, a slow burn of anger rising at the unfamiliar scars that now mar his beautiful skin.

I don't know what happened to him, but if I ever find out who did that, I'll kill them with my bare hands, I swear to God.

"Did they break any bones?" My voice is low, but even.

"His nose. His arm. Recent, but healed by the time we acquired him."

"Acquired," I repeat. Not rescued. Not recovered. Not exfiltrated. In other words, Seagrave still sees Mason as a risk.

I get that. I understand his reasoning and his fear. But he's not right. He can't be right, because that would be the final blow that absolutely destroys me.

"No head injuries," he continues, his voice bland. "That's not the cause of his memory loss."

"I wasn't even thinking about that. I was just—"

I sigh, overwhelmed by the sight of him and the situation. But no matter how horrible everything is, that is my husband in there. *Mason.* The dark hair that appears so thick and coarse, but is as soft as silk to my fingers. Those deep-set eyes that can steal my breath with a single glance. His rugged face highlighted by the slight, kissable cleft in his chin.

And his body. Tall and muscular and vibrant and *mine.*

We'll get past this. Somehow, I'm going to get him back.

As if he can hear my thoughts, Mason turns and walks toward the mirror. Toward *me.* He stops in front of it, completely naked, his head tilted slightly down so that our eyes meet, though I know he can't see me. My pulse kicks up, and I let my gaze roam over every delicious inch of him, soaking him up like candy.

"That's Mason," I whisper, my attention focused especially on the tribal band tattoo on his left arm. Mason doesn't like rings—not since he saw his cousin's finger get ripped off after the seventeen-year-old got his hand caught in construction equipment during a summer job. Instead of a ring to symbolize our marriage, he'd chosen to get a tattoo. I'd considered doing the same, but in the end, I'd gone with my platinum band.

I press my palm against the glass and sigh. "He may not realize it, but that's definitely Mason."

Seagrave's back is still to the glass, so I can easily see the way his forehead creases as he studies me. "If you're about to give me a run down on specific physical attributes, don't bother. I've gotten a full report from the med team already."

I smirk. "I definitely recognize every inch," I say, choosing not to comment on the spider web of scars that make me want to weep. "But that wasn't what I meant. I'm saying that he's Mason. With Mason's habits. His—I don't know— *programming*."

"Programming?"

I shake my head quickly. "I don't mean he's gone all *Manchurian Candidate* on us. I just mean that people develop certain patterns over a lifetime. He hasn't forgotten those. Even if he's forgotten where they came from. That has to be a good sign, right?"

"He walked naked into a room that he may well believe is private. So what? Tell me what exactly that means to you."

"Defiance," I say, grinning at my bare-naked husband still standing in front of the mirror, looking hard at us even though I know that all he sees is himself. "We both know he understands what that mirror is—don't try to tell me you think otherwise. So that's one clue. Here's another—Mason never leaves the bathroom naked. He always wears a towel or dresses in the bathroom."

That, in fact, is a quirk that I've always found unfortunate since the man has an incredible body. But he shared a room with his sister until he was fourteen and now the towel habit is deeply ingrained. He's broken pattern only twice in our marriage—our wedding night and the night before he left on this mission. Mostly because I'd cajoled him into—and out of—the shower with me.

Not that I'm going to share those details with Seagrave.

"But he's *not* Mason," Seagrave says. "That's the point. That's why he's breaking pattern. No towel. No old habits."

"Maybe. Or maybe this is his way of flipping you the bird."

I watch as Seagrave's mouth curves into a frown. He spins the chair, then stares at Mason, who's still standing in front of the mirror. "He knows we're here. And so he's purposely acting against instinct, knowing full well I'd be watching."

At first, I think he's mocking my theory. Then I realize he means it. "You agree with me."

"That he knows we're behind the mirror and that he is, as you say, flipping us off? Yes. I do." Seagrave's shoulders rise and fall. "But as to whether he's in defiance of the habit of the towel, too ... well, that I can't be sure of."

I shrug. "Fair enough," I say. "It's enough that I'm certain."

I think about what he's just said. "Why do you say he knows about the mirror?"

"We weren't twiddling our thumbs in the days before I called you. We've been doing a series of tests and interviews. He recognized his Special Forces tattoo. He admits to a level of familiarity regarding intelligence work, though no specific assignments."

"Familiarity," I repeat. "Like habits. Behavior."

"Yes."

"So he knows he's an agent. A spy."

"Or that he was. But what we didn't know— and what he couldn't tell us—was if he'd been compromised."

I feel the blood rush to my face. "Brainwashing. Triggers." I think about my *Manchurian Candidate* quip and wish I'd said nothing. The idea that some enemy of the state or vile mobster brainwashed my husband to blow a gasket when he sees a particular pattern or hears a trigger phrase or verse ... well, the possibility is too horrible to even think about.

"No," Seagrave says gently. "He's undergone hours of testing and interviews with Dr. Tam, and we've reached almost one hundred percent confidence that he hasn't been compromised that way."

I nod slowly. I trust the SOC's staff psychiatrist, but in the intelligence world, nothing ever reaches one hundred percent certainty.

"I want to see him now," I say simply.

"I'm not sure that's a good idea today."

"You've run your tests. You've run your evaluations. You've had him for over four days. It's time to open a window for him to his actual life."

"I don't disagree."

For a moment, I'm confused. Then I exhale loudly. "Right. This isn't about him. You think I can't handle it. You think it's going to break me if I walk into that room and he doesn't know who I am."

"Won't it?"

"No," I lie, but I can see on his face that he doesn't believe me. I can't get angry about that, though, since I'm not sure I believe it myself.

"I told you on the phone this was an informational visit only," he continues.

"Please, Anderson," I say, feeling a hot tear trace a path down my cheek. "I need this. I need to go in there. I need to see my husband."

I watch his face. The way his shoulders dip slightly. Anderson Seagrave is a good man, and I know he's only trying to protect me. But I'm done in. At this point, every moment I'm not in that room with Mason is hell. And when I see Seagrave nod, I know he's finally realized that, too.

"All right, Denise," he says. "You have ten minutes."

I start to protest, but he lifts a finger, reminding me that he's the one calling the shots here.

"Ten minutes," he repeats. "And there are a few conditions as well."

4

___

I PAUSE OUTSIDE THE DOOR, trying to gather myself. I press my hand over my queasy stomach and try to will my nerves under control. I don't completely succeed, but I'm also not willing to wait any longer. With a deep breath for courage, I reach out and rap on the door.

Almost immediately, Mason's voice filters through the speaker system. "What the fuck, Seagrave? You know damn well I can't let you in."

I mentally kick myself, then tap in the code, wait for the locking mechanism to disengage, and push the door open. I step inside, then freeze when I see him, forcing myself not to whimper with the anguish that washes over me.

His back is to me, and I catch sight of the black band of his briefs peeking out from the waistband.

He's pulling on a shirt, and I watch as the muscles in his back ripple, the urge to touch him—to hold him—so powerful that it's almost painful.

It had been hard enough to view this medieval nightmare of crisscrossing scars through the one-way glass. Now, the sight has completely broken me, and I have to fight the urge to sob on his behalf. I want to hold him close and soothe him, and I crave the caress of his breath against my ear as he whispers softly, promising me that we'll get through this together.

Most of all, I want to release my fears and lose myself in the arms of the husband who loved me.

But that's not the man I'm looking at.

Not anymore. Maybe not ever again...

Oh, God.

"Are you okay?"

I look up, only in that moment realizing that I've shifted my attention to the floor in an unconscious effort to hide my tear-filled eyes. I sniff and manage a wobbly smile. He's looking at me with such tenderness and concern that I truly can't wrap my head around the fact that this man doesn't know me.

With a mental curse, I wipe it away. I'm better trained than this. But my reaction isn't about work. It's about my husband. It's about Mason Walker. Who likes to jog with me on the beach at sunset and spend lazy summer mornings in bed sharing a carafe of coffee as we watch old film noir movies or big budget fantasy flicks.

But now they tell me he doesn't remember any of that.

It's bullshit. It *has* to be bullshit. Because despite the years of training. Despite having actually taken a bullet not once, but twice. Despite having some serious covert creds, I can't wrap my head around the words Seagrave kept pounding into me. That the man on the other side of this room is going to look me straight in the eye and not have a clue who I am.

That can't be right. He has to know me, because that's the only version of reality that my fragile heart is willing to accept. Seagrave has to be wrong, and I take a step toward Mason, certain that any second now I'll see the polite confusion on his face shift into loving relief.

He'll whisper my name, his voice thick with tears, and then he'll sprint across the room and pull me against him with such force that we'll both fall to the ground, holding each other as we sob with relief and joy.

That, of course, doesn't happen.

Instead, he grabs a box of tissues from the dresser and walks toward me, extending the container like a peace offering. I'm left handed, so when I reach for the tissue, my simple platinum wedding band gleams under the fluorescent lights.

I see his eyes dip to it before returning to my face. *This is it*, I think. *This is the trigger that restores his memory.*

"I'm going out on a limb and guessing that we know each other," he says, shattering my hope. "Or knew. I'm still a little uncertain about which is more grammatically correct under the circumstances." His mouth curves into an ironic smile and I laugh despite myself. Then I want to cry all over again, because Mason could always make me laugh with his stupid, random jokes.

A fresh tear trickles down my cheek, as if determined to completely eradicate that tiny bubble of levity, but I manage to hold the smile. "Yeah," I say, as I study his face for any sign of recognition. "We know each other."

"Present tense. I like it." I watch his gaze flick over me. "You look like someone I want in my present and not just in my past."

"Do I?" My voice is strangled, and it's all I can do to get the question out without crying. "Do you have any idea who I am?" All I want in that moment is for him to throw me a bone. Some tiny hint of recognition. Some flash of reaction in those deep brown eyes I know so well.

But there's nothing.

Nothing except a calm assessment, an apolo-

getic shake of his head, and then the flat, emotionless gaze of a man trained to hide all expression. "I
don't. I'm sorry. But if we're playing the elimination
game, I can rule out Seagrave, Dr. Tam, and a few
of the med techs."

"That's a start," I say, trying to keep my voice
light.

"After that, I'm at a loss. But maybe there are a
few things I know."

A flicker of hope tickles in my chest, like a tiny
bird fluttering its wings. "What do you mean?"

"We must have been close."

I nod, mute.

He grins, like a little boy who's just won a
cookie. As he moves to sit on the edge of the bed, he
gestures for me to take the single chair by the small
table, I do, grateful to sit.

"I've spent the last few days studying every
inch of my face, and I don't see a resemblance
between us," he says. "Which means we're not rela-
tives, right?"

"No," I whisper. "No shared blood at all." I
swallow, then force a smile. "Is that all?"

"I'm just getting started." His grin lights his
face in a way that I hadn't seen while watching
through the window. *That's for me*, I think. *If
nothing else, I've brought him a tiny hint of joy.*

I relax a bit, returning the grin. "Enlighten me."

"You're married," he says, as I realize that my

thumb has been caressing my ring. "Which means you're not my girlfriend." His gaze skims over me, quick but thorough. Then he flashes a familiar half-smile, the one that makes his hidden dimple pop into view. "Of course, we could be having an affair..."

For a moment, the possibility hangs in the air, heavy with the memory of his body on top of mine, his eyes seeing straight into my soul. At least that's what pops into my head. I have no idea what he's thinking.

I really wish I did.

"Do you think we are?" I ask, pleased that my voice betrays no emotion. Thank God for government training. "Having an affair?"

He hesitates before answering, his eyes never leaving my face. "No."

"Oh?" My voice stays level, reflecting none of my insecurities. *Doesn't he find me attractive? What happened to our connection? That spark that had flared the very first time we met?* "Why not?"

His gaze dips to my ring finger. "Because I'm not the type of guy who sleeps with a married woman. And I doubt I was even when I knew my name. Plus, I know you aren't the kind to cheat."

"You know that?" I raise my brows. "How?"

"Your ring."

At first I don't understand. Then I realize that I've been fiddling with it constantly. Rubbing it with my thumb. Spinning it. Touching it in some way or another.

It's not just a ring. It's a symbol. It's my way back to Mason.

And the irony is that the man sitting in front of me doesn't even have a clue.

"A woman so completely focused on the symbol of her marriage wouldn't cheat."

I'm not sure I agree with that as a blanket statement, but he's right about me. So I simply nod. "You still haven't said how we know each other. You've said we're close and we're not sleeping together. So far, you're two for two. But what about the rest?"

He holds up a finger. "I'm close with your husband, right?"

"Well, not anymore," I say, both deflecting the question and broadening his grin.

"You make a good point." He leans forward, his elbows on his knees and his chin resting on two steepled fingers. It's a completely classic Mason pose, and I have to work to hold my stiff smile in place.

"Was I close with your husband?"

I nod slowly. "That would be a fair statement."

"Fair, but not entirely accurate?"

"Are we playing Twenty Questions now?"

He laughs, but the sound is hollow. "At the moment, my life *is* a game of Twenty Questions."

I nod, conceding the point. "Correct. Fair, but not entirely accurate."

"All right. That means he and I weren't partners, were we?"

"No, you weren't."

"Which means that you and I were."

I lurch back, my mouth opening in surprise. "How did you work that out?"

"So, I'm right. Good. If I was wrong I was going to have to rethink everything."

"I'm serious," I press. "How did you know?" Does he remember that part of our life? Is he seeing little flashes of our first few years together? I swallow, trying not to be too hopeful. But if he's started to remember that, what else might he remember?

"I'll trade you. Tell me my name, and I'll tell you how."

It would be so easy. All I have to do is spit it out.

Granted, the moment I do, agents will burst in through the door and drag me off to military prison. Probably. And even if that doesn't happen, I'll have completely destroyed Seagrave's trust in me. Which isn't something I can live with. I respect the man too much.

Not only that, but I've been trying to foster a working relationship between the SSA and Seagrave's operation. Go against his direct orders and that will never happen. And Seagrave was crystal clear with his instructions—I can't tell Mason his name. I can't tell him our relationship. I *can* tell him that we worked in the field as partners. But that's as far as I'm allowed to take it.

I'm not crazy about the parameters, but I would have agreed to anything to get through that door. Now that I'm in, I'm not going to risk being dragged out again.

"I take it by your silence that you're not going to tell me," he says. "It's okay. I didn't really expect that you would."

"If it helps, I was debating. But I'm pretty sure I'd end up chained in the dungeon for the next decade if I spill. And I just started re-watching *Game of Thrones*. It would suck to have to stop midway through season one."

Mason and I watched the show together until he went away, and I search his eyes for a flicker of recognition, but I don't see a thing. My shoulders droop with disappointment, but maybe it's for the best. According to Seagrave, Dr. Tam insisted that any specific reference to his name, his relationship to me, or any past assignment runs the risk of short-circuiting his brain, which could end up blocking the information for good.

"She explained it with medical speak and a fifty page brief," Seagrave had added when he gave me the rundown. "But that's about what it amounts to. Something traumatic happened, and we're assuming that event is tied to his discovery of key information that could lead to us shutting down that terrorist cell once and for all. We can't risk burying that information forever."

Maybe not. But at the moment, I care a hell of a lot more about Mason than I do about a terrorist cell. But only in my heart. My training is too ingrained, and no way would I compromise the country's security or undermine all the work that Mason did while he was gone.

So instead of telling him his name, I volley the question back to him. "What are you calling yourself?"

"Jack Sawyer. It amused Seagrave. I guess it amuses you, too," he adds, obviously noticing my grin.

"You always were a fan of *Lost*. Do you remember the show?"

"I do. Life on that freakish island seems more real at the moment than my own." He stands, then goes and gets a cup of coffee from the Keurig in the corner of the room. "Want?"

I nod, and a few moments later he brings me a Styrofoam cup filled with the magical elixir. Our fingers brush as I take it, and an unexpected shock of awareness ricochets through me at this first contact in what feels like forever.

I tense, hoping he doesn't notice, and at the

same time delighting in the flood of memories that even this slight contact with him revives.

Mason—no, I need to call him Jack—returns to the bed and sits again, slowly sipping his coffee. As far as I can tell, he's completely unaffected by the brush of skin against skin.

"Your turn," he says, and it takes me a second to realize he wants to know my name.

"Denise. Denise Marshall." I've always used my maiden name professionally, so it easily rolls off my tongue, even though what I want is to tell him that my name is Denise Marshall Walker, and why the hell doesn't he remember that?

"And your husband?"

I hesitate only a second. Then I look him straight in the eye. "Mason. Mason Walker."

For a moment, the name hangs in the silence. Then he says, "Is he dead?"

I'm unable to hold back the small, strangled noise that escapes my lips. "He—he's been gone a long time."

He nods sympathetically, and I'm terribly afraid he's going to ask me a more probing question. One I really can't answer. So I fire my own question off first. "How did you know we were partners? You still haven't told me."

"Well, apparently I'm a hot shit intelligence officer."

It's the right thing to say, as a laugh bubbles out

of me, lightening the mood. "Can't argue with that, but I still want to know your reasoning."

"I was close to him, but you said we weren't partners. If we'd been just run-of-the-mill friends he wouldn't know about my work."

"Not everyone in intelligence works undercover."

"But I did. Or at least, I'm playing the odds and saying I did." He sweeps his arm, indicating the room. "If not, all this seems like overkill."

Since I can't argue with that, I don't. "How do you know that he was aware of your work?"

"A guess, honestly. But you know. And if I wasn't Mason's partner, the next best guess to get you into this room is that you're in intelligence too, and that—"

"—we're partners. Yeah. I get it."

And I do. It's cold, hard reasoning, which has always been one of Mason's strong suits. Right now, though, he's reasoned me right out of his arms and into another's. I'm his friend. His colleague. His partner.

But I'm not his lover, and I'm not his wife.

He's erased me. Somehow, his mind really has erased me along with everything else, and there's not a damn thing I can do about it.

I can't wrap my arms around him and weep. I can't twine my fingers through his hair as my mouth finds his.

I can't kiss him back to reality as if I'm a fairy tale princess and he's a prince trapped in a hundred year sleep.

I can't even tell him the truth.

All I can do is cry, but I'm not even allowed to do that.

"You have to hold it together," Seagrave had said. "You're a professional, Agent Marshall. If I let you walk into that room, I expect you to behave like one."

The memory whips through my head, and I draw in a resigned breath as I once again focus all my attention on Mason.

Correction: Jack.

He's Jack Sawyer. I'm Denise Marshall. And never the twain shall meet.

"How long have you been in the private sector?" he asks, interrupting my pity party and making me look up sharply.

"How do you know I am?"

"Because if we were still partners, you would have popped into my cell before now. You're still in the business, though. Just more on the civilian side of things."

"Guess you really are a hot shit intelligence officer."

"I know something else, too," he says with a grin. "We made a damn good team."

"You don't know that."

"Sure I do," he says. "I don't remember it, but I feel it. We were good together, weren't we, Denise?"

"Yeah." My voice catches. "We made one hell of an awesome team."

5

"THAT's about the saddest thing I've ever heard," my friend Cass says, glancing up from where she's doing the final touches on a wrist tattoo of a single domino with four dots on one side of the tile and two on the other.

I've just finished telling her and Sylvia—who's getting the ink— that I saw my husband this afternoon, and he didn't have even an iota of an inkling of a clue that I'm his wife.

"Believe me," I say. "I know."

"Are you supposed to be telling us this?" Cass adds. "Isn't this one of those situations where you can tell us, but then you have to kill us?"

"Yes," I say, looking from her to Sylvia. "As soon as you finish Syl's wrist, I'm going to take you both out."

"Well, hell," Syl says with a put-upon sigh.

"What's the point of getting a new tattoo if I don't have time to show it to anyone?"

"That's true," Cass says. "Whacking us would be just plain rude."

I exhale loudly and flop down into the big leather armchair that's been tucked in this corner of Totally Tattoo for all the years I've known Cass. I keep my expression bland, but inside I'm grinning. I knew my friends would make me feel better. "Fine. You live. But that means you both owe me a drink." I glance at the kitty cat clock with the swishing tail. "As soon as the big hand gets to the twelve, I expect my due compensation."

"I can't believe I'm saying this, but I'll have to take a rain check." Syl offers me an apologetic smile. "I'm so sorry I can't stay. Because honestly, Denny, if anyone deserves a drink today, it's you."

"I won't argue with that," I say. "And I forgive you. Big plans?"

Her huge smile is answer enough. It lights up her face and makes her eyes twinkle. She wears her hair short, like Audrey Hepburn in *Sabrina*, and the style complements her elfin face.

"We're dropping the kids off with Nikki and Damien for the week," she tells me. "Then Jackson and I are heading to the airport."

"That's right," Cass says. "The museum dedication in Reykjavik, right?"

Syl nods. "I've never been to Iceland, and Jackson's giving a speech and getting an award. It should be a fabulous week."

A world-famous architect, Jackson Steele is also Damien's half-brother. And Sylvia, in addition to being Jackson's wife, is a high-level exec with Stark Real Estate Development.

Considering I now work for the Stark Security Agency, I find it completely ironic that I met Sylvia through Cass and not through Damien. Especially since Cass isn't a billionaire, doesn't work for any Stark subsidiary, and doesn't know squat about the intelligence community.

On the contrary, Cass is just Cass—one of the best tattoo artists I've ever met, which isn't saying much since I still haven't summoned the nerve to get a tattoo. But back when Mason got his tribal band, I did a ton of research on local parlors and learned that Totally Tattoo is one of the best.

The studio's been around for over three decades, and Cass has been working at the place in various capacities since she was a kid. Back then, her dad ran it. And from what she tells me, she and Syl met when they were teenagers, hit it off, and have been lifelong besties.

When Mason and I came in, the plan was for us to get matching ink. After watching the process with Mason, though, I'd chickened out. I may be a badass in the espionage world, but that doesn't mean I want to voluntarily get stabbed with a zillion little needles.

Cass took my wishy-washiness in stride, which was probably the second thing about her that impressed me. The first, of course, was her looks. With her ever-changing hair—today it's dark with pink tips—her brilliant green eyes, and the magnificent tattoo of an exotic bird that marks her shoulder, Cass has always been exceptional.

Since I felt guilty for bailing on my ink and leaving Cass with a big gap at the end of her Friday calendar, Mason and I took her out for a beer. After that, we started hanging out a lot. Me, Mason, Cass, and her girlfriend, Siobhan.

That's part of why I feel no guilt for sharing Mason's secrets. I know Cass loves him, too. Not like I do, but our friendship is strong, and when that first month without Mason dragged into two, five, ten, it was to Cass's house that I'd go when I needed a reality check or a shoulder to cry on.

That shoulder is the reason I came here today instead of going straight to my house in Silver Lake. I need a hug. I need to talk. I need...

Honestly, I need Mason. But since that isn't going to happen, a friend is the next best thing, which is exactly what I tell her when we're finally settled at Blacklist, the Venice Beach bar just a few blocks from Cass's shop.

"The bottom line is that I couldn't bring myself

to go straight home," I tell her as I sniff my bourbon at the long oak bar, then push it away. "I didn't want to walk into that house without him, which is stupid, since I've been going home to an empty house for over two years now."

"But before it was empty because he was away working, but you knew that he was wishing he was there with you. And that made it important." She traces her finger thoughtfully along the rim of her wine glass. "Because it belonged to both of you."

"It still belongs to both of us," I say defensively.

"I know," Cass says gently. "But it's hard to be in a place after the meaning changes." She looks down at her wine, her head tilted so that her hair falls in a curtain of curls, partially shielding her face. I expect her to brush it back, and I frown when she doesn't.

"Cass?"

She takes a sip of wine, shakes her head, and tucks her hair behind her ear. What she doesn't do is look straight at me, and in that moment my gut twists and I realize I'm the worst friend ever.

"What happened?" I say. "Is Siobhan going to be stuck in Chicago longer than you thought?" After organizing a few successful fine arts exhibitions in the LA area, Siobhan got invited to work on a touring show, and she's been traveling for months. The last I heard, she was in Chicago for the final three-week run.

I assume Cass is just missing her, so I'm unprepared when she lifts her head, meets my eyes, and says flatly. "She's staying."

"Staying? So, what? She wants you to move to Chicago?"

"No," Cass says. "She doesn't want me there at all. I'm pretty sure Anthony doesn't want me there either."

"Anthony." The name comes out flat, and I say nothing else. I don't have to. I know where this is leading.

"At least Siobhan will finally make her dad happy. He hated when she dumped her boyfriend and came back to me."

That was before my time, but I've heard about how Cass and Siobhan had split up, then got back together. But from what Sylvia told me, those two were meant to be, and Siobhan's return had been both a happy surprise and inevitable.

"Does Syl know?"

Cass shakes her head. "She knows that I've been irritated with how little Siobhan was checking in, but I just wrote that off to her being so busy. This is a new development—yesterday, actually. At least from my perspective. Apparently from Siobhan and Anthony's point of view, it's been almost four months in the making." She shrugs. "I thought about telling Syl at lunch today, but I didn't want to drop all this on her right before she heads to Iceland."

I get that. The news hit me with the force of an anvil, and Syl has known Siobhan for years—and witnessed their first break-up and reconciliation. She's going to be knocked sideways second only to Cass herself.

I take her hand and squeeze. "I'm so sorry."

"I appreciate that, but I really didn't mean for this outing to be about me. After all, if we're comparing pain, I'm going to say that you win."

I'm not entirely sure that's true. As much as it hurts for Mason not to know me, I can't even imagine how horrible I'd feel if he'd willingly walked away from me. At least this way, I know that it wasn't his decision.

"True," Cass says when I tell her that. "But I still think it's worse for you. I could fly to Chicago if I wanted. Put up a fight. You can't. Because even if you tell him who you are, he doesn't remember it. So there's no solid ground for the two of you to stand on. From his perspective, it would be like you were arguing about some characters in a TV show. Vaguely familiar, but nothing to do with him." She lifts a shoulder apologetically. "At least if Siobhan and I have it out, we both know what the stakes are."

I let her words flow over me, then nod. "You're right. I'm definitely the one getting screwed here."

She laughs, as I'd hoped. And even though I meant what I said one hundred percent, I laugh, too.

"Of all the things I imagined when we got married, this was never on my radar. I mean, I thought about when we would have kids. And what we would do if we retired. I worried I couldn't handle it if he got sent out on assignment with another woman. You know, the usual stuff. But it never once occurred to me that I'd be totally erased from his life. It's—it's like being hollow, and I can't wrap my head around it."

"And it's worse because you can't tell him."

I nod, then reach for my drink before remembering I don't want it.

"What?"

"Just not in the mood for alcohol, I guess."

"Here, take my water." She pushes it to me. "But that wasn't what I meant. There's something else on your mind."

I shake my head, part of me not wanting to talk about it, and the other part not knowing how to put what I'm feeling into words.

"You thought he would know," she says softly. "That he would snap back when he saw you. You thought it would be like a fairy tale, and you'd step into the secret cave and rescue the wounded prince."

"You make me sound like a fool."

She flashes a sad little smile. "I don't mean to. I think I'd feel the same way. Anybody would. What you're going through—it's not exactly normal."

"Maybe I just did it wrong," I quip. "I mean, in the fairy tales, it's always a kiss that works the magic."

Beside me, Cass grins. "Maybe you should try that."

"I wish I had the nerve," I admit. "But I have a feeling Seagrave doesn't share my romantic streak. I'd end up getting banned from the SOC, and Mason would be confused—possibly turned on—but none the wiser."

"I'm sorry," she says, all levity evaporating from her voice.

"Thanks." The real truth is that I don't know what to do with myself now. Despite my rather hairy childhood, I've always believed that things would turn out all right. That my father abandoning me and my mom wasn't an omen. That—just like my mother told me—if I kept a positive outlook, everything would be okay. I just had to keep the faith.

And so I did. Even when cancer settled into her bones. Even when she died despite promising that she'd never leave me. That she'd fight it, and she'd win.

Even with all her promises, she lost the battle. But I still clung to that stupid, fucking optimism.

I'd kept the faith, and when Mason came into my life, I truly believed that he was my reward.

But now he's gone, too. And I can't seem to wrap my head around the randomness of the world. Like it's nothing more than a game of chance. Dice or cards or...

I frown, turning to Cass as I remember Sylvia's tattoo. The domino wasn't the first—far from it. In fact, the first time we went to the beach together, I was surprised to see how many she had. "Memories," she'd told me after I commented on her ink. "And a bit of therapy. A map of triumphs and milestones that I hold close."

"What was the point of the domino?" I ask Cass, then realize I know the answer as soon as the question leaves my mouth. "Because of the business center," I answer.

The Domino is a relatively new business park in Santa Monica. Specifically, it's a co-development between Stark Real Estate and Steele Development, which means that Jackson and Sylvia worked on it together. And I can't blame her for wanting to memorialize that in ink.

In fact, the more I think about it, the more I think that it's a very good idea. And despite my aversion to tiny needles, I shift on the bar stool to face Cass directly. "Can we go now?" I ask. "There's something I want you to do for me."

6

His DREAMS HAD BEEN FILLED with a green-eyed beauty, and Jack woke with her still on his mind. And he hated himself for it.

He'd dreamed of the soft brush of her blond hair against his bare chest. The gentle pressure of her full lips against his skin. The flash in her feline eyes as she'd tilted her head up, then practically purred as she eased down his body, her soft hands exploring his skin, her generous mouth doing such extraordinary things before she straddled his hips and rode him all the way to heaven.

He'd awakened worn out and sated, the memory of her scent clinging to him as tightly as the hot, twisted bed sheets.

He tried to tell himself that his dream lover had been an anonymous girl. A fantasy woman. The blond-haired, green-eyed siren of his earlier dream

in the hotel. But it wasn't. The woman who'd so
sweetly tormented him in the night wasn't an
ephemeral fantasy. She was Denise Marshall. And
he had no business allowing her into his dreams,
much less fantasizing about her lips on his cock.

She was his former partner. A professional, just
like he supposedly was, although damned if he
could remember any aspects of his career. And she
wasn't just his partner; she was another man's wife.
A man who was gone.

A man she wanted back.

He'd stood right here in this room and assured
her that he was honorable. That he would never
take what belonged to another man. That he would
respect her pain and loss.

And all of that was bullshit, because damned if
he didn't fuck her in his dream.

Yesterday, he hadn't known what kind of man
he was. Not really. How could he have?

Today, he knew.

"Perhaps you're being too hard on yourself,"
Dr. Tam said when he met her in therapy later that
morning. She wore a plain gray suit, her shirt
buttoned up to her neck. Her dark hair was cut
short, revealing small ears that contrasted the
lovely, huge eyes that hid behind the large, plastic
frames of her glasses.

He guessed her to be in her late fifties, and he
knew from Seagrave that in addition to her work

with field agents, she conducted independent research and was a frequent lecturer at medical schools around the globe.

Jack didn't care about any of that. If she could peel back the curtain to reveal his memories, she was useful. Her credentials were just so much noise.

"Fantasy is an important aspect of life," she continued, her eyes never leaving his face. "An important part of being human."

"I already knew I was human," he told her dryly. "Now I know I'm an asshole, too."

"Because you made love to a woman in a dream?"

"Fine," he said. "You're right. I'm making too much of it."

The words were a lie, of course. He didn't know why, but Denise Marshall had gotten under his skin. She was a constant in his thoughts, so much that she felt like a talisman. As if her kiss could restore him. As if the only way he could find peace was in her arms.

It was bullshit, and he knew it. She was beautiful and he was lost. Lost in the world. In his own head. And he didn't need Dr. Tam to tell him that he was clinging to her as a connection to his past. His former partner. His friend. He'd elevated her in his mind and turned her into something she wasn't.

He got it. He didn't need therapy to explain it. And he damn sure didn't need to share it.

He dragged his fingers through his hair. "Look, I'm sorry. But like I said, you're right. I'm drowning in self-pity, but we both know I'm not exactly sure-footed here. My entire world is inside this building. My little prison. This tiny room. Seagrave's office. At least he has a view."

The room that was his new home had no view; just that damn mirror through which Seagrave and Tam and everyone else could watch him as if he was a goddamn hamster in a cage. And this office he was in now, while cozy with its walls of book-shelves and comfortable chairs and sofas, was nothing more than a disguised surgery center— where Dr. Tam used her words instead of knives to cut into his brain.

Only Seagrave's office had a view. Not a lovely one—just a few rooftops and downtown structures. But at least there was sunshine.

"The accommodations are a bit bland," she said. "But you understand why, I assume?"

"Less stimulation in my environment, more stimulation in my head." He leaned back in the overstuffed armchair. "That's the theory, anyway. I think it's bullshit."

Her brows rose over the tops of her tortoise-shell frames. "Oh?"

"How the hell can I recover my life if I can't

experience my life?"

"We've had this discussion, Agent Sawyer."

He made a scoffing noise that she must have heard, but she continued without missing a beat.

"We don't know if your memory loss was due to physical trauma, mental trauma, or a combination of both. We don't know if your memory was intentionally wiped, perhaps through drug manipulation or hypnosis. In short, we don't know anything except that you were a key player in an important investigation. You discovered something both urgent and dangerous. You signaled that you would be making contact with key intel, and three weeks later you called Colonel Seagrave from a hotel in Victorville, seemingly with no memory of yourself, the information, or what had happened to you."

"Seemingly?"

"Surely you can understand why we must proceed with caution."

He did, of course. Grudgingly he nodded. He understood everything she was saying, but that didn't make it any easier. He'd been inside these walls for over a week now. It had been days since he'd seen Denise Marshall. In person, anyway. God knew she'd been showing up in his head regularly enough.

And it had been less than twenty-four hours since they'd told him he'd made contact, warning about an urgent threat. He disagreed with their rationale for waiting, but there wasn't a goddamn thing he could do about it. He was a prisoner here. A mind for them to probe. An unknown entity with no name, no resources, and nowhere else to go.

In other words, he was at their mercy.

The thought was not a pleasant one.

"You have a job, you know," Dr. Tam said, studying him with those intelligent eyes.

"Do I?"

"You're not a prisoner, Jack. You're an asset."

"If I'm an asset, the world is fucked." The fact that he said it with a smirk didn't mean he believed it any less.

"I want to talk about what you do remember. A truck you said."

"You know what I said. We've been over this multiple times."

"You recall being thrown out of a truck. You don't remember the face of whoever tossed you. You aren't even sure if the person was male."

"I remember movement. I remember the impact when I hit the street. I remember the sting in my palms and the needle stabs to my eyes when I blinked from the sun. I remember a black shirt and the impression that it was a man standing in that open cargo door. I remember all of that, but I'm not sure about a single fact."

"But you did walk, and you did end up in a motel in Victorville. That's verifiable."

"Has anyone here been able to locate the truck? Traffic cameras? Any satellites that happened to be taking snapshots? Any cars that passed me who called in a sighting of some battered man walking down the road?"

"If we'd found anything, we would have told you."

"Would you?" He dug his fingers into the padded armrests. "You haven't even told me what agency this is. I'm going on faith that this is a government operation. Well, faith and observation."

"Faith?"

"Apparently I worked for you. For this. I don't like to think I was working for the bad guys."

"We could be an independent organization of good guys."

"Possible. But there was a paystub on your desk yesterday—old fashioned, by the way. Most people just get an email. But clearly government issue."

She almost laughed, and he liked her more in that moment. "The funds are direct deposited. But I haven't gone paperless. I file the stubs. I suppose that makes you right. I'm old-fashioned."

"Convenient for me. As for Seagrave, there are quite a number of military commendations hanging on his walls. I doubt a man with that much cred with the military would chuck it all to go private."

"You're in the main office of the Western Division of the Sensitive Operations Command. The SOC is a covert, off-the-books paramilitary and intelligence organization that operates independently with oversight from the NSC."

"You're telling me just like that? I thought you didn't want me to have details about my life."

"I want you to trust me, Agent Sawyer. I need you to trust me—and Colonel Seagrave—to give you what you need. And to guide you as we think best."

"In other words, you just tossed me a bone."

"And you caught it." She smiled at him, easy and friendly, and the tension that had been building inside him dissipated a bit. He didn't understand her approach or agree with her choices, but he wasn't a shrink. At least, he didn't think he was. And for the moment, at least, he would trust her.

He spread his hands. "Alright. Go for it. Ask me questions. Get into my head. Do your worst."

"How about we both do our best?"

He nodded. One crisp tilt of his head.

"I'd like to go back to the truck. You've told me everything you recall?"

He closed his eyes and let it all play back. "I could smell exhaust. I was bounced around. The truck had a roll-up door. And there were at least two people, because the truck pulled away as the guy who tossed me was still standing in the cargo area."

"And your first memory?"

"The motion. Swaying. My hands tied behind my back. My ankles bound. My back aching from trying to stay seated. I was on a bench of some sort. You already know all of this."

"You remember nothing prior to that? Nothing before the motion of the truck?"

"No."

"So what does that tell you?"

"Not much, but it raises a hell of a lot of questions."

"Such as?"

He drew in a breath, then met her eyes. "The biggest, of course, is whether the memory is real."

She tilted her head. "You think it might have been planted?"

"I think I don't know you people any better than I know myself."

She surprised him by smiling broadly. "And now, Agent Sawyer, you're beginning to live up to your reputation. Yes, that is a risk. It's also possible that older memories are resurfacing." She reached for a remote and clicked on a wall-mounted television.

He turned, frowning as the screen popped on, revealing a mission report with all names redacted.

"That report's over a decade old," he said, skimming the paragraphs that summarized a mission in which the reporting agent had been held captive, then tossed from the back of a cargo van. "I filed this?"

"You did."

"So you're saying that I might be pulling up old memories. Dumping them into the present?"

"It's a possibility we can't overlook."

"Then how did I end up here? Like this?" He held out his hands, still red from the fading abrasions.

"Escape. Given up for dead and left at the side of the road. We may never know."

"We won't unless I remember. Why won't you help me remember?"

"Agent Sawyer, we've discussed—" She cut herself off with a shake of her head. "Jack." She began again, more gently. "I know it's difficult, but you need to trust me. Telling you your past runs the risk of destroying that past. We must approach our work in small increments. Otherwise we risk burying your secrets permanently."

He sat up straighter. "And if that's a risk I'm willing to take?"

She leaned back in her chair, studying him. Then she seemed to make a decision. She reached for her tablet, tapped the screen a few times, and a new image popped onto the television screen. A video of a man. He was sitting on his knees rocking back and forth. "And then," he said. "And then and then and then."

The video changed. Another man, this one sitting on the edge of a cot, staring blankly into space, a smile on his face.

Another. A man playing chess against himself, muttering. "That's all he does," Dr. Tam says. "He plays chess. I think he's trying to work it out. That somewhere inside his mind, he thinks that if he can beat himself, he'll get out of his own head. But if you're playing yourself, you can't beat yourself."

Jack felt cold. "Who are these men?"

"They could be you."

He swallowed. "Agents you pushed. Who were force fed memories."

"I didn't push them," she said. "I would have advised against that course. They were sent to me afterwards, with the hope that I could help. But I can't."

"Oh, God." His gut clenched.

"I can tell you this much—you are an agent of this organization, and you took an oath upon joining. This risk is not yours to take. Your memory and your mental health are under my protection, and that is a responsibility I take very seriously even if you do not."

He nodded slowly, hating what she was saying but also realizing he was in no position to argue. "Okay, but at least tell me what you can. How did I make contact? Was I working undercover? How long had I been in place? Do we have other assets in the field?"

He knew all the questions to ask. He knew how the job worked. He knew what he did as an agent. He just didn't know what he'd actually *done.*

And right at that moment, he felt more frustrated than he'd ever felt in his life.

At least as far as he could remember...

"I want answers."

"So do we all," she said. "That's why you're here. That's why we're having these talks. So that I can guide you. So that we can take it slowly and not miss anything. Not bury anything."

"What if I don't want to go slowly?"

"You were a good agent once. You valued the mission over self. Over family."

"I'm not the same person I was. Aren't you the one telling me so?"

"I'm the one trying to help you find that self again." She looked at him over the rim of her glasses. "Are you telling me that's no longer your code?"

He wanted to say yes, that was exactly what he was telling her. He wanted to demand that she do anything and everything to excavate his damn memories, and fuck the risks.

But he said nothing. She was right. He couldn't —*wouldn't*—risk burying whatever dark secrets he'd stored away.

"We'll do it your way," he said. "But I can't live like this. You want me to remember my life? Then I need to be allowed to live it."

He watched, his heart pounding, as she nodded slowly. "I don't disagree. I can speak to Colonel Seagrave. But I think we both know that you can't return to active duty. Until we know what's hidden in that head of yours, your clearance won't be reinstated. The issues SOC agents deal with are far too sensitive."

She was right, of course. And when he insisted that she let him put the issue to Colonel Seagrave himself, the older man simply repeated the doctor's concerns.

"You may have literally just fallen off the turnip truck, but you're not completely ignorant of how we work," Seagrave told him when Jack was escorted to the older man's office. "As much as I need what's in your head to protect national security, I can't risk that same security by letting a man without a memory run around like a loose cannon."

Jack nodded, then took a sip of the coffee Seagrave had offered him. "You're right, of course," he said. "But what about matters not related to national security?"

For a moment, older man simply studied him. Then he put down his coffee cup, leaned back in his chair, steepled his fingers beneath his chin and asked, "What exactly did you have in mind?"

7

RYAN HUNTER SITS at the head of the conference table, his fingers dancing over a keyboard as he skims a screen, then lifts his face and surveys the table. Lean, with chestnut brown hair and commanding blue eyes, Ryan is a natural leader. "Where do we stand, Noble? Your team ready to go?"

A lanky man, Winston Noble's wind-worn face speaks of the West Texas plains where he used to work as the sheriff before moving to California for reasons that I still don't know, and don't intend to ask. Not after seeing the haunted look in his eyes whenever his past is mentioned. He has a slow, easy way about him, and his thick Texas twang disguises a sharp intellect. Winston's a man that no one sees coming. More than that, he's one hell of a nice guy and an excellent leader. One I'd serve under without hesitation.

"I'd like to join the team," I say, swallowing the bite of dry toast I'd been nibbling on. The daughter of a Chinese diplomat was snatched during a family vacation in Washington, DC. The call came in at six this morning. It's eight now, and Winston's crew is wheels-up at nine. Under the internal rules of the SSA, Quince and I are both still on Local Assignment Status for another thirty-six hours, a policy designed to ensure that agents recover sufficiently following a rigorous mission.

I'm hoping that Ryan will overlook that fact. Because knowing that Mason is back in LA and holed up in an SOC observation room where I can't see him without command level approval from Seagrave is absolutely messing with my head.

I've barely slept for the last two nights, and when I do, I dream of my husband. I rub my wrist where Mason's newly tattooed name is hidden under the cuff of my starched, white button down. I'd thought the permanent reminder would act as a talisman and give me some peace. So far, it hasn't helped.

I want him back so desperately, but the truth is that even if he walked into the room this very second, he still wouldn't be Mason. He'd be Jack Sawyer. And I'm having a hell of a time dealing with that. More, honestly, than I would have expected, but the stress is taking a toll on my stomach, and I've been waking up queasy and unsettled.

Thus my breakfast of dry toast and apple juice instead of my usual black coffee and a power bar.

From the end of the table, Ryan meets my eyes, his gaze sympathetic but firm. "You're needed here, Denise. Besides, Winston and Leah are set to go. And Trevor is already on the ground in DC."

I start to argue, but across the table, Leah gently shakes her head. I worked with Leah on Stark International's security team before moving over to the more specialized and elite SSA. And while I really want to flip her the bird and snap that she doesn't have any right to tell me when to back off a mission, I also know that she's right. So is Ryan. So are they all.

Because the only reason I want to go to DC is to run away from my own hollow heart. But that's not something I can escape from anyway.

"Good luck," I say instead. "You have me here for tech support if you need it."

"When don't we need you, darlin'?" Winston asks. "You're the computer whisperer, aren't you?" He grins and the room laughs, including me. I worked in the field with Mason for years, and more recently with Quince. But what I really love is squeezing information out of bits and bytes.

"Go on," Ryan says, dismissing Winston and his team with a nod of his head. He turns his attention to Liam and Quince. "You've got your assignments. Any issues?"

"Any other day I'd complain that reviewing surveillance tapes is bloody boring," Quince says. "But under the circumstances, I'm content with a nine-to-five assignment."

Ryan grins. "Enjoy your evenings while you have them."

Quince glances at me. I know exactly how his evening will be going. At home with Eliza. I roll my eyes in response to his wink, hoping he can't tell that underneath my happiness for him, I'm a jealous, lonely mess.

"Foster?" Ryan turns his attention to Liam, a tall black man with a solid build, military bearing, and a dry sense of humor.

Originally from New York, Liam Foster came to the SSA from his post as the head of security for the Sykes chain of department stores. A pedigree that I thought was ludicrous until I learned that the security job was only a blind. Legitimate work, yes, but hardly his focus. And definitely not the line on his resume that landed him at the SSA.

I should have known there was more to him from the first moment I met him. After all, a department store gig wasn't exactly the kind of job that hardened a man. And despite his kind nature, Liam is definitely hard. Turns out that Liam served in the military for years. And after that he was second in command of Deliverance, a once-secret vigilante organization that tracked down kidnap victims, mostly children, and did whatever was necessary to rescue the victims and bring the perpetrators to justice.

He's smart, competent, and loyal, and we've become good friends.

"I'm set. Got a meeting during B-shift," he adds. The SSA operates on a twenty-four hour schedule, with teams of agents reporting every three hours. "I'll be on the job after that."

Ryan nods assent as Liam packs up his things. He and his team are working a standard protection detail for a rising pop star whose manager insists she needs protection despite the star's protests.

He pauses at the door, then turns back to me, one thick finger aimed my direction. I sit up straighter, wondering what the hell I've done to draw his fire, but all he does is smile gently, nod, and head out the door.

"He's right," Ryan says, when the door clicks closed.

"About what? He didn't say a word."

Neither does Ryan. I roll my eyes. "It's like having a bucket full of older brothers."

Ryan chuckles. "I'm not sure Leah and the other women will appreciate that."

"Siblings," I say. "For an only child, I'm

surrounded by siblings." I don't add that it's nice. Odd, but nice.

I take another bite of my toast, my queasiness finally starting to fade. "I'm going to go review Winston's mission specs," I say as I begin to gather my things. "I can start setting up some parameters, maybe even get some additional intel by the time they land in DC."

I stand, but Ryan motions me back down. "That's a good idea, but we need to talk about Cerise Sinclair."

I settle back into my chair. "Did something happen?"

In her early twenties, Cerise Sinclair is one of Los Angeles's pretty faces who grew up with money, has a trust fund as a cushion, and pays her daily bills off the income from being a social media influencer. A year ago, she bought a cozy little house in the Hollywood Hills without giving a thought to security. She has three vacant lots surrounding her, all with steep terrain, but not so unfriendly that a determined stalker couldn't walk there. And considering how much of her personal life she shares on social media—and how often she shares those details in only a bikini—she's collected quite a few ardent followers. Some of whom seem to think her posts are something akin to foreplay.

Before Quince and I dove headlong into the search for Eliza's sister and a missing princess, I'd consulted with Cerise on the installation of a security system for the property. The system is top notch and, as far as I know, hasn't registered any breaches to the home's perimeter.

Ryan shakes his head. "There've been no attempts to enter the residence, but Cerise asked if you could swing by. She didn't say why, but…"

He trails off, but I understand. Cerise may be a little high-maintenance, but she's both a client and one of Ryan's personal acquaintances, having come to the SSA via Ryan's wife, Jamie, who had interviewed Cerise a while back for a television news segment about the growing popularity of social media.

I glance at my watch. "I can go now and then devote the rest of the day to getting through my backlog and doing research for Winston's team."

Ryan's phone vibrates on the table, and he glances down as I start to stand. "She's in San Diego for the day, and asked that you come this evening," he says as he taps out a quick reply to the incoming text. "Just as well. I want you to take a partner with you."

I settle back into my chair, studying him. "To go to Cerise's? Why?"

"New man on the team. Might as well ease him in."

"Ease him in? Since when is this the kind of operation that eases anybody in?" Though relatively new, the SSA has already developed a reputation for complex jobs, many with international components. We're not a training facility.

Ryan ignores me, instead pushing the button on the desk's console that shifts the conference room's status from locked to open. The light above the door clicks to green and I watch as Damien Stark pulls open the door and steps in, all strength and command and poise. He's flanked by Seagrave and Mason, with Quince and Liam bringing up the rear.

I glance at Ryan, realize my mouth is hanging open, and shut it. I turn my attention to Quince. We've worked together enough now that I've gotten good at reading his face. But he looks as confused as I do, and I realize that Damien must have asked him and Liam to join the meeting, probably figuring I needed a buffer.

I'm just not sure what exactly I need buffering from.

"Denise," Mason says, his too-familiar smile both delighting me and making tears prick my eyes. He steps toward me, his hand extended. "It's really good to see you again."

I take his hand automatically, realizing in that instant that except for a light brush when he passed me coffee, it's the first time we've touched since his return, and I have to force myself not to squeeze tight and tug him closer. On the contrary, I gently pull my hand free, my heart pounding in my chest as my whole body sings, begging for more than this simple brush of hand over hand.

"New?" he asks, as I slide my now-free hand into the pocket of my jacket. I must look confused, because he nods toward the pocket. "Your wrist," he says. "The tattoo."

Without thinking, I pull my hand out of my pocket. The cuff has pushed up and is gripping my forearm, revealing my wrist and the single word inked in Cass's clean, simple font: MASON.

"I'm sorry," he adds, and I shake my head in confusion. "You didn't have that when we met. I can't help but think I said something that made you sad."

"I—" I swallow and try again. "It wasn't anything you said. Where Mason's concerned, I'm always sad. I just realized that I wanted a tangible reminder."

"One of Denise's good friends is a tattoo artist," Damien explains, then gestures for us all to take our seats.

I remain standing, my attention alternating between Damien and Ryan. "Can I speak to you two outside before we get started?" My smile is so sweet it's a wonder everyone in the room doesn't develop diabetes. "I was just about to update Ryan on a crisis that's developed in the Michelson matter."

There is no Michelson matter, but to both men's credit, they simply nod. Damien stands, then gestures for the door.

I'm about to step that direction when Mason also rises. "Wait a moment. Please."

His attention is entirely on me, and I feel his gaze burning through me, sending a tumble of emotions roiling through me. I want so badly to be with this man, and yet I'm afraid I'll reveal too much to him and make things worse.

I'm furious with Damien and Ryan for putting me in this position. Seagrave, too, and that bastard hasn't even said a word. He's just sitting there like some chess master moving us around as if we were pieces on a board.

Mason's the only one I'm not irritated with, even though he's the one who frustrates me the most, since he's the one around whom I must watch myself, putting on my Academy Award winning performance when all I want to do is hold him close and tell him the truth.

I say none of that, of course. Instead, I look to Mason and say, very simply, "What is it?"

"If there really is a Michelson case that needs your attention, then by all means, don't let me stop you."

I start to take a step toward the door.

"But if you just want to get your two bosses past that door so that you can rip them new assholes, then you're about to attack the wrong people."

I stop moving, cross my arms, and stare at the stranger who is my husband.

"I arranged this," he says. "If it makes you uncomfortable, please don't blame Mr. Stark or Mr. Hunter. Or Colonel Seagrave, for that matter."

Beside him, Seagrave grunts, but says nothing else.

"Go on."

"You know that Dr. Tam thinks that any direct revelations as to my past might be detrimental to my ability to pull out my memories, especially the memories of my last mission. Which, I'm beginning to realize, was an even more crucial assignment than I'd originally believed."

He says the last with an eye to Seagrave. I knew nothing about his mission other than how long it took him away from me. But I did know how much the government trusted my husband and his skills, so learning that the mission was key comes as no shock.

He looks at me as if waiting for me to ask a question. I don't. I just twirl my hand in a *get on with it* gesture.

The corner of his mouth twitches, and I feel a pang in my heart, because this is an all too familiar scene. Mason going on about something at length when I'm already caught up, and me impatiently urging him to wrap it up.

"If the SOC wants my memories but can't give me the canvas on which to paint them, then it makes sense that I should go back out in the field. Step as much into my old life as possible."

"Work with me, you mean." The words both excite and terrify me. "I'm not sure how much that would help. It's been years since we worked as partners."

He nods. "I know. But right now, you're the best connection I've got."

I look helplessly at Liam and Quince, both of whom look sympathetic, but offer no practical help. As for Seagrave, his expression remains entirely blank.

"You approve of this? You and Dr. Tam? You're not afraid that Ma—the man he was before Jack Sawyer won't get buried?" I hold Seagrave's eyes, certain he understands my question: *If I do this, am I going to lose any hope of getting my husband back?*

"We think our Mr. Sawyer might have a point," Seagrave says.

"And you two?" I say, turning to Damien and Ryan, who know full well what this will do to me.

"Even if he's forgotten who he is, he still has skills," Ryan says slowly. "The man will be an asset."

"And working together may well be therapeutic," Damien adds, and I know damn well he means that it might be therapeutic for me as much as for Mason.

"I realize it's strange," Mason—*Jack*—says. "I even know it's going to be awkward for you. I don't have any excuse. All I can tell you is that I'm selfish. I want my life back, and I will go to the mat with all of you to get this chance. Denise," he says softly, "please help me."

I draw in a strangled breath, then look at the ground so he won't see my tears. I'm better than this. I'm not some emotional twit who cries all the time. But apparently where Mason is concerned, I am.

"Why me? Why not just return to the field?"

"Because we were partners," he says. "And because I trust you."

I shouldn't have asked. His words are too hard to hear. But they also drive home the simple truth that I'm all out of objections. More than that, I want this. As dangerous as it is to my heart and as hard as it will be not to accidentally reveal too much of our past, I want this chance to once again work with my husband.

"Okay."

His brows lift in surprise. "Okay? Really?"

"Do you want me to reconsider?"

He laughs and shakes his head as I glance over

at Quince who's grinning. We sound, I'm sure, like a quarreling couple.

"We'll go see Cerise Sinclair together this evening. In the meantime, I can give you the file to read." I frown. "I was going to run some errands before meeting Cerise. I can pick you up. Are you going to be staying in your room at the SOC?"

"Yes," Seagraves says.

"Absolutely not," Jack says. He faces Seagrave dead-on. "I'll check in regularly. I'll report to Dr. Tam daily. But you will not hold me prisoner. And if you don't like it, you're going to have to arrest me or kill me."

I hold my breath until Seagrave nods. "Where will you stay?"

For a moment, I actually consider offering him our house. Fortunately, Liam jumps in before I make that ridiculous mistake. "He can stay with me. Assuming you don't mind the beach?"

I watch as Jack's face light's up. We bought property inland because it was the only way to afford a house big enough to raise the family we eventually wanted. But my husband loves the beach.

"No problem. I've always wanted to live by the beach." He grins at all of us. "Or, at least, I think I have."

8

"NICE PLACE," Jack said, standing at the windowed back wall of Liam's beachfront condo. The condo sparkled and still had that new car smell that signified either fresh construction or a recent remodel.

"It's been around since the nineties," Liam said when Jack asked the question. "Most of the units were remodeled at least a decade ago. But this one was owned by an elderly woman who lived with her six cats—and no, I'm not exaggerating. When she passed away, the family didn't want to bother with it—they live in Idaho—and they put it on the market without any updates. Got a few nibbles but everyone haggled. I made a cash offer, then had Jackson draw up some plans. Then I hired Syl to act as a contractor, and the rest is history."

He shrugged and grinned, looking pleased with

himself. "Got it reappraised after the remodel, and even with my outlay of cash, I'm still in the black. That plus an ocean view. I consider it a win."

"Not bad," Jack said. "Syl and Jackson?" He almost hesitated to ask the question. Probably someone he should remember.

"Jackson Steele. He's a pretty famous architect. Ring any bells?"

"Not even a tingle."

"Jackson's Damien's half-brother. He designed The Domino, actually."

"*That* I remember. The business park where the SSA is located. Was in the news for a few years while it was in development, right?"

Liam nodded. "I'm impressed," he said as he headed into the kitchen. "Coffee?"

"Thanks. Black is good." He moved to the back wall composed of glass sliders. "It's weird what I remember. I know who's president. I remember the oceans and continents, and I know the plot of at least a half dozen *Star Wars* movies."

Liam laughed. "Not surprised. Denise is a huge *Star Wars* fan."

Jack frowned, then looked back over his shoulder, and saw a flicker of something cross over Liam's face. Like he was irritated with himself.

"Denise? So, she and I saw a lot of the movies together?"

"You were partners," Liam said evenly, his

attention on the coffee pot. "And you both like action movies and fantasy."

"Huh." Jack turned back toward the ocean, wondering what it was about Liam's response that made him feel so off. Like he should remember something. Like maybe he wasn't as honorable a guy as he liked to think and he'd taken his partner to the movies, not simply as casual friends, but for the pleasure of sitting next to her in the dark, their fingers brushing over the popcorn.

Fucking hell...

"Were Denise and I—"

From over the pass-through bar, Liam looked at him, his expression bland. "Say again?"

"Nothing. Just wondering if we worked well together."

"I never worked with the two of you, but from what she says, you guys made a great team."

He nodded, pleased that he'd managed to divert his own misstep before Liam noticed. And irritated that his thoughts had zeroed in on Denise Marshall with such laser-like intensity. Not because she was his partner, but, damn him, because he craved her.

There. He said it. Maybe not out loud, but he'd voiced the words in his head. Words he'd been dancing around since the first moment she'd walked into his little cell of a room at the SOC.

And now here he was, about to start working in close proximity to her.

All of which made him a fucking idiot, because the part of his body that he needed to kick-start was the memory centers of his brain. Not his damn cock. And the last thing he wanted to do was insult her or the memory of her husband.

If he was a better man, he would have stayed away. Not approached Seagrave with his plan to spur his memory at all. But he couldn't deny that spending time with her had been at least as appealing as the possibility of sparking his memory. And definitely more certain.

He sighed, looking out over the Pacific. "Sometimes I wonder if I forgot myself because I'm just that much of an asshole."

Liam frowned. "Come again?"

He waved the words away. "Sorry. Pity party. Ignore me."

"Yeah, well, if anyone deserves one, it's you." He stepped out from behind the counter with two mugs and handed one to Jack.

"Thanks. And thanks for letting me stay here. You sure I'm not putting you out? Wife? Girlfriend?"

"Just me." There was a hard edge to Liam's voice. The kind of edge that hinted at secrets. And had Jack shifting the conversation. He might be curious, but he wasn't about to piss off his host.

Especially not since he hoped that host would grow into a friend.

Liam cleared his throat. "Let's get you settled, then I need to head back for my team meeting. Denise is picking you up this evening right?"

Jack nodded, then held up the duffel that contained all his belongings in the world. "I'd like to own more than one pair of jeans and an extra pair of skivvies. Thought I'd grab an Uber and pull out the shiny new ID and credit card Seagrave arranged for me. That is, if you don't mind giving me a spare key."

"It's a keypad lock," Liam said, telling him the code. "And no need for a ride share. You can handle a bike?"

"Let me guess. A Harley?"

"If that's your poison. There's one in the garage. A Ducati, too, along with a few other beauties. Keys are on the hook by the fridge. But don't touch the Bonneville. I just finished restoring her, and I always take the inaugural ride."

Jack's grin stretched so wide his cheeks hurt. "Liam, my man, I think I'm going to like crashing here."

———

He didn't need much. Considering he had no closet of his own, Jack only intended to buy the bare minimum. A clean pair of jeans without rips in the knees. A couple of decent T-shirts so he didn't look like he'd raided his grandfather's closet. Figure of speech, that. He didn't even know if he had a grandfather.

Shoes. A razor. A toothbrush.

Nothing but the essentials. Get in, get out, get back to Liam's and do a little prep work on Cerise Sinclair, thanks to Ryan agreeing to shoot the encrypted files to the spare laptop Liam had left for him. Not strictly necessary—Ryan had assured him the matter was simple enough that Denise could brief him on the way—but Jack didn't intend to slack. If he was on the team, he was doing the job.

Besides, Denise had already seen him at his worst. He wanted her to know that he was also sharp, efficient, and always prepared.

He remembered that there was a mall in Century City, an unremarkable memory for most people, but one that had him fighting the urge to do a victory dance. It turned out to be of the Pyrrhic variety, however, because he quickly learned how much he hated shopping. The only point was to acquire clothes and other necessities, and yet as far as he could tell, the stores wanted to make the process a multimedia experience.

And if one more rail thin woman asked to spray him with some new cologne that she assured him was manly, he feared he'd have to break something.

He ended up escaping with a single pair of jeans, a gray Henley, a sport coat, shoes, and a package of underwear. After that, he hit a drugstore for bathroom essentials. As he was heading toward the checkout, he passed a display of condoms—and immediately his mind filled with images of Denise Marshall. Not X-rated. Not even NC-17. But definitely a strong R-rating.

He was in so goddamn much trouble.

He drew a deep breath, told himself that he had bigger things to worry about than getting laid, lectured himself on the importance of being a professional, and then got the hell away from the display as fast as he possibly could.

By the time the doorbell rang at six that evening, he'd cleaned up, changed, reviewed the Sinclair file, and resisted the urge to plug Denise and Mason's names into Google.

For a while, anyway.

He'd originally justified the urge by telling himself that she knew a hell of a lot more about him than he knew about her. But that was bullshit, of course. What he really wanted was to see what made her tick. *Who* made her tick.

He wanted to find out about Mason—and he wanted to find out almost as much as he didn't want to be the kind of asshole who'd do that.

So he'd backed away from the computer.

And then, dammit, he'd come to terms with the

thought of being a prick. He'd run five searches and he didn't find a thing. Not one single thing. Not a name. Not a picture. Not a half-assed remark in someone else's Twitter stream.

Nothing.

So he ran more. Looked deeper. Harder.

Crickets. Not even a hint.

Which mean that Mason had been a ghost. A high-level operative who was placed in key, long-term, undercover missions. The kind of guy who, for every one of him, there were at least fifty other agents parked at computers across the world whose job entailed nothing more than making sure he was completely erased from the web, the deep web, the dark web, and all the layers in-between.

More than that, it meant that Mason could still be alive.

He frowned, trying to remember his earlier conversation with Denise. She still wore his ring, and she'd told him—*what?*

Not that her husband was dead. All Denise had said was that he'd been gone for a very long time. Jack had assumed the rest.

With a sigh, he leaned back in his chair, and once again condemned himself as a prick. He'd just learned that his partner's husband—a man who by all accounts had been his friend—might well be alive. He should be happy. He should be scheming ways to learn the truth, even if it pissed off

Seagrave and the rest of them. Because God knew Jack didn't have anything to lose at this point.

He should be doing anything other sitting there numb and feeling like a little boy who just learned that Christmas was canceled.

Asshole.

Yeah, that's right. He needed to just own it. He was a fucked-up, horny, prick who hadn't been laid in God knew how long. He met a woman he was attracted to—a woman who turned out to be off-limits—and that fact offended his apparently Neanderthal sensibilities.

Well, too bad for him.

Because in the grand scheme of things, he had a lot more important things to worry about. Like, oh, who he was and what he'd been working on. Everything else could wait, and if that meant he took two cold showers a day, then so be it.

For that matter, he should probably take one right now...

Ding!

He frowned, the sharp chime of the doorbell reminding him that he was all out of time. "Coming!" he called before stopping by the bathroom to splash some cold water on his face.

Then he hurried down the stairs, only to stop short when he saw her standing in the entrance hall.

"Sorry," she said. "I was already inside by the

time I realized you'd probably said *coming*, not *come in*."

"It's all good," he said. "I'd offer you something to eat or drink, but it's not my kitchen, not my food."

"No worries." Her grin lit up her eyes making them spark like green flame. Christ, but she was lovely. "But if you need a tour of Liam's kitchen, I'm happy to walk you through."

A nip of jealousy grabbed hold of him, like some irritating little mongrel he couldn't shake loose. "You hang out here a lot?"

"I'm the plant and fish girl." She laughed, obviously in response to his expression. "I stay here when Liam's out of town. I like walking on the beach. And I'm not all that crazy about my house anymore." She met his eyes, then looked away quickly, as if she didn't want him to see her secrets.

"The house you shared with Mason."

"We never got around to fixing it up. And it's lonely without—him."

He had the impression she'd been about to say something else, though he couldn't imagine what. "And that ties in to plants and fish how?"

"You obviously haven't seen Liam's room. Come on."

She took the stairs two at a time, passing the open door to his bedroom, and continuing up to the master bedroom that took up the entire third floor.

The minute he stepped through the door, he understood what she meant. Small potted plants dotted the room, but it was the outdoors that truly drew his attention. The balcony was covered with greenery. Not in an overbearing way, but in a way that made the outdoor space welcoming and pleasant for anyone who wanted to sit out there and watch the surf.

He thought of Liam—big, muscular Liam—sitting at the small metal table sipping coffee, and had to grin.

"Bet if you had to guess what was on his balcony you would have gone with a weight bench and a punching bag."

"Pretty much," he agreed. "And the fish?"

"Oh, the fish are especially cool." She cocked her head, and then led him into the huge master bath, where one entire wall was a giant seawater fish tank filled with stunning, colorful sea life.

"That's incredible."

"I know, right? When I stay here to plant and fish-sit, I sleep in the guest room. But I told Liam that he had to let me use the master bath. It's just too fun."

"Jackson Steele did this?"

"Liam told you about the remodel? Yeah. I keep thinking I'll ask Jackson to come up with something equally awesome for my house. But then..." She didn't shrug, but her overly casual smile worked equally as well as a dismissal.

He didn't take the bait. "You didn't want to work on the house alone."

She turned back toward the fish, and for a moment, he thought she wasn't going to answer. He was about to apologize for pushing too hard, when she said very softly. "No. No, I was wa—"

"Waiting for Mason to come home? He's alive, isn't he?"

She'd shifted, returning her attention to him. "I never said he was dead."

"But you knew I'd think it. And for awhile, I think you believed it."

Her brow furrowed as she studied him. "What makes you say that?"

"You looked so haunted when you'd said he'd been gone a long time. Anyway, it doesn't matter. The point is that he's not dead, is he?"

"No." Her throat moved as she swallowed. "He's not."

"I'm glad for you." He meant the words. He had no desire to hurt her. But they still left him hollow. "He was on an undercover assignment, right? Deep cover?"

"How do you know that?"

"A guess, but clearly a good one. If he was in deep cover, how can you be sure he's alive? Has he made contact?"

She drew in a breath, then looked him straight in the eyes. "Yes," she said. "Twice. And you know enough about that world to know I shouldn't be talking about it. Which means this conversation is done."

"Fair enough."

She glanced at her phone, then frowned. "We need to hurry if we're going to meet Cerise on time."

"Want me to drive?" He still had the Ducati's key in his pocket, and now he dangled it. He was teasing, of course. He knew damn well they'd take her car.

Which was why her delighted laugh and eager nod threw him completely off guard. So off that he couldn't prevent the words that burst into his head, terrifying in their truth—*Damn, but he could fall hard for this woman.*

9

"I FORGOT about the hills and curves," I shout as I cling to Mason—*Jack!*—while he expertly navigates the Hollywood Hills. "Take your next left, then an immediate right."

He may have lost his memory, but he hasn't lost his skill on a bike, and I'd be lying if I said I wasn't enjoying this chance to hold onto my husband. His well-muscled body fits perfectly against mine, and I keep my arms tight around him, my chin resting on his shoulder as we sail over streets carved from these tree-covered hills.

Cerise's house sits at the rise of one of the steepest hills, and I press my thighs more firmly against Jack's hips, holding on as we creep up the hill at an obscene angle. Her place is lovely—three levels of stucco and wood with an incredible view of Universal Studios and the valley beyond—but access is a challenge, and this isn't a route I'd want to navigate daily.

Nor is it a home I'd want if I was worrying about stalkers. It may be hard to get to, but it's also hard to leave. Her road is a dead end, and her only neighbor is an elderly man who spent his youth working on television sitcoms.

The three lots that surround her property are for sale, but so far no buyer has been interested in tackling the engineering nightmare that comes with building on such steep lots, particularly with the hassle of getting equipment up these narrow streets.

"Still," Jack says when I run all of that by him, "that's one hell of a view."

He's right. And for a moment we stand at the side of the road in front of the bike, looking past the house to the view beyond. "Some consolation for living up here," I say. "All the same, I think I'd choose the beach."

"Or your place?"

I frown. I love my house—I do. But I love a vision of it that may never come to fruition. And that's not something I want to talk about with Jack. Especially not with Jack.

Instead, I divert the conversation, lifting a shoulder and saying simply, "Neither hills nor beach. I'm a sad example of a real estate maven."

"I don't think you're a sad example of anything." There's something soft and familiar in his voice, and I turn without thinking to face him, then draw in a tight breath at the look in his eye. A familiar glint of humor and passion. The kind of look that was usually followed by a swift tug on my arm to pull me close, a firm grip on my ass, and the kind of hot kiss that would melt me right into bed.

I swallow a strangled gasp and yank my gaze away, suddenly fascinated with the cuff of my jeans.

"Denise, I—"

The rumble and squeak of the rising garage door cuts off his words, and I silently thank Cerise for her ill-timed appearance. She's standing inside the garage, and she bends down to slip under the door, then waves at us.

The wind has caught her silky, black hair, and she pushes a wild curl out of her eyes. "What on earth are you doing out here? I saw you pull up and got tired of waiting. Your bike?" she asks, eyeing Mason in a way that makes my girl parts sit up and start growling.

"Cerise," I say, forcing myself to be polite, "this is Jack Sawyer, my new partner. I wanted to introduce you and let him take a peek at the equipment. And we both want to hear whatever it is you wanted to talk about. Ryan was rather vague."

"Oh, sure." She hugs herself and flashes an

extremely photogenic smile at Jack. I tense, forcing myself not to sidle next to him and hook my arm possessively through his.

"Are you having trouble with the system?" I ask as she leads us inside through the garage.

"Not really," she says with a small frown. "I don't think to check the video that often, but since the feed goes direct to your monitoring station, I feel pretty confident." She looks over her shoulder as we move down the back hall toward the main living area. "I know setting me up was small potatoes for Stark Security, but it's made me feel a lot safer knowing your staff monitors the feed."

"That's the point," I say. She's right, of course. For the most part, the SSA takes on high-end assignments. But Damien's always been adamant about the SSA being service-oriented. Which is why we also provide basic security service for celebrities at events and home security for anyone who walks through the door and can afford the equipment and monthly fee. And a few people who can't, if Damien or Ryan approve the cost, as I've seen them do for a number of near-destitute women who were being harassed by their ex-husbands or boyfriends.

"No one's been too obnoxious in person," Cerise continues, "but some of the online comments..." She trails off, her nose wrinkling.

"I get it," I assure her. I'm not online much, but I have a very good imagination. "So, all in all you feel safe up here? You're pretty isolated."

"That's part of what I like," she says. "I really do love this place. That's why—" She cuts herself off with a shake of her head. "I'm probably just being paranoid."

"It's usually someone who thinks they're paranoid who gets kicked in the nuts," Jack says.

"Well, then I'm safe," Cerise quips, making me laugh.

"What do you think you're being paranoid about?" Jack asks.

She drags her finger through her hair. "I saw someone last night, way down the hill. But he was just out of camera range. I checked the feed, and it cut off before the dip. Right there," she adds, pointing down. "It's not even my property, which is why I figure I shouldn't worry about it. Probably a homeless person. Or maybe the owner was walking the property. Thinking about clearing brush or something. The sun was behind the hills, but it wasn't pitch black yet."

"Maybe," I say. I don't mention that the lot is currently owned by the bank. So there's no owner who could be wandering it at night.

"Peter said it was probably a coyote and not a man at all," she adds, a blush rising on her fair skin.

"But he said I should call you if that would make me feel better."

I grin, amused. "Peter?"

Her whole face lights up at the question. "He's fabulous. We've been seeing each other on and off for a while, but now..." She trails off and sighs happily. "Well, I think he wants to get serious."

"That's great," I say. "Congratulations."

"Thanks." She hooks a thumb toward the kitchen. "Do you want some wine? I'd just opened a bottle before you got here."

We agree, and she returns a moment later with three glasses hung by the stems in one hand and a bottle of red in the other.

"To you and Peter," I say after she pours.

"And to tightening up your camera array," Jack adds.

"Oh, I almost forgot," she says after taking a long sip. "I'm meeting Peter tonight at Wester-field's. I told him all about how you worked with me to get the house security set up, and how I feel so much safer now, and we thought it would be fun if you came, too." She looks at Jack. "Even better now that you'll have a date."

"Ah, well..." Jack looks at me, his expression decidedly uncomfortable. My stomach does that unpleasant flipping thing again, but why wouldn't I be a little nauseous at the realization that my own husband is disgusted by the idea of going out with me?

I stiffen as I say, "I don't think we—"

"Of course, we'll come," Jack says, talking boldly over me. "We'd be thrilled."

10

I PARTED ways with Jack after we returned to Liam's so that I could go home and change. Now, I arrive at the West Hollywood club alone. The line, as always, is down the block, but mine is one of the names permanently on the VIP list—a perk of working for Damien Stark, who owns the popular hotspot. Not that he comes often anymore. With two little girls, I don't think he and Nikki frequent the club scene.

I step inside, then pause, letting the music wash over me. I glance around for Jack, but don't see him. I do, however, catch sight of Cass. With a grin, I head that direction.

"Hey, stranger," I say, letting her pull me into a hug. "Am I interrupting a date?" I look around for a girl who might be with Cass, hoping that she's moving on after the bullshit with Siobhan. But she shakes her head and gives me *the look*.

"I'm not even playing the field," she says. "I only came for the awesome company."

"So this isn't a coincidence?" At the same time I ask the question, Quince and Eliza approach, and I actually clap my hands, delighted.

Quince is carrying two drinks, one of which he passes to Cass before hooking his free arm around my shoulders and giving me a squeeze.

"Hell of a way to start the weekend, eh?" His British accent is more pronounced than usual, so I figure this isn't his first drink of the evening.

I look between the three of them. "This isn't a coincidence, right? Not that I'm complaining."

"Cerise called," Cass says simply. "Said she'd invited you and Jack and that I should come down, too. Then she asked me to invite Syl and Jamie and their guys, but obviously Syl's already left the country."

"So Jamie and Ryan are coming?"

"That would be big, fat no."

She's grinning when she says it, and I narrow my eyes, wondering at the joke. "Well?" I prod.

"Oh, right. Jamie's exact quote was that she already had Ryan naked, and that while we were all a lot of fun, he was better."

I slam my hands over my ears in mock horror. "I did *not* need to hear that about my boss."

"You asked," Cass says.

"And I should have known better," I admit. I love Jamie, but the woman has no filter at all. "Where's Cerise?"

"Around here somewhere," Quince says. "She's got her boyfriend with her, so you might check dark corners."

Beside him, Eliza gives him an elbow nudge.

"What?" he asks. "You know I'm right."

Cass laughs, then points at Quince and Eliza while still talking to me. "I didn't know they'd be here. So I consider them a perk. And a comedy show, too. All rolled into one."

"Funny girl," Quince says, making Cass grin.

Quince drags over an extra chair, and we all squeeze in around the small cocktail table. Cass slides her drink my direction. "Want to share until we can get a waiter's attention?"

I take it, ready to start Friday right, but just the smell of the whiskey makes my stomach roll, and I decide to stick with water, hoping that whatever bug has taken up residence in my stomach gets bored and moves out quickly.

Still, probably best to stay sober, especially since Jack should be here soon.

As if he's reading my mind, Quince says, "How are you coping?"

I shrug. "I disarmed a nuclear weapon once. Did you know that?"

He shakes his head.

"That was easier."

"Denny..."

I manage a half-smile, feeling even more sorry for myself at the sound of my name on his lips. Not that I mind Quince adopting the nickname. But it was Mason who first started calling me Denny, and his are the lips I want to hear it from.

Beside Quince, Eliza leans forward. "I'm so sorry you have to deal with this."

"I appreciate that," I say, and I mean it. But at the same time I don't want to talk about how hard it is. Because that just makes it harder.

In an effort to deflect the attention off me—and because I'm legitimately curious—I ask if they've heard from Emma. Eliza's sister was at the center of the case Quince and I just wrapped. Now she's in Europe, returning a kidnapped princess to her monarch father.

"I talked to her this morning," Eliza says. "So far, the trip's gone smoothly."

"Has she decided what she's going to do?" Emma's a private investigator with a seriously badass covert ops background. Basically, my job is as boring as alphabetizing an old-fashioned card catalog compared to some of the stuff Emma has handled in the course of her career.

Which means she'd be a hell of an asset to the

SSA, and I really hope she decides to come on board.

Meanwhile, I look around for my not-covert, not-badass client, and finally see her talking with a guy on the far side of the room. They're in shadows, so I can't see his face, but something about him looks familiar. I'm about to stand up and go talk with them when I catch sight of Jack heading my way from the other side of the room. And, of course, the sight of him erases every other thought from my head.

I'm not even exaggerating. Nor am I surprised.

The first time I saw Mason, I'd been walking into an NSC briefing at the Pentagon. A room full of the most powerful people in the country, including me, newly-anointed to go out into the world to fight terrorism at its root.

But did I act the part of the well-trained badass?

Well, actually, I did. That's where the "well-trained" part comes in. Because the moment I saw Mason sitting at that table, all rational thought left my head. Suddenly, I was just a girl in high school crushing on the cute guy. The smart guy. The clever guy. *The perfect guy*.

And when I found out that he felt the same way about me...

Well, for Mason and me, there was no slow burn. We were combustible from the first moment we were together. And it kills me—absolutely slays me—that he can walk so casually across this club, sidle up to me, and say nothing more engaging than, "Fancy meeting you here."

Honestly, it's not even that cute a line.

Where's the man who could make me come with a heated look?

Who'd tug me into a dark corner for stolen kisses or even naughtier moments?

The man who could shut that all down during a mission, then release every trapped desire the moment we wrapped, fucking me for hours in our bed until we were both exhausted and sated?

I want that man back as much as I want the guy who'd drink wine with me on the sofa while we watched reruns of *Firefly*. The guy who'd bore me to tears spending hours in Home Depot comparing paint colors for the bathroom. The guy who knew how to grill a steak better than any five star chef.

In other words, I want my husband. Mason, not Jack. The man who remembers he loves me. The man with whom I'd shared a life. A history. The man who knew my secrets and my fears, my hopes and desires.

But Mason is gone, and it's Jack standing beside me. Jack with whom I have to play a role, when all I want is to go home and cry.

"Denise?" He's peering at me, his brow furrowed. "You okay?"

"Tired," I say. "And sober. I've got a stomach bug or something and alcohol is not sitting well."

He flashes a grin, revealing his dimple. "That is a tragedy. How about I take the edge off and—"

We don't get to the *and*.

Instead, we're interrupted by the arrival of Cerise and her companion.

He isn't in the shadows now—in fact the whole club fills with wild, flashing lights. The beams bounce with the music as they crisscross the dance floor, illuminating every inch of his all-too familiar face.

"Peter," I squeal as I throw myself into his outstretched arms.

"Denise!" He hugs me tight, then pushes me away so that his hands are on my shoulders and I'm grinning up at him like an idiot. "I had no idea you were in LA."

"Same," I say. "This is amazing."

"I'm sorry," Cerise says. "You know each other?"

Peter and I exchange glances. And with perfect timing, we look back at Cerise. "Nope," we say, then start laughing all over again.

11

I'm STILL GRINNING when Jack approaches, but my smile fades when I see the way he's rubbing his temples. Peter's hand rests on my shoulder, and I slip out from under his touch, then approach Jack, lightly brushing his arm as I try to read the expression in his eyes. "Are you okay?"

He gives a little half-shake of his head, his expression one of mild annoyance. Not at me, I don't think, but at his own discomfort. "I think it's the damn lights. They started flashing, and it's like needles to my eyes."

"You're not prone to migraines," I say.

"Aren't I?"

I bite back a wince, realizing how close I came to giving away too much. But it's reasonable that I'd know if my partner suffered from migraines. Still, I need to be more careful.

Now, though, I just shrug. "Not that I've seen before."

"Probably a symptom," he says. "My already battered brain doesn't like the crazy disco lights."

"Trust me," I say dryly. "It's not just you. Welcome to Friday at a club." I sweep my arm out to encompass the entire room, noticing as I do that Cerise has moved a few feet away and is laughing with a group of women I've never met before.

"Speaking of welcome," Peter says, waving for Jack's attention. "It's great to see you again, M—"

"*Jack,*" I say firmly, speaking loudly on top of Peter before he can announce Mason's real name. "Jack, this is Peter."

"Am I missing the joke?" Peter asks, looking between the two of us.

"Jack's having a little trouble with his memory."

"Which is the polite way of saying that I'm a blank slate," he puts in. "And we're sharing this information why?"

"It's okay. Peter and I worked together for about a year in Washington before I moved over to the SOC."

"Obviously, I don't remember you," Jack says. "Sorry about that."

Peter shakes his head. "No worries. I would say your little problem is an occupational hazard, but the truth is that I haven't seen this before. Heard of it. But I always assumed the stories were urban legend."

"A story they tell about bad little agents?" Jack quips, making Peter laugh.

"Is that what you were?"

Jack shrugs. "How the hell do I know?"

Peter chuckles. "I see you kept your sense of humor."

"Did we work together, too?"

Peter shakes his head. "No. We only met the one time when you two got m—"

"Medals of commendation," I interrupt, shooting Peter a sharp glance, in response to which he looks sufficiently contrite. We don't actually have any medals of commendation, and even if we did I don't know why Peter would have come to the ceremony. But thankfully Jack doesn't seem interested in the point. Or in Peter or I for that matter. On the contrary, he's looking at something across the room, his brow furrowed as if in confusion.

"The lights still?" There's no laser light show at the moment, but there is a colorful disco ball that's casting moving circles of light on the walls and floor.

"Mind if I borrow Denise for a second?" Jack says, to which Peter shrugs and says he'll go freshen his drink.

"What's going on?" I ask, waving off Cass who's started to head in our direction.

"I'm not sure." He nods toward the dance floor. "When the lights started, I thought I saw..."

"What?"

He shakes his head. "I don't know. A face."

"A face?"

He meets my eyes. "A face."

"We're in a club. There are a lot of faces."

"I don't know why it struck me. I can't even find it again in the crowd. I'm not even sure if it was a man or a woman, much less real. Maybe it was just a shadow. A mirage in the dark."

"But you don't think so." It's a statement, not a question.

"I think it's a memory. I think there's someone here with us that I remember. Or that my mind is trying to remember."

"From your past? Or from your mission?" I'm assuming the latter. And I'm trying not to let my feelings get hurt because he's semi-remembered a shadowy face before he remembered his wife.

"From my torture," he says flatly. "I saw that face, and my blood ran cold."

My hurt feelings are pushed away by guilt, and I take his hand. "We'll find him. We'll find him," I repeat, "and we'll get some answers."

"I'm going to make a few rounds through the club, then I'm going to head back to Liam's. I know tomorrow's Saturday, but I'd like to work. Maybe go over some of our old files. See if that triggers any new memories. Okay?"

"Of course. Meet you in the office around ten?"

"I'll be there," he says, then slips into the dark.

I stand there for a moment, letting the beat of the music pound through me. I want to follow him. I want to take his shoulders and look into his eyes and tell him everything.

But I can't. And I hate how impotent I feel.

I turn with a sigh, intending to go to the bar for a tonic and lime. Instead, I find Peter behind me. "You okay?"

"Sure. Where's Cerise?"

"Ladies' room." He holds out his hand. "Dance?"

I shake my head. "Not in the mood."

"A pity. I am."

"I'm sure Cerise will be up for it when she gets back. I like her a lot," I tell Peter. "But she doesn't seem to be your type."

"That's because you were always my type."

I mentally kick myself. I should never have opened that door. Peter and I worked in the same field office and got along great. But the times we partnered for a mission together, I was never at my best. I could feel the attraction rolling off him. And while Mason's interest in me never got in the way of our work, it was a distraction with Peter. The difference, of course, was that I wasn't in love with

Peter, and so I didn't trust him the way you trust a true partner. And Mason always was a true partner, even before we became involved.

"Peter..."

He holds his hands out in surrender. "I know. Just friends. Don't worry. I'm over you. I'm just stating a fact. And Cerise is a doll. I really do adore her."

"I'm glad to hear it. She's not just a client. She's a friend."

"So why aren't you telling him the truth?"

It's a total flip in the conversation, but I follow his thread easily. "You know I can't give you details. Let's just say it's protocol."

He nods, then steps back, his eyes looking me up and down. I'm wearing jeans and a plain white tank top, and the heat in Peter's eyes is the kind I want to see in Jack's.

His gaze stops at my wrist, where Mason's name has been recently inked. "Who does he think that is?"

I draw in a shaky breath. "My husband. Who may or may not be dead."

"Makes it rough for you, doesn't it?"

This time, I can't follow his thoughts, because everything about my life and Mason is rough right now. "What do you mean?"

"I saw the way he looked at you. Guy's hot for you. And looks to me like you want him, too."

I swallow. "Where are you going with this?"

"Same place you are—nowhere. Because you're too honorable a woman to cheat on your husband. Which means that you can't cheat with your husband. No matter how much you want to." He's got about six inches on me, and he uses the tip of his finger to tilt my chin up. He locks his gaze with mine and flashes a wicked grin. "Or are you planning to fuck him anyway?"

With effort, I resist the urge to reach up and slap his face. Instead, I say, "This is why you and I never got together. I prefer my men with a bit of character."

"What can I say? You bring out the worst in me."

"Try to keep it inside," I say, then turn and walk away. I don't see Quince or Eliza, but Cass is laughing with a cute blonde by the bar. I catch her eye, then point toward the door. She lifts her hand to her ear in a "call me" gesture, and I nod. I'll give her a buzz tomorrow. Right now, I'm heading home.

On the sidewalk, I lean against a signpost as I tap my phone and order an Uber. It's five minutes away, and I take a moment to close my eyes, draw a breath, and enjoy the sounds of the night.

The cool steel of a blade presses against my throat and my eyes fly open. I stay perfectly still, trying not to breathe, and cursing myself for inexplicably dropping my guard.

Whoever is holding the knife is behind me. About my height, and his hand doesn't shake, so it's clear he knows how to handle a knife.

When he leans in close to my ear, I catch the smell of jalapeños and tequila, and I make a note to have one of the tech team pull the receipts from Westerfield's and use the security feed to match them with patrons. Maybe I'll get lucky.

"I'm not the only one who can get to you," the man whispers. "Keep that in mind. Tell him he needs to remember. If he wants you to stay safe—to stay alive—he needs to give back what he took. Tell him."

"Who?"

"Cunt," he says, and I gasp as the knife presses harder. There will be a thin line of blood on my neck, I'm certain of it. "You know who." But then, as if he wants to be sure there's no confusion, he whispers, "Mason Walker. You tell him. You tell him you're a dead woman walking unless he comes through."

Something hard smacks my head, knocking me forward at the same time he yanks the knife away. An instant later, he shoves the back of my neck and I fall to my knees as a black Lexus squeals to a halt, and he turns just enough for me to see greasy hair, bushy eyebrows, and a bulbous nose. Then he leaps in. The car races away down Sunset Boulevard, the Arkansas plate undoubtedly stolen.

I stumble to my feet at the same time my Uber arrives, and I climb in, draw a breath, and pull out my phone.

12

It was almost three in the morning, and Jack still hadn't made it back to Liam's place. He'd left Westerfield's intending to return to the Malibu condo, but instead he'd let the bike take him where it wanted to go.

Or, more accurately, where his subconscious wanted to go.

He assumed he'd lived in LA before they'd stolen his memory, but no one had specifically told him that. Hell, no one had told him shit. And even though he knew the reasons, it was still damn hard to stomach.

So he drove the streets of Los Angeles County, praying that some spark of familiarity would strike him.

He recognized a lot of things. Malls. Restaurants. Tourist attractions. He remembered The

Getty Center and the Santa Monica Pier, the MOCA downtown, and Rodeo Drive in Beverly Hills.

He didn't wander the hiking trails off Laurel Canyon, but he had a feeling that if he did, he'd remember every twist and turn. And when he closed his eyes he could almost remember the swell of music bursting from the Hollywood Bowl amphitheater.

Goddammit, he wanted his mind back. His life back.

Unbidden, Denise popped into his thoughts, and he swerved the bike onto one of the Mulholland Drive turnouts, killed the engine, and let his head fall down to rest on the handlebars.

There it was—a living, breathing reason why he had to get his memory back, and sooner rather than later. Because damned if he didn't want her. If he hadn't wanted her from the first moment he'd seen her. And the hunger for her was only getting stronger with each passing minute.

He'd stood in that club tonight surrounded by beautiful women in revealing dresses and low-cut shirts, and he hadn't felt the slightest twinge of interest. Then he saw Denise in her simple jeans and plain white tank top and he'd just about lost his shit. The way the denim hugged the curve of her ass. The way the white of the tank contrasted her tan skin. The hint of bra he could see when she bent to put her drink on the table. The sweet curve of her lips when she smiled at him.

His fingers had itched to touch her, and he'd closed his eyes and imagined what every silky inch of her body would feel like against his fingers, his lips, his cock.

And when he'd seen her with Peter ... well, that had really fueled the fire.

God, he was an asshole.

She trusted him as her partner. She was helping him pull his life back together. Most of all, she belonged to another man. And yet there he was, fantasizing about getting her naked and beneath him.

No. He drew in a breath and sat up straight. *No, that wasn't entirely true.* He wanted her—damned if he didn't—but not just physically. He wanted to be with her. Wanted to talk with her, walk with her. Laugh at silly things and soothe her through the sad ones.

He didn't know if this was new or if he'd been enthralled by her for months. All he knew was that whatever barriers had held him back before seemed to be crumbling.

Most of all, he knew that if he wasn't careful, this uncontrollable infatuation would be the death knell of a friendship that he cherished.

A wave of exhaustion overtook him, and he yawned deeply, then pulled out his phone to check the time, only then realizing that he'd turned the thing off in the club and forgot to turn it back on. What was the point considering he'd been with Denny, and barely even knew half a dozen other people?

Even so, he switched it back on. Almost immediately it emitted a cacophony of buzzes and pings signaling missed texts and phone calls.

He glanced at the screen, saw that almost all the calls and messages came from Liam, and started to dial his host back, feeling like an ass for making Liam worry about his whereabouts.

The call hadn't even connected before headlights appeared behind him. He ended the call, then turned, squinting into the lights from an SUV that he couldn't identify in the glare. The door opened, and a mountain of a man stepped out.

Jack didn't have a weapon, but he flipped on the bike's ignition, prepared to speed away if he needed to.

The man walked forward, his back to the SUV's headlights so that his face was in shadows. "Christ, Jack. What the fuck have you been doing?"

Liam.

"I tried calling, but your phone's off. I had to log into the tracker I keep on the Ducati. I've been tailing you for almost an hour. What the hell are you doing riding in circles around the damn city?"

Jack dismounted, trying to process everything

Liam was saying. "I should have called—sorry. I just needed a ride in the fresh air to blow out some of the shit floating around in my head."

"I hear you, and normally I wouldn't play babysitter, but Denise was freaked when she couldn't get a hold of you, so I—"

"Wait. What?" He took a step toward Liam. "What happened? Why was she calling? Why was she freaked?"

"Somebody attacked her outside the club. A man, she says. She's fine," he added quickly, holding up a hand to forestall Jack's burst of terror and fury. "But she said it might have been your face?" He shook his head. "She didn't explain, but she did say that you'd understand. And that the bastard told her that you needed to remember. That you needed to return what you took. Ring any bells?"

"Not a goddamn one." And now Jack was kicking himself for not trying harder to track the Face down in the club.

"Well, I told her I'd find you."

"I need to go to her."

Liam took a step toward him. "No, she's asleep. As soon as the bike pinged on the tracking map, I called. Said I'd catch up to you and that she should get some sleep. I finally got her to agree—she sounded bone tired—and she said she'd see you at the office at ten."

Jack nodded slowly, considering. "Fine. Then I'll show up at her house at eight."

"Jack..."

"Best I can do, man. May as well not even bother arguing."

Liam chuckled. "Fine. I'll let Denise shoot you down. God knows she's capable."

"Hey," Jack said. "Thanks for running me to ground. Sorry to lead you all over the city. I had a lot of thinking to do."

"No surprise there. Just glad I found you."

"How'd your job go tonight? Security for Ellie Love, right? I heard on the radio that the concert was a sell-out. I like a few of her songs. She as good live as they say?"

Liam shook his head, looking a little frazzled. Jack didn't know him well, but he had a feeling that frazzled wasn't a usual state for Liam. "For such a tiny woman, she's got some serious pipes. And one hell of a lot of talent. She's also a royal pain in the ass with some serious attitude, but as it's SSA policy not to speak ill of a client, you didn't hear it from me."

Jack chuckled. "Sorry about that."

Liam shook his head, looking both amused and exasperated. "Honestly, man, I still don't know what to think of her, and I didn't see a damn thing that suggested a threat, so I don't know what game she or her manager was playing. But the woman's like a damn force of nature, and woe to anybody who tries to get her to do something she doesn't want to do. But at least it's over. A one-night gig and the cord was cut. I don't expect she'll be back in LA until she puts out her next album."

"And maybe then she'll hire some other security company."

Liam's teeth shone in the moonlight with his smile. "We can hope." He pointed at the bike. "Stay out as long as you want, but keep your damn phone on, okay?"

"Deal," Jack said, then waited until Liam and his SUV disappeared over the hill.

Then he dialed the phone, feeling absolutely no guilt when a groggy voice answered with a sleepy, "Hello?"

"It's Jack," he said. "How soon can you meet me?"

———

Despite seeing him at four in the morning, Dr. Tam looked completely awake and perfectly put together. Jack had to give her props; she hadn't protested when he'd insisted on the early morning emergency session.

Then again, he had a sneaking suspicion that he might be the most pressing unanswered question at the SOC at the moment, so helping him was in everyone's best interest.

"So this man, this face, triggered a reaction," Dr. Tam commented. "But you don't have any specific memory?"

"None. And I need to know where I've seen him. I need to figure out who he is. Name. Location. Anything. This fucker attacked Denise and he's going to do more unless I reveal something I don't even remember. So, dammit, make me remember. Use hypnosis if you need to."

Dr. Tam leaned forward, her elbows on her knees. "Jack, we've talked about this. Walking you through your memories—something you reported or something we can find in hypnosis—is dangerous. We could literally short-circuit your memory centers. You've seen the videos."

"I saw. But I've also poked around online, and despite what happened to those men, the technique has a high success rate."

"You poked around online?" Her brows rose above her glasses. "You managed to log into the government's confidential files regarding memory work and treatment with affected intelligence officers? Because my guess is that you're looking at bullshit articles that your phone pulled up with Google. I know you're good at your job, Mr. Sawyer, and with time, I'm sure you could find the right files. But you haven't found them yet, or you'd know I'm telling you the truth."

She was right, of course. And while he wanted to shout curses and demand she do anything and everything to make him whole, he wasn't quite that rash. "All right. Then explain to me the difference. Why is someone like me who's trained to control their mind, reactions, and emotions more susceptible to melting down than some traveling salesmen whose mind got wiped after his car went over a bridge?"

"You just answered your own question."

He shook his head. "I guess I'm not as smart as you think I am. Spell it out for me."

She took off her glasses and rubbed the bridge of her nose. "You may not remember it, but your training was quite extensive. You learned how to withstand torture, both physical and mental. And because of your affiliation with the SOC, that training went further and deeper than most of our intelligence officers ever experience."

"And that's good, right?"

"Of course. But no program can render you entirely immune to torture. At some point, you reach a limit. You reached yours, Mr. Sawyer. For purposes of this discussion, we'll say you snapped."

He swallowed, hating that his own failure to hold it together had led to this condition. "Go on."

"In our salesman, that snap happened much

sooner. He barely fought it at all. The bad guy—in this case the accident and nature—didn't have to torture him too much before he reached his limit. To make the concept visual, we'll say that he sunk three inches into the hole."

"I'm listening."

"In contrast, you fought and fought and by the time you snapped, you were six feet under. His little hole is easy to climb out of. Yours, not so much. You try, and you end up pulling more dirt down on top of you. If you don't climb out slowly and methodically, you'll end up buried alive. Do it right, and you can find yourself on the green, hugging all those memories close." She looked hard at his face, staring him down. "Don't bury yourself."

"So, what are you saying? I shouldn't even try? Shouldn't talk to people I used to know or go places I used to visit?"

She shook her head. "No, no. I'm not saying that. But you have to move with care. Go too fast or dive to deep and—"

"What?"

"You'll feel it. When I say you could lose those memories forever, it's not just a psychological break, there's a physical one, too. You can burst a vessel, damage a lobe. You could end up with a migraine that keeps you down for a few days or fried synapses that put you in a catatonic state for the rest of your life. It's not an exact science, Jack. And the bottom line is that you were on that mission for a reason. We need to know what you know. And we can't risk losing all that intel forever."

He nodded, recalling the headache that had come on so unexpectedly at the club. Wasn't that about the time he first noticed the face? Had that memory been pounding hard to get back in?

"Tell me you understand," Dr. Tam demanded. "And promise me you won't be reckless."

"I understand. And I don't know myself well enough to know if I'm the reckless sort."

"Jack..."

He stood and shrugged. "I'm not going to let them hurt her."

"That's a noble outcome," she said. "But protect her with your brawn, Agent Sawyer. And keep your mind intact."

———

He was free of Dr. Tam and on his way to Denise's house by five-thirty. He'd been up all night, and was too exhausted to think straight, so he decided to wait an hour before waking her for the conversation about their work and his mind.

Unfortunately, it was hard to nap on a motorcycle, and she had no furniture on her front porch.

Undeterred, he slipped through the gate and into the backyard, pleased that it wasn't any trouble to do so, and also irritated that someone with a job where she saw all types of nastiness in the world didn't bother to lock her back gate. Or the glass and screen door of her patio sunroom, he added a few moments later.

At least the door between the patio and the kitchen was locked tight. He considered picking the lock—both to judge the level of security and to prove that he at least remembered *that*—but he was too damn tired. So instead he moved to the eastern wall, laid down on a lounge chair with forest green cushions, closed his eyes, and drifted off almost immediately.

The next thing he knew, the sun was spilling over him, a gentle hand was on his shoulder, and when he opened his eyes he was looking into Denny's beautiful face.

"Denny," he murmured, and heard her gasp in response.

He pushed himself up onto an elbow. "You okay?"

"I—yes. What are you doing out here, anyway? You should have just knocked. Or let yourself in." She grinned. "We both know you could have, even with my alarm system."

He sat up, matching her grin and relieved that she didn't seem annoyed that he'd camped out on her patio. "I was completely wiped, and I didn't see the point in bothering you, especially when this patio's perfectly comfortable."

"All right." She'd been standing beside him. Now she settled herself on the cushion by his legs as he sat up to give her more room. "That explains why you crashed on the patio. Now tell my why you came here at all."

"I need you to walk me through our missions. Hell, our lives. How we started working together. What you know about my background before the SOC. Any details of the last job I was on. Introduce me to our sources. Pull files so I can review mission briefs. Arrange meetings with mutual friends. Start from the first thing you know about me and take me step by step through to today."

He rattled the words off, afraid that if he paused at all she'd shut him down. She didn't. But she did stand and move to window, her back to him, the morning breeze through the screen catching the loose waves of her golden hair.

"Denny?" He frowned, noticing that he'd called her by the nickname. He liked it, though. It felt right. "Denny," he repeated. "Are you listening? I need you to do this for me."

"Why? What changed? I thought you were supposed to take it slowly."

"I saw Dr. Tam this morning." Not a lie. "And I

need to jumpstart my memory." Also not a lie. Not technically, anyway.

She turned around, her arms crossed in front of her chest, and studied him. "You talked to Liam."

"I'm not going to put you at risk because my mind is Swiss cheese."

"I'm not a civilian. I can take care of myself."

"Not disagreeing. But even if some asshole hadn't attacked you, we still need to know what's trapped in my head."

She nodded slowly, as if considering. "So you want to move faster. Amp up our efforts to get the memory ball rolling. Not just put you back into your life, but sit down and tell you specific stories about your past and hope it all sticks."

"Exactly. Essentially what we've been doing, but kicked up a notch. Before, it was almost academic. They'd dumped me like garbage, but where was the rush? Now, we know there's something in my head they want. Which means I caught wind of something specific they're up to. We need to know what. And the sooner the better."

She crossed the patio to him, then stood right in front of him. She bent, cupped his face, then kissed him ever-so-gently on the mouth.

Then she pulled back, a sad little smile touching her lips as she said, very simply, "No."

13

I SHOULDN'T HAVE KISSED him.

I don't know what the hell I was thinking, but I know that I absolutely shouldn't have kissed him. It was just an innocent peck. A friendly touch. But, dammit, it opened a door I should have kept firmly shut.

Now, my lips tingle from the memory. I can still recall his scent. Can still hear the way he drew in a sharp breath in surprise at my boldness.

Most of all, I want more. Want *him*.

It's as if I struck a match and now my whole body is on fire, every hormone buzzing and humming. My nipples are tight. My skin so sensitive. I flipped a switch that I had no right to touch, but the truth is that I don't regret it at all.

I'd felt so helpless after Seagrave's call had awakened me. The colonel had given me the entire rundown of Mason's meeting with Dr. Tam. And knowing that Mason intended to take such extreme risks because he was worried about me, was like getting a hard punch to my gut.

"He stormed out," Seagrave had told me. "I imagine he needed time to think, but I don't like leaving him alone that long."

Neither did I, and the relief that had washed over me when I found him here at our house—right where he belongs—was like sunshine blooming inside me.

He was Mason in that moment, not Jack. He was my husband, asleep in our home, his focus on protecting me.

And then he'd called me Denny, and it had taken all of my strength not to cry.

It was all too much, and I'd needed that one, tiny kiss to ground me.

Still, I shouldn't have done it. I shouldn't have opened that door.

Now, I lean against the kitchen counter and draw a breath, gathering myself. In front of me, the coffee maker's automatic timer triggers, and I hear the gurgle and hiss as it starts to brew.

Behind me, I hear Mason open the door.

"No?" He says the word as if no time at all has passed. As if I haven't wandered down long roads in my mind, only to come back here to my kitchen and my problems. "You can't just shut me down with a no."

"Yeah, I can." I draw a breath and then turn to face him. His expression of determined frustration is so familiar that I almost laugh. I really do know this man so well. "You want to dig deep into your past? Peachy keen. But you can't do it alone because, hello, you don't remember your past. So, yeah, I can say no. And that's exactly what I'm saying."

"Then I'll find someone else." He takes a step toward me. His jeans are dusty, his T-shirt wrinkled. His jaw is shadowed with stubble and his hair goes every which direction. He looks tired and irritated and amazing, and all I want to do is pull him into my arms, kiss him, and tell him to shut up about doing stupid things.

"No," I repeat. "You won't."

"Why the hell not?"

He's only inches away, his eyes boring into mine as if he can read the answer on my soul. I reach up without thinking and cup his face, his stubble scratchy against my palm. I see the spark flare in his eyes, and I draw in a breath, feeling it —*fighting it*—too.

"I know what could happen," I tell him gently. "Seagrave's call woke me up and he told me everything."

He starts to turn away, but I lift my other hand

and hold him in place, my gaze never wavering. "It's amazing that you would take that risk for me, but I won't let you. I won't let you risk losing yourself."

"That's not your decision to make."

"And," I add, ignoring him, "I can't handle the thought of losing you that way. I've already lost most of you. Don't steal the rest from me because of some bullshit sense of chivalry."

For a moment, we just look at each other, the air thick between us. Then he takes a step back. I lower my hands, releasing his face.

He reaches out and, very gently, runs the tip of his finger over the thin, red cut that the Face's blade left on my neck. "I don't like seeing you in danger."

"I'm not crazy about it either, but it comes with the job description."

He sighs, then sits in his usual spot at our breakfast table. "This whole situation is fucked up."

"No argument from me." I sit across from him, just like I have for so many mornings. "Thank you," I say.

His brow furrows. "For what?"

"For being willing to take such a huge risk for me. Just because I won't let you go through with it doesn't mean I don't appreciate it."

His mouth curves into a wry grin. "You're welcome," he says, then stands up and heads to the coffee maker. I stay seated, thinking about another risk he took about four months ago on Valentine's Day, our anniversary. A day when he broke cover to come to me, knowing how desperately I was missing him.

Not that he ever admitted that it was him. And not that I saw him. Our reunion had rules, and one was that I was blindfolded.

But I know my husband's body. His touch.

And I know that it was him who made love to me that night. That one magical respite in a sea of days and months and years apart.

"You're smiling," he says as he returns to the table with coffee for both of us.

"Why shouldn't I be? It's a lovely day, and I woke up to find one of my favorite people on my patio."

He laughs. "I don't know, Denny. Sounds like you're too easy to please."

"Denny," I repeat as I lift my coffee cup. I look at him over the rim. "Mason used to call me that. He was about the only one who would until Quince decided to take it up."

I shouldn't be telling him this. It's edging too close to the truth. But I can't seem to help myself.

"Does it bother you?"

I press my lips together in an effort to battle back the tears that threaten. Then I shake my head. "No."

Almost as a diversion, I lift the cup to my lips,

breathing in the coffee scent I usually love, but I realize I don't want it and put the cup back down.

After a moment, I notice that Mason's staring at me, his brow furrowed. *Jack*, I remind myself. But it's getting harder and harder to remember.

"What?" I ask as he continues to study me.

"Coffee."

My brows rise. "Yes. Good call. What was your first clue? The smell? Or the glass container of grounds sitting next to the machine?"

He ignores my sarcasm, and when he speaks, his voice is low and a little unsteady. "I remember," he says. "I remember you and coffee. Always a cup in your hand. Always making jokes about needing your caffeine hit."

I sit back, my body going cold as my stomach churns.

He cocks his head, looking at me. "You haven't taken even one sip. Are you feeling okay?"

I ignore the question. "You remember? You're not just piecing together things you've seen since you showed up at the SSA?"

"I don't kn—" He cuts himself off, and I watch as a violent shiver cuts through him. He's looking down at the table, his hands tightening on the edge. When he lifts his face, there's triumph in his eyes. "I remember."

A shock of joy cuts through me and my throat

goes dry. "Everything?" My voice is raspy, my entire being on edge.

He shakes his head, the triumph fading, and I feel like a total heel. "No. No, not everything. Hardly anything, I suppose."

I reach across the table and take his hand, squeezing hard. "That's okay," I say. "You remember coffee. And me. I think that's a hell of a good start."

His mouth twitches, then curves into a smile. "Yeah," he says. "I suppose it is."

"So you remember my coffee habit. What about yours?"

For a second, he looks blank. Then his face clears. "I don't have one. Not a habit, anyway. I drink a single cup in the morning, then I switch to smoothies. Greens and protein. I make them myself..." He trails off, shifting in his chair as his gaze locks onto the Vitamix that sits near the coffee maker. He frowns, and for a moment I wonder if he's putting it together. If he's realizing that he's Mason. That he's my husband.

But he just frowns and says, "A contraption like that. Every morning. Right?"

I shrug, trying to look nonchalant. "As far as I know."

"Okay. Good. This is good. What else?"

"We're not going to push, remember?"

"That wasn't a push," he says. "That was a

memory. A real, live, fucking memory."

I get up and take my coffee to the sink, then dump it. My back's to him, and I allow myself a bright smile and a silent sigh of relief. Maybe his memory really will come back. Maybe—

"Hey."

I whirl around to find him right behind me. Immediately, my pulse kicks up, and I pray he doesn't notice.

"What's up with that?" he asks, nodding toward the sink.

"What do you mean?"

"I remember coffee and so you dump it?"

He's teasing, I know, but I feel unreasonably defensive anyway. "I'm not changing my habit because I want to mess with your head."

He lifts his hands in supplication. "Sorry. Didn't mean to—"

"No, I'm the one who's sorry. I've got some sort of stomach bug, and it's been lingering. I shouldn't have snapped. Feeling bad is making me moody." I take a deep breath, willing myself to feel better. "It'll pass," I add. "It always does."

Something important flits into my mind, then flits right back out again. A thought. Something I should heed. But damned if I can lock onto it.

Frustrated, I shake my head, then focus on Mason. "Listen," I say, "I have an idea."

He takes a step back, his hands sliding into the

pockets of his jeans. "I'm listening."

"I'm not going to tell you stories about the past like I'm some modern version of Homer," I begin.

"But?"

I roll my eyes, but I'm secretly delighted by the interruption. Because that's exactly how Mason would interrupt.

"*But*," I continue, "you and I did a lot of stuff together, even outside work. And I'm thinking maybe we should cover some of that ground. See if it trips any memories."

"You mean play hooky today." His smile lights his face, and I match it.

"That's exactly what I mean."

"Lead the way."

"Really?" I plan to start with the beach, and I know that lunch will be on the agenda. One of the places that Mason and I haunted regularly. I take a quick look at Jack, then frown. "You look like you slept in your clothes."

"That would be because I did."

I smirk. "Do you want something else to wear?"

"Do you have something?"

"You and Mason are about the same size," I say casually. "You can borrow whatever you want."

He stays still for a moment, and I begin to fear that I've somehow gone too far. But then he nods and smiles. "Let me borrow the shower, too, and we have a deal."

14

"You REMEMBER how to ride a bike well enough," I say, as we both bring our bicycles to a stop. We've been riding for the last hour, first on the Venice Beach bike path, and then through the cute little neighborhoods of the coastal LA-area town.

"Let's walk for a bit," he says. "I saw someplace I want to check out."

"Someplace you remember?"

"Maybe."

I'd been about to suggest food, but since his plan sounds promising, I decide to ignore my growling stomach, appeasing it with only a long swig of water from my bottle. The bikes are ours—not that Mason realizes that he's riding his own bike—and we brought them here from Silver Lake on the rack that's a semi-permanent fixture on the back of my Highlander.

Now, we lock them back onto the car, and I follow Mason's lead as he weaves us back toward Windward, one of the main streets that runs perpendicular to the ocean.

He twists and turns and obviously knows where he's going. I'm honestly not paying that much attention. Instead, I'm lost in my thoughts, wondering how he can remember his way around a town but not his wife.

Which is why I'm completely blown away when he stops at a corner, points down the street, and says, "There. We passed it earlier, and I want to go in."

He's pointing at Totally Tattoo.

"Do you remember that place?" My mouth is so dry it's hard to get the question out.

"Honestly? I'm not sure. I think so. I thought we could go in and ask them if that's where I got this." He taps the tribal band below the sleeve of the Grateful Dead T-shirt he "borrowed" from Mason.

I follow him toward the shop, forcing myself not to cross my fingers. I want so bad for it all to flood back. Maybe it's foolish, but I can't help but think that if he just finds the right key, all of his memories will ease back into their proper little boxes.

Could our wedding tattoo be that key?

All the chairs in the parlor are full, but Cass

herself isn't doing anyone's art. Instead, she's sitting at the counter, her laptop open and a scowl on her face.

"What a warm and welcoming look for those of us entering the shop," I say with a laugh.

"Hey, you two," she says, glancing up. Her hair has streaks of magenta today, and she's wearing it in a ponytail, probably to keep it out of her way as she works.

"Bookkeeping?" I ask.

"The devil's work," she says. "I'm absolutely sure of it." She smiles at Mason, and I hope she remembers that for the time being, he's Jack. "Did you have fun at Westerfield's?"

"I did," he says, his eyes cutting to me. As for Cass, her gaze shifts between Jack and me, and she looks a little too much like a girl with a secret. Honestly, I love Cass, but it's a good thing she doesn't work in my profession.

"I didn't realize this was your place," Jack says. "Denny told you about my memory?"

Cass's eyes widen as she looks at me, obviously unsure if she's allowed to be in the know. I nod, and she visibly exhales. "Yeah. No offense, but it's like something in a movie."

"I suppose this is the town for it," he says. "I was wondering what you know about this." He taps the tattoo, and once again Cass looks to me.

Jack laughs. "Never mind. Got my answer."

"Oh, shit. I'm sorry," she says to me. "Was I not supposed to say anything?"

"You didn't say anything," Jack points out.

"It's fine," I tell her. "Jack remembered your storefront and thought this might be where he got the tattoo. It's fine that you confirmed, but you can't tell him anything else about it." I look at her hard, willing her to understand. "It's important that all the memories come from him. No prompting."

"Sure. Right. I've totally got it."

"I just want to know when you—" Jack begins, but I cut him off with a shake of my head.

"No," I say. "Take a seat, soak up the atmosphere, meditate if you want to. But nobody is going to just plop facts in your lap. Okay?"

He doesn't answer, but he does walk to a display wall and start looking at photos of some of the ink the shop's turned out.

"Can I talk to you for a sec?" Cass asks me. "You're okay for a bit, right, Jack?"

"I'll be here," he says wryly. "Lost in my memories."

I roll my eyes and follow her into the back storeroom.

"What's up?" I ask, expecting to hear a blow by blow of her evening with the cute blonde she was talking to at Westerfield's.

Instead, she says, "Are you ever planning on telling me? I mean, I get that you didn't want to talk about it before, what with him being gone. But now that he's back and he can't even know … I guess I just figured you'd need someone to talk to."

My stomach twists, but I'm not sure if it's nausea or dread. "What are you talking about?" But even as I ask the question, I know.

Cass leans forward. "Seriously?"

"I can't be." I shake my head. "I can't possibly be pregnant."

"Wait. Whoa. Back up. You really didn't think about it before? And yes you can. Four months ago, remember? He was here. With you. On Valentine's Day." Her brow furrows. "Are you telling me you've had your period since then? Because if that's the case, then maybe you're just sick, and—"

"I haven't," I say, feeling like the world's biggest fool. "I never got them regularly, and I'm on the pill so I never thought about it."

"And I'm guessing you weren't that careful about the pill, what with Mason being gone."

I nod. "And I don't keep track on a calendar because why bother? It's not like I've had sex in forever."

"Except for Valentine's Day." She takes my hands. "Is this good or bad?"

I look up into her blurry face and realize I'm crying. I pull one hand free and wipe my tears, then suck in a watery breath. "Good," I say. "Of course it's good. Mason's child. But—"

"You can't tell him."

I shake my head. "I can't tell Mason because he doesn't know he's Mason. And I can't tell Jack because he knows how long Mason's been gone." I choke out an ironic laugh. "I don't want him to think I cheated on my husband."

"I'm sorry."

"It's kind of a mess."

"But a good mess," she says, pulling me into a hug as I nod. "You should take a test just to be sure."

"I will. But I'm sure." Now that we've said it out loud, I don't know how I could have been so blind for so long. I can only assume that my subconscious didn't want to think about being pregnant without Mason here to go through it with me. Denial. Big time.

And now that he is here ... well, part of me still wants to ignore it while another part of me wants to sing with joy.

"Ready to go out and face him?" she asks. "Or do you want to sneak out the back and I can say you were kidnapped by fairies?"

"A nice offer, but I'll go with door number one." I draw a breath, square my shoulders, and head back out.

"What do you think?" he says, pointing to a picture of a guy with a shaved head and a tattoo of a tree going up the back of his neck to burst into leaves on his scalp. "Is it me?"

It's kind of cool in theory. But Mason, it's not.

"Come on," I say, taking his hand as he grins. "I want an ice cream and a walk in the surf."

He glances over at Cass. "How do I say no to that?"

"I don't think you do," she says. She wiggles her fingers in a goodbye gesture, then adds, "If you remember more about getting the band and want to ask me questions, you know where to find me. And don't worry," she adds to me, "I won't tell any more than I'm supposed to."

I nod. But I don't know if she's talking about the tattoo, the baby, or both.

"Is this something else we use to do," Jack asks later as we walk through the surf. I have my shoes in one hand. The other swings beside me, and more than once it's bumped Jack's free hand. It feels flirty, like we're on a date. And under the circumstances, I like the way I feel a little more than I should.

Which, of course, is totally unfair. He's my husband. I'm supposed to be able to hold his hand and romp in the surf. I'm supposed to be able to tell him about our baby. I'm supposed to be able to stop and kiss him. I'm supposed to be able to say, "I love you."

But I can't. Not yet.

And today especially, that breaks my heart.

"Are you okay?"

I realize I've slowed down and have fallen behind him.

"Yeah. I am. Sorry. I've just been thinking."

"Me too." He tilts his head inland. "Can I buy you dinner?"

"Sure." It occurs to me that Seagrave must have set up a full Jack Sawyer identity, which would include Jack Sawyer credit cards and bank accounts. I hadn't thought about it before, and those aren't the kind of details that usually escape me.

What do they call it? Baby brain?

We walk silently to Blacklist, a restaurant Mason and I frequent when we're in the area. Usually, we sit at one of the sidewalk tables, but today he leads me inside to a small table in a dark corner.

We order, then sit in an awkward silence until the waiter returns with our food. Cheese fries to share, a sparkling water for me, and a beer for Jack. He takes a sip, looking like a man seeking liquid courage, then puts his glass down.

"What's going on?" I ask, hearing trepidation in my own voice.

"We need to talk," he says, and I wonder if he overheard Cass and me talking about the baby. And about who he really is.

For a moment, I'm giddy. Because if that's the case, then Dr. Tam was wrong. He had the truth dumped on him, and his brain is just fine.

Then he says, "I know you loved your husband," and my little fantasy goes *poof*, replaced by my hard, sharp-edged, strange reality.

"I did," I say. "I do."

"Of course. I didn't mean to suggest—" He cuts off the words. "My point is that I know that. And I'd never try to suggest that you don't love Mason or that you should try to get over him."

I frown, not understanding where he's going with this.

"I should probably just keep my mouth shut, but we know I have to get my memory back, right?"

I nod.

"And that means I have to look at all my memories."

"Jack, I'm really not following you."

He sighs. "Look, I don't want to make you uncomfortable. I don't want to ruin our friendship. I'm asking you this because we *are* friends. Because even if this is something you want to leave behind, I trust you to give me an honest answer, okay?"

"You're kind of freaking me out."

"Okay?" he repeats, and I nod.

"Yes. Of course. Okay."

He draws a breath, then looks down at his hands where he's been ripping his napkin into tiny shreds. I still have no idea what he's going to say, but I definitely know that he's nervous.

"Before when we worked together—even when Mason was around—was there ... I mean, were we ... oh, hell. Were we having an affair?"

I'd been about to take a sip of my water. Now I freeze, the glass suspended there. Slowly, I return it to the table. "Why do you ask that?"

He sighs. "Vague memories. The way Cass looked between us—as if there was more connection than just partners. The way I see you looking at me sometimes. The clothes in your closet that fit me and don't feel like another man's clothes. The Vitamix that makes me wonder if I left it at your house to make my mornings easier. The way I knew where you were going to sit at the breakfast table. The way—"

"Okay. I get it."

"—the way your kiss this morning felt like—"

"Like what?" I whisper when he cuts himself off, leaving silence hanging between us.

He hesitates, his focus on the napkin shreds. Then he lifts his eyes to mine. "Like coming home."

"Jack, I—" I take a long sip of water, then stand, my mind racing. "Excuse me," I say, then hurry to the ladies' room before he can stop me.

In the small space, I clutch the counter and lean forward, staring at myself in the mirror as his question swirls through my mind. Literally, the answer is no, because I've never cheated on my husband, and Jack ... Mason, whoever he is, wouldn't ever betray a friend. And I don't want him thinking that he's the kind of man that would.

But the core of his question—the *are we together* part—well, the answer to that is yes.

Except I can't tell him so without risking destroying him. Literally destroying him, since, "Why no, honey, we're not having an affair because we're married," is exactly the kind of memory trigger that Dr. Tam is certain would set off a horrible chain reaction.

Bottom line, I have to lie. I have to tell this man I love and am desperately attracted to that I don't want him. That I've never wanted him. Because he's Jack and I'm married to Mason, and neither of those men are the type who would cheat with their partner or a friend's wife.

With a sigh, I press my hand over my belly. "Your mommy is a mess," I say. "And Daddy's not doing too great either."

I draw in a breath for courage, open the door, and step out into the dark alcove that separates the dining area from the kitchen and restrooms.

I don't see him until he says, "Denny." Then I turn and find him in the farthest corner. And, because I'm a fool, I go to him.

I start to speak, but before I can utter a word, he takes my wrist and pulls me close. I only have time to gasp before his arm is wrapped tight around my waist and his mouth closes over mine. And, damn me, I can't help it. I melt into his embrace. My mouth opens to his and our kiss is deep and hot and oh, so wild.

It's everything I want, everything I need, and I feel the surge of our connection pulsing through me. I want him so badly. Want to feel his hands on my breasts, between my legs. I want to feel him moving inside me, making me wild and wet. I want to forget everything except the reality of his touch, and when I explode, I want to return to a world where my husband knows me and himself.

But that won't happen, and it's the memory of that truth that has me pulling away.

"Jack, please, we—"

"I remembered something else, too," he says, gently brushing my hair out of my face. "I remembered making love to you."

A lump of tears sticks in my throat, and all I can do is shake my head helplessly. I don't know what to say. I don't know what to do.

And so I take the coward's way out, and bolt.

I pause at the entrance to the dining room and look back. "I can't," I say, a sob stuck in my throat. "And I'm sorry, but you're going to have to find your own way home."

I'M A WRECK. A sniveling, teary-eyed mess who clearly doesn't know what she wants and is utterly incapable of navigating a personal crisis.

I also should never have gotten behind the wheel of my car, and it's only by some miracle that I got home safe and sound, because God knows my mind wasn't on the road, and I could barely see through the tears that kept leaking from my eyes.

I made it, though. And I'd burst into the house, raced to my bedroom, threw off my clothes, and slid all the way under the covers. My plan was to sleep through the rest of the summer and on into Christmas. Then, like a groundhog, I'd peek out and decide if it was safe to emerge.

Of course, I hadn't factored in little things like eating and giving birth. All I wanted to do was sleep off my misery like a horrible hangover.

He wanted me. I wanted him.

And I couldn't have him.

Why?

Why, why, why?

The question keeps circling in my mind, and the more it bounces around in my head, the more I lose sight of the answer. I know I'd had reasons to walk away, but what were they?

That I don't want to cheat on my husband? That one is laughable. Mason is my husband, no matter what his name.

That I don't want him to see me as a woman willing to cheat? Maybe, but to what end? I've never been unfaithful, and under the circumstances, Jack can hardly think ill of me.

That I don't want Jack to see himself as the kind of man who could seduce a married woman, a co-worker, a friend? Maybe, but again, to what end? If his memory comes back, he'll understand. And if he never remembers his past? Well, in that case there won't be any danger of a visit from a cuckolded husband.

Every reason I consider and shoot down makes me feel foolish for walking away from him. Foolish and empty, because damned if I don't crave him so much I feel hollow.

And yet...

I close my eyes and let the truth wash over me —I want him, and yet I run. But I don't understand what it is I'm afraid of.

I toss and turn in the bed, but I can't sleep for even an hour, much less until Christmas. Annoyed, I slip out from between the sheets, tug on my bathrobe, and pad barefoot into the kitchen.

Coffee, wine, and whiskey are all out of the question, so I settle for hot chocolate. I haven't made it in ages, but I have milk and a tin of real cocoa that I bought last winter. I even have some whipped topping in the fridge, left over from a recent craving for ice cream with bananas and caramel. A craving that had seemed inexplicable at the time, but now makes perfect sense.

I stir the chocolate into the milk, then wait until it just starts to bubble around the edges. Then I pour it into the huge Disneyland mug that Mason bought on our first and only trip to the park. I add a squirt of whipped cream, put the mug on the table, and then head to the pantry in the hopes that I have a package of Oreos. Honestly, I should have planned my descent into self-pity better.

As it turns out, my quest is successful. Shocking, really, since without Mason in the house, my shopping list doesn't usually include sweets. But I've been shopping on autopilot lately, and apparently the little dude or dudette growing inside me is making some of my choices.

"Good job," I say, patting my belly with one hand and carrying the Oreos with the other. "What are we going to tell your daddy, and when are we going to tell him?"

Excellent questions, and not ones I feel like contemplating at the moment. Because unless Mason miraculously gets his memory back, I know that the first thing I have to do is set a meeting with Seagrave and Dr. Tam. I want Mason—or Jack—to know his child. But I don't want to fry his mind while telling him the truth. And the idea of him being Uncle Jack instead of Daddy just doesn't seem fair.

Frustrated, I break open an Oreo, then eat the un-iced half as I wait for the cocoa to cool. I'm just about to lift the mug for a tiny test sip when a rap on the kitchen door makes me jump.

I hurry to the wall switch, flip on the light for the covered patio, and find Mason standing on the other side of the kitchen door, peering at me through one of the six panes of glass he'd installed himself.

I should tell him to go away; I'm too raw to do this tonight.

I should, but I don't.

Instead, I open the door, greeting him with, "What the hell are you doing sneaking in through back patio again?"

"I wasn't sneaking, I swear."

"Most people arrive in the front."

"Your lights were off. I wanted to see if you

were still up, and I figured if the lights were off back here I'd leave you a note on the porch. But the light was on, and there you were, and so I came in."

"You shouldn't have," I say, suddenly very aware that I have nothing on under my robe. "And I shouldn't have let you in."

"Maybe not. But since you did..." He trails off, his head tilted a bit to the side and a cocky grin dancing on his mouth.

I shouldn't take the bait, but I do. "What?" I demand as I tighten my sash.

"Since you did, the least you can do is share your Oreos."

Mason, I think, feeling both delighted and a little weak in the knees.

I stand up straighter, and keep my expression stern. "That seems awfully extreme. I mean, we're talking Oreos. There are some sacrifices a woman shouldn't be expected to make." I allow myself a slow grin, and he smiles back.

"I promise I'll make it up to you with the pleasure of my company."

"Sit," I say. "I'll get you some cocoa. Unless you'd rather have bourbon?" Bourbon and Oreos is Mason's favorite late night snack. I've always thought it's a bizarre combination, but he swears by it.

Now, I watch his face, but see nothing other

than an adventurous acceptance. "I'm game. Will you join me?"

I shake my head. "It's a cocoa night for me. But for you..." I trail off as I grab a bottle of Knob Creek from one of the lower cabinets. I put it on the table, bring him a glass, and watch as he slams a shot back.

I lift my brows. "It's supposed to be savored with the cookies."

"I'll do that, too. I needed a bit of fortification for what I need to say."

"Oh." I pull out my chair and sit down. "So we're to that part already."

He takes another sip, this time pairing it with an Oreo. "That really is remarkably good," he says, then stands up again. "And completely beside the point." He draws in a breath. "I should never have followed you in the restaurant. And I definitely shouldn't have kissed you. I probably shouldn't have even asked you if there was ever a thing between us. I pushed boundaries. I made you uncomfortable. And I'm sorry. Truly sorry. It won't happen again."

"Oh." This isn't at all what I expected, and I want to say something else, but I honestly don't know what, and an awkward silence hangs between us, all the more awkward because I've never for a moment felt uncomfortable around Mason.

"Right." He clears his throat. "Well, I should

get back to Malibu. Liam's going to start to wonder if I forgot the way there along with everything else."

He turns to leave, and as I watch him go, it hits me, and I know what it is I'm afraid of. That he's going to disappear from me just like my father did. Like my mother did. And, yes, like Mason did.

My father walked away, but Mom didn't want to leave me. She hadn't been given a choice. Neither had Mason. One day he was here, and the next he was gone. He's back now—not whole, not yet—but he's *here*.

And my deepest, darkest fear is that he's going to disappear all over again. Losing him once almost killed me. Twice will do me in.

So there it is, the reason I don't want to get close now. It's not because of Dr. Tam's rules about his memory or any misplaced notions of fidelity as applied to amnesia victims. It's because I'm protecting my heart.

But in that moment, I realize how much more I'll lose by not going for it. Even if it's only a month, a week, a day's worth of memories, that will be that much more to keep for our baby. Even if he forgets everything. Even if he disappears for another two years, I'll have a little bit more of him than I did before.

But oh, dear God, I hope to hell he doesn't disappear.

He pauses at the kitchen door, then turns back with an apologetic smile. "Thanks for the snack. I'll see you at work tomorrow. And I'll behave myself from now on."

I just stare, by mouth literally gaping open, stuck in that horrible place between what I want and what I fear. But then he pulls open the door and leaves the bright kitchen for the patio, and I can't stand it any longer.

I race after him and grab his hand before he can push open the screen door that leads into the back-yard. "Wait!"

He stops. "Denny?"

"I can't," I say. "I can't let you walk away. Not knowing that you might end up staying away forever."

Confusion washes over his face. "I don't know what you're—"

"Dammit, Jack," I say, untying the sash on my robe and then shrugging it off my shoulders. I stand there naked, my heart pounding in my chest as I watch his face, illuminated now only by the light from the kitchen seeping out through the windows. "Just touch me."

"Denny." His voice is thick with a desire so familiar I don't know if I want to cry or celebrate. "Dear Christ, you're beautiful."

"Look all you want," I say, taking his hand once

again and this time putting it on my breast. "But you have to be touching me, too."

"I like your terms," he says, his eyes on mine as his thumb brushes my hard nipple, sending rocket flares of need coursing through me. I make a whimpering sound, and bite my lower lip, fighting the urge to beg him to kiss me. I want that kiss, yes, but mostly I want the pleasure of losing myself as Mason explores my body for the zillionth—and the first—time.

He doesn't disappoint.

"Close your eyes," he whispers, and I do as he says. He continues to tease my nipple with his thumb, adding his other hand as well, so that both my breasts are getting his full attention. Then I feel his lips brush my temple, followed by the whisper of breath against my ear before his tongue traces the curve. I shiver in response, biting my lower lip.

He chuckles, the sound soft and low, then kisses his way down my jaw before brushing his lips over mine. "That's my job," he murmurs, before kissing me so sweetly, the gentle pressure turning demanding when he pulls away, his teeth tugging on my bottom lip and sending a coil of heat all the way through my body, from my greedy mouth all the way to my pussy.

I whimper, then shift my stance, spreading my legs and relishing the sensation of the air between my thighs. I'm wet and needy, and I'm craving his fingers, his mouth. He's taking his damn time, though, and so far he hasn't even ventured south of my breasts.

"Jack...please."

"Please, what?"

"Touch me," I beg.

"I am touching you." His lips move against my ear as he talks. "I want to hear what you want." As he speaks, one hand slides down, moving south on my belly. "Tell me how to touch you, Denny. Tell me what you like."

"This," I say, and I've never spoken truer words. I'm opening up after a long hibernation. I'm back in my husband's arms, and I don't even care that he doesn't know it. He's bringing me back to life, just like a princess in a fairy tale. "This," I repeat. "I want all of this. And more."

"Me, too." His voice is a growl. Rough. Edgy. And I know that he's as desperate as I am.

"Denny," he says as he drops to his knees. "I have to taste you."

I tremble, overwhelmed with desire as his hands cup my thighs, and he slowly eases them up until his thumbs are teasing the tender skin between my sex and my legs. He tilts his head up and meets my eyes just long enough for me to see the hunger on his face. Then he gently strokes my clit with his tongue, sending shockwaves of pleasure rushing through me, so intense it's a wonder my legs don't collapse beneath me.

I whimper when he pauses, then suck in a sharp breath when he orders, "Play with your nipples."

My body tightens in response. Mason isn't usually this demanding, but I like it. I want to arouse him as deeply as he's aroused me. I want to hear what he wants, share his fantasies. Hell, I want to *be* his fantasy.

I want to surrender to his every whim, and that's why I eagerly tease and pinch my nipples as he laves my clit with his tongue, his hands cupping my ass as he holds me firmly in place.

I could stay like that forever, but Mason changes the game. His hand on my rear shifts, and he slides it between my ass cheeks, then further still until his fingertips find my core. I'm incredibly wet, and he thrusts inside me as I grind against him, craving every pleasure and sensation that he is giving me.

Too soon, he pulls his hand away, then teases his wet fingertip along my perineum before stroking the tight muscle of my ass. I gasp at the unfamiliar sensation, but I can't deny that it feels fucking incredible.

"You like that." It's a statement, not a question.

"Yes. God, yes."

But it's as if my admission is a indictment,

because he stops. I whimper, and he stands, his expression teasing and devious. "I like the look on your face," he tells me. "As if you want to beg, but don't want to give me the satisfaction."

"I'll beg," I say. "I'll do anything you want me to."

"I like the sound of that," he says, then kisses me hard and deep. It's a wild kiss, all tongue and teeth and violent demand.

When he pulls away, we're both breathing hard. "You should beg. You should tell me everything you want, every naughty thought, every wild fantasy. Because all I want is to satisfy you. To feel you surrender. To hear you scream. I want to make you explode, Denny. And then I want to do it all over again."

I stroke his face, his stubble rough against my palm. "Who are you?" I whisper.

Mason's not shy in bed—not by a long shot. But this intensity is so much more. I don't know if it's because of our time apart or his new boldness, but I've never been so turned on in my life, and every one of his touches sends shivers through me.

He smiles in response to my question. "I'm the man who's making love to you."

"Yes," I say. "Oh, yes, you are."

He takes my hand and tugs me to the small sofa under the windows that look into the kitchen. He sits, then holds up a hand to stop me when I start to go toward him. "Wait. I want to see you."

"I'm hard to miss. I'm right in front of you and very naked."

His mouth twitches. "Touch yourself."

My pulse kicks up, and a delicious heat settles more firmly between my legs. "What?"

"You heard me." He moves his hand to his cock, stroking it through the denim of his jeans. Even from where I stand, I can tell how hard he is. And I can feel how wet I am.

"Denny," he says. "I want to watch."

It's such a simple statement compared to the intensity of his gaze, and I find I can neither protest nor resist. He wants to watch, and damned if I don't want to perform. Want to feel his eyes on me as I play with my clit. Want to watch the motion of his hand quicken on his thick cock as I thrust a finger in my pussy, then suck my sex-slicked finger.

I want wildness. Fantasy. Desire.

I don't know. Maybe I want to make up for lost time.

Mostly, I just want Mason, and as he watches, I close my eyes and slowly slide my hand down, then start to tease my hard, slick clit.

"Baby," he murmurs, the need in his voice so intense it sounds as though it's laced with pain.

I'm wet—so wet—and it's all because of him. I slip my fingers inside myself, and as I do, he tells me to open my eyes. I comply, and the passion on his face rocks through me, the precursor to a wild explosion.

He sees it and I watch as his hand tightens on his straining cock.

"Take off your clothes," I say.

"Why?"

"Because it's my turn. Because I want you."

He doesn't make a move, so I climb onto his lap, straddling him, then rub myself over the bulge in the denim.

I whimper, and he laughs. "I like watching you."

"Yeah? Would you like fucking me, too?"

He doesn't answer aloud, but he unbuttons his fly, then slowly takes his cock out. He's huge and hard, and I stroke myself over the length of him as he groans, then closes his eyes and tilts his head back as he holds my rear and guides my movements.

He's harder than I've ever seen him, and tonight we've been wilder than ever before. "What are we doing?" I ask, as I continue to rock my hips and he teases my rear with his forefinger. "We've never—"

"What?"

I gasp as his finger explores me more intimately, my whole body craving him, wanting to be filled by him.

"This," I say when I can force out the words. "Everything."

"So I was right. You. Me. The past. We did have a thing. This isn't our first time."

I swallow, trapped in my own obfuscation. "You know it isn't. And please, please, right now I just want—"

"Tell me."

"I want you inside me. Please, Jack. Please fuck me."

"I don't have a condom," he says, breathing hard.

"It's okay," I say. "It'll be fine. Just please, don't stop."

I start to shift, rising up so that I'm no longer riding his shaft. I want the head. I want all of him inside me.

"Denny, I don't think—"

"I'm on the pill," I say, which isn't technically accurate anymore, but he's also not going to get me any more pregnant than I already am.

"Denny..." He looks into my eyes, his gentle and sad. "We can't risk it. I'm not worried about a baby—"

"Then what?"

"I don't know what they did to me. I don't know what *I* did. And I won't risk you—"

I kiss him, then smile when I pull away and look into his confused eyes. "It's okay," I assure him. "Seagrave and his team did every test imaginable on you. You're clean, I promise."

I think that will reassure him, but he looks even more confused. "Why on earth would they tell you that?"

Because as your wife they thought I might want to know.

"We're partners."

"Yes, but that doesn't—"

"Jack," I say firmly. "Do you want to debate privacy policy at the SOC, or do you want to fuck me?"

Shock flickers in his eyes, changing swiftly to amusement.

"Trust me, sweetheart, debating is the last thing on my mind."

"I'm very glad to hear it."

He cups my neck, then pulls my face down for a hard kiss, with tongue and teeth and heat, and so wild and deep it's almost fucking. But not close enough, because what I want is Mason. My body is on fire, craving release. Needing satisfaction.

"I can't wait any longer," I tell him.

"Me either."

I bite my lower lip, then shift my hips until I feel the head of his cock against my core. His hands are on my hips, and I let him maneuver me, lifting and lowering me as he teases himself and me, barely slipping inside me, then pulling out, then repeating again in a maddening ritual that has me going absolutely crazy.

Him, too. I can tell from his face. From the ecstasy etched on his features.

"More," he demands, releasing my hips and giving me full control. I take it greedily, impaling myself over and over again as my body tightens, every atom in me pulling together, readying for a wild explosion.

Tighter and tighter, faster and faster.

Inside me, Mason's close, too. He's as tight as a spring, and I want to explode with him. I want us to come together, to be together. I want—

The world shatters around me.

I rock back, my body on fire, my husband's name on my lips. "Mason! Oh, God, Mason!"

And then I realize what I've done.

His body goes tense as my eyes fly open in shock and embarrassment. "Jack," I say. "I didn't mean—"

He stands up, then tugs on his jeans as I wince, feeling like an absolute shit.

"I'm sorry," I say as he shakes his head, then reaches down, grabs my robe, and tosses it to me.

"No, I'm the one who's sorry." He drags his fingers through his hair as I slide the robe on and pull it tightly closed. "I can't be what you need. I can't be a stand-in for your husband."

I shake my head. "You're not. I swear you're not. It just slipped out. It didn't mean anything—"

"Dammit, Denny, it meant everything."

Hot tears spill down my cheeks, because it's happening just as I feared. I'm losing him all over again. "Please," I whisper, but he just shakes his head.

"I don't want to be the kind of man who cheats on a friend. And you're not the kind of woman who cheats on her husband. I don't know what kind of madness grabbed us before, but—"

He cuts himself off, his brow furrowing as he lifts his face to mine, a wild, almost feral look in his eyes. "You're not the kind of woman who cheats," he repeats, then reaches out for my left hand so quickly that I gasp with shock. "Not you," he says, rubbing the pad of his thumb over the platinum band the way I do when I'm lost in thought.

He draws in a stuttering breath, then squares his shoulders as he looks straight at me. "You didn't cheat tonight, did you?"

Fear and joy war for space in my heart. Is he saying what I think he's saying? "Jack, I don't—"

He presses a finger to my lips and shakes his head. "I'm not Jack," he says. "I'm your husband. I'm Mason."

16

HE WAS MASON.

Mason Walker, not Jack Sawyer.

Mason Walker, former Special Forces soldier turned covert operative for the Sensitive Operations Command. Not that he remembered any of that. But he knew it was true. Just as he knew that he was married to Denise Marshall. *Denny.* The woman who'd made his heart stop from the first moment he'd seen her inside that goddamn little cell at the SOC.

The same woman who was looking at him now as if he were a lit fuse, and any moment he would burst apart. He stifled a wince. Considering the state of some of the amnesia victims Dr. Tam had showed him, he supposed that wasn't an unreasonable fear. Right now, though, he felt fine. All he wanted was his life back.

He drew in a breath. "This is our house? We own it together?"

Her eyes widened a bit, but she nodded.

"When did we buy it?"

"I don't think I should just tell you—"

"Yes," he said stepping closer to her. "You should."

"Dr. Tam said—"

"No." He shook his head. "I know the risk. I know the concern. But my head feels fine."

She shook her head, and a single tear spilled down her cheek, making his heart crack open. "I can't," she said in a voice clogged with tears. "I get that you're angry with me, but I'm so goddamn happy to have you back. *You.* And I can't risk that. I just can't."

Oh, God, she was killing him.

"I'm not angry with you," he said, using his forefinger to tilt her chin up. "I'm relieved. Confused. Thrilled. Awed."

"Awed?"

"That you belong to me. That the woman I've fantasized about since the first moment I saw her actually belongs to me."

"It was hell having you gone," she whispered. "I'm used to missions, but that one went long, and I didn't hear anything and…" She trailed off with a shudder. "It was hell," she repeated. "And then you came back, and … well, that was hell, too. I was so thrilled to know that you were alive. Thrilled to have you with me again. But it was a whole new level of hell, Mason. It really was."

She sniffled, then brushed tears away with her fingertips before using the sleeve of her robe to wipe her nose. "Sorry. I'm kind of a mess. I'm exhausted and, well, let's just say it's been an unusual day."

"It definitely has."

He took her hand. "Come with me."

He led her inside, a throbbing need building inside him. Not sexual—not entirely. But demanding and urgent.

"This is our kitchen?"

"Such that it is," she said. "We got new appliances because you like—*liked*—to cook. But the countertops and new floors and all that..." She trailed off with a shrug.

"You were waiting for me to come back."

"We wanted to do it together, the way we'd done the back porch. Room by room, a year or so of weekends. And then we'd have a new house by our anniversary." Her voice cracked as she spoke.

"I'm sorry."

She shook her head vehemently. "No. Don't be. We both love our work. I still do, even with everything that's happened. And despite leaving the SOC to move over to Stark. What we both do, it's important. You may not remember what you were doing, but I promise you it was something vital. And we bought this house knowing that anything could happen. We could get transferred to another country. We could end up on a long-term undercover assignment. One of us could get whacked on the head and end up with amnesia." She said the last with a sad little laugh, but he couldn't bring himself to smile in return.

She cleared her throat. "Anyway, the point is that we knew the risks. And we knew that we might never be able to settle down like civilians. This part?" She swept her hand to encompass the room, the house. "The part where I couldn't deal? That was all on me." Her lips twitched with humor. "I guess I loved you even more than I realized."

He moved closer, then cupped her chin and gently tilted her face up. Then he kissed her. Just a gentle brush of lips on lips, but it set him on fire, and when he stepped back he was breathing hard. And he knew exactly what he wanted. Her. His life. *Everything*.

"We'll finish the house," he said. "We'll finish it together. We can start tomorrow."

Something bright shone in her eyes. "Really?"

"It belongs to me, too."

"Right. Of course. It does." Her voice was soft. Breathy.

"So do you."

"I do."

The words—a vow—sliced through him, hot and demanding.

"Take off your robe," he said, barely able to hear his own voice over the pounding of his pulse in his ears.

"What?"

"You heard me." He moved closer, knowing he was pushing limits, but also knowing that he had to. That it was right here and right now that would either make this shadow life real for him, or leave him outside the glass looking in.

She was breathing hard, her lips slightly parted as she studied him, as if trying to read his mind.

"You're my wife, aren't you? You belong to me as much as this house? This furniture?" He reached for the loose end of the sash. "Love, honor, *obey*."

She met his eyes, hers sparkling with mischief. "Actually, we left the obey part out of our vows."

"And if I want it back in?"

Her brows rose. "Do you?"

"Do I want to know that this is still real to you? Me? This marriage? Do I want to know—truly know—that you belong to me, wholly and completely? Do I want to know that there is nothing you won't do if I ask, just as there is nothing I won't do for you? Yes, wife. I want that."

She didn't answer him, not in so many words, but the color rose on her face and she was breathing hard when she closed her hand over his and tugged the sash loose. She moved her shoulders, and the robe slithered to the ground, leaving him holding only a white cloth sash in his hand, dangling down to where it was tethered to a puddle of crisp, white terrycloth.

He dropped the sash.

For a moment, he simply stood there, taking in every inch of her. Before, she'd been a woman he desired. But that desire had been mixed with guilt. He'd not only coveted another man's wife, he'd pulled out his cock and fucked her.

Except he hadn't.

The woman he'd craved was his. His woman. His partner, his friend.

His wife.

His life.

Wasn't that the way it was supposed to work? And in his case, it was more true than usual, since the sum total of his known life was so small. But Denny was at the heart of it, and he had the feeling she always had been, even when his life was as wide as the world.

"I love you," she said. She stood naked and unabashed in front of him. "God, Mason, I love you so much."

The words warmed him. Centered him.

He supposed that to another man in his position they might be terrifying. But not him. Not with her. Denise Marshall was saying those words to him, and even though his mind had been erased, he felt like the luckiest man in the world.

"Upstairs," he said. "I want you in our bedroom."

For a moment, she didn't move. Then a smile lit her face. "Yes, sir," she said, then walked out of the sunroom ahead of him.

He followed, enjoying the view of her heart-shaped ass and the way her hips swayed.

His, he thought, and still couldn't quite believe it.

When he got to the bedroom, he found her on the bed, ankles crossed, arms stretched wide. "Like a feast for me," he said.

"Oh, I think I'll enjoy it, too."

"Wife," he said, then drew in a breath. "My beautiful wife."

As he watched, her cheeks turned rosy from her pleased blush.

"Husband," she countered, holding out her hand. "Will you make love to me?"

"Oh, yes," he promised, climbing onto the bed. But first he wanted to explore every inch of her. Wanted to listen to her breathing quicken as his fingertips traced her skin. As his lips tasted every inch. As he discovered a smattering of freckles on her shoulder and a diamond-shaped birthmark that seemed to float right over the indentation between her torso and her thigh.

She had a kissable dent at the base of her neck, and it also was her most ticklish point. And when he ran his forefinger under the arch of her foot, she just about leaped off the bed.

"You're extraordinary," he said finally, though he wasn't through exploring her. Hell, he'd probably never be through. Right then, though, he wanted more. He wanted to kiss her. To lose himself inside her. And then, after they'd both exploded in each other's arms, they'd drift off to sleep together.

That's what he wanted, he thought, as his cock slipped deep into her tight, hot core. What he craved, he thought as he moved inside her, their bodies joined. One heart, one soul. One memory.

Her. Them.

In that moment, that was all there was.

And the true miracle of the moment was that he knew without a shadow of a doubt, that she felt the same way, too.

17

I WAKE to find Mason beside me, propped on an elbow as he looks down on me, his expression so tender it almost hurts my heart.

"Good morning, wife," he says, and I smile and snuggle close in response.

"Can we just stay like this for a week or two? Surely the universe owes us that much."

"Sounds good to me," he says, his fingertip gently stroking my bare arm. "I'm not ashamed to say I'm exhausted. It takes a lot out of a man to be deflowered by his wife."

I burst out laughing. "Deflowered. You? Hardly."

He sits up, pulling me up with him. "Ah, ah. No arguing. Especially when I'm right. That was the first time for me, after all. At least as far as I can recall."

I grin, because he's right. And then, inexplicably, I start to cry.

Or maybe not so inexplicable. Baby hormones, after all.

But all the hormones are doing is stealing my self-control. The worry and fears are real. As are my tears.

"Hey," he says, pulling me to him. "Hey, we're going to be just fine."

I suck in a ragged breath. "Are we?" I ask, and then kick myself because I don't want to have this conversation right now. And yet it looks like we're going to be having this conversation. Right now.

"What do you mean?"

"I just—it's just—Oh, hell, Mason. You're here, and I love you, and I'm your wife, and from my perspective, that's all amazing."

I mean every word, but I'm going to have to bite the bullet and reveal a little bit more of my heart if I don't want Mason to think I'm a crazy person.

He scoots back so that he's leaning against the headboard. I shift, too, so that I'm sitting cross-legged in front of him, the sheet pulled up to cover me since I feel so damn exposed.

"Denny," he says, his voice tense. "What's going on?"

"I'm just afraid," I say.

"That I won't get my memory back?"

I nod. "And that you can't—come on, Mason. You don't remember me. You don't remember yourself. You're here in this bed because you're my husband, but what if you're not the same person now? What if you don't want to be here?"

What if you don't want a baby when you don't even remember its mother?

I push the thought away.

"I'm sorry," I say. "You have so much to deal with and now I dump this on you, but—"

"You're afraid," he says simply as he reaches out to hold my hands. "Of course you are. Your husband came back and he doesn't even know you."

I make a harsh sound. "Yeah. That about sums it up."

He scoots closer, pulling me toward him as he does so that our hips touch and I can lean into his outstretched arms.

"I'm sorry," I say again. "This shouldn't be about me. Not after everything you've—"

"The hell it shouldn't." His lips brush my forehead. "Here's the thing, though. We made a vow to each other, right? For better or for worse? Are you saying we should bolt just because we're skirting up against the worst?"

"I don't know," I say, honestly. "People leave. They leave all the damn time."

"I'm not leaving." His voice is hard. Intense. A

statement and a promise. "Hell, even with amnesia, I came back. And here's something else—I do love you. And I expect that will deepen over time."

"You don't even know me."

"I know your core. Your heart. I know I like what I've seen. I know that I trust my gut, and so far it seems to me that Mason Walker is a pretty decent guy."

I grin. "He is."

"And he loved you. Which makes me pretty sure I love you, too. Or I will. Right now, it might just be all about the sex."

Now he's teasing me. "The sex is definitely worth sticking around for," I say, meeting his smile.

"Definitely." He taps the end of my nose, something the old Mason used to do, and happy butterflies dance in my soul. "Did you know I remember movies?" he asks. "A lot of movies."

"Um..." I have no idea where that came from. "I knew about TV shows. I mean, you remember *Lost*."

"And I remember *When Harry Met Sally*. All those real life interviews. One of them was an arranged marriage, and they did just fine. So why can't we? I mean, if we want to?"

And there it is. He's just voiced the heart of what's terrifying me. "Do you want to?"

"Oh, yes," he says, and there is no denying the depth of passion in his voice. Or in his kiss when he bends and kisses me ever so sweetly. "Don't ever doubt that I love you. Not now. Not ever."

I bite my lower lip as I nod. "Okay. Don't ever make me doubt it."

"Deal." He tugs my sheet down and gently cups my breasts. "In fact, I'll go one better," he adds as slowly slides one hand down my belly. "How about I show you?"

————

"Feeling better?" he asks me, two orgasms later.

I nod, then roll over onto my stomach. I prop myself up on my elbows and just look at him, this man I missed so much. Who has, miraculously, come back to me. And who means to stay.

I still need to tell him about the baby, obviously, but I don't feel any guilt about waiting. He's had a lot of reality thrown at him in the last few days, and it's not like I'm going to go into labor this afternoon.

Plus, I need to talk to Seagrave and Dr. Tam. I got pregnant when Mason snuck back to me during his operation. And that's a pretty intense memory. If I tell him, are we risking blowing the circuits in his mind?

I don't know, but I'm not about to do anything that puts Mason at risk. Which means the baby and I are in a holding pattern for now.

Meanwhile, I have a job, and he's still supposed

to be shadowing me at work. If that kick-starts his memory, then all the better.

"We should get up," I say. "We're supposed to be at work. Chasing bad guys. Filing reports. Getting the details from Liam about his concert prima donna."

"And yet I'm not racing for the shower." He runs his fingers lazily over my bare arm. "Was I always such a rule breaker?"

"You were a soldier, so no."

He smirks. "Amnesia agrees with me."

I laugh, which changes quickly to a moan as he flips me over, then straddles me, his mouth closing hard over mine. "Again?" I bite his lip. "You're an insatiable rule breaker."

"Is this a problem for you?"

"Really not," I say, and wrap my arms around his neck right as his phone chimes.

He scowls as he rolls toward the side table. "Only a handful of people have that number, and I probably shouldn't ignore any of them. Sawyer," he says, as he presses the button to start a speaker call.

"You want to tell me why my bike is parked outside Denise's house?" It's Liam's voice, and I sit bolt upright, feeling as guilty as a student caught kissing in the janitor's closet.

"Because we're still in bed. And naked."

There's a pause, then Liam says, "Probably

more information than I needed," and I try very hard not to laugh.

"Turns out she's my wife."

I hear Liam's sharp intake of breath. "You remember?"

"Actually, no. Not a goddamn thing. But apparently it's true. And right now, I'm enjoying being blissfully ignorant. Or I was, until you interrupted."

Liam sighs. "Definitely TMI."

"You outside?" Mason asks. "Because you could have just knocked."

"Got worried. Just in case you forgot who you were again. Would be a shame to lose such a nice bike."

"On the contrary, I'm feeling remarkably self-aware."

"Uh-huh. Ryan says to get your asses to the office."

He winks at me. "Apparently we're in trouble with teacher."

"We're on our way," I shout over him, then smack him in the shoulder as he laughs and ends the call. "I think we shocked him," I say.

"I doubt that."

I shrug. "I don't know. I adore Liam, but I'm not sure he dates. I don't think I've ever heard him talk about going out with anybody." Then again, he's best friends with Dallas Sykes, so I doubt anything could shock Liam.

"Maybe he has a secret lover tucked away somewhere. And maybe," he adds as he tugs me out of bed, "I don't want to talk about Liam while I have you naked in the shower."

18

"You have your memory back," Ryan said, clapping Mason on the back as he slid into a chair next to Denny. "That's incredible. How the hell did it happen?"

"Apparently through the wildfire of rumors," Mason said, his gaze landing on Liam. "I said I knew my name. That's about it."

Liam leaned back in his chair, clearly unperturbed. "It's a start."

"How'd you remember it?" Quince asked.

Mason bit back a smile as he recalled how Denny had screamed his name in bed. Beside him, Denny scrolled through her text messages with her left hand as her right closed over his thigh. Her fingers dug deep into his flesh in a not so subtle warning.

"Just something Denny said." He smiled at the team. "It just clicked."

He pressed his hand over hers before she could pull it away, wanting to keep the contact.

"Here's hoping for more pieces of the puzzle," Ryan said. "As for today's briefing, we need—"

"I'm sorry," Denny said, sliding her chair back and tugging her hand free. He was on his feet, too, pushed into action by the worry etched on her face.

"I just got a ping on Cerise's system. Someone's on her property right now."

"Go," Ryan said. "Check in later."

They both nodded assent, and hurried to the garage. They'd come on Liam's bike, which turned out to be fortuitous considering the early morning snarl of traffic. "I'm going to get me one of these," Mason said as they dismounted at Cerise's house, where an LAPD patrol car was already parked.

This time, Cerise didn't step out to greet them, and when they knocked on the front door, a shadow passed over the peephole before the lock clicked and the door opened. At the same time, a car skidded to a halt in front of the house, and Denny spun. Her hand, Mason noted, was on her weapon.

"I hoped you'd beat me here," Peter said as he sprinted for the door. "Tell me the system notified you directly, and you're not here because Cerise called you, terrified, like she called me."

"The system," Denise assured him. "And it called the police, too."

"They're in the backyard," Cerise said, biting her lower lip as she stood on her front patio. "Two cops. But the guy was already gone."

"You have the feed?" Peter asked Denny.

She nodded. "I can download it to my phone. But it'll be clearer on Cerise's monitoring system. Can we go inside?"

"Huh? Oh, yes. Of course." Cerise stepped back in, then signaled for them all to follow.

The system was set up to play the feed through Cerise's home entertainment center, and Mason watched as Denny turned on the television, selected the proper input, then rewound the video.

"I'm putting it at forty seconds prior to the time-stamp on the alert I received," she said. "Let's see what was happening then."

"Definitely an improvement on coverage," Mason said as the image filled the screen. "No more blind spots. And see? Right there. Movement in that bush."

"I see it," Denny said, moving to stand beside him.

"See!" Cerise squealed the word, then pointed to the shadow of a man as he crawled up the steep incline of the lot behind her house. The sun hung low in the sky, and the vegetation made the area even darker. But as he moved up the hill, more light found him, and the man's features became clearer.

Denny stood beside Mason, their arms brushing as they studied the feed. So he both felt and heard her shocked reaction when the man looked up, and the camera caught him. *The Face.*

Cerise's intruder was the man from the club. More important, he was the man who attacked Denny, who gave her the long, thin injury over which she now pressed her hand.

Behind him, Peter was talking to Cerise. "Do you know him? Is he the same man you saw before?"

Mason was only half-listening. How could he hear over the rage that was bubbling up inside him?

He turned, then met Denny's gaze. She didn't look scared. On the contrary, she looked furious.

And he knew in that moment they were thinking the same thing. They were going to find the Face—and then they were going to do whatever was necessary to figure out what the fuck was going on.

———

It took some time to get Cerise settled. She didn't want to leave her home, but she also didn't want to be alone, and Peter assured her he'd stay the night. Or as long as she needed.

"We're going to assign a team to stay outside the property, too," Denny said. "They'll either act as a deterrent or they'll be first responders if he comes back."

Cerise nodded. "Thanks. I think that would make me feel better. At least for a few days."

"Go open a bottle of wine," Peter suggested with a hug. "I'm going to walk Denise and Jack out."

At the end of the sidewalk, his gentle demeanor changed to one of hardened fury. "The minute I find out who's fucking with her—"

He cut himself off, then drew in a breath as he looked between the two of them. "Who is that asshole, and what's going on?"

"A good question," Denny said, her face all hard lines and grim determination. She met Mason's eyes. "We're going to find out."

"Find out?" Peter's brow rose. "Dammit, Denise, I saw your face. You two know something. You've seen him before. Who is he?"

She started to reply, but Mason jumped in first. "When we know, you'll know."

Peter studied Mason's face, then nodded. "Fine. Good." He sighed. "I want her feeling safe." He pointed between the two of them. "Call me."

As soon as he disappeared back into the house, Denny raised a brow. "I've worked with him. He's a solid agent."

"Doesn't mean we need to pull him into this loop. It's not his rodeo," he added when she raised a brow. "And I don't think Mr. Face has a damn thing to do with Cerise."

She nodded. "I was thinking the same thing. It was one thing for you to notice him at the club. I mean, maybe his face was familiar because you saw him walking down the road as we were driving up, and it had nothing to do with your amnesia at all."

"But..." He tapped his own throat.

"Yeah. Exactly. The assault on me."

"So this guy's been stalking Cerise in order to keep an eye on you or get your attention," Mason said, turning the possibility over in his mind.

"More than that. Maybe he wants *your* attention. The message he gave me was for you."

He let that sit awhile and then shook his head. "Except Cerise's first incident was before I was on the team. It doesn't make sense."

She exhaled. "Then we keep poking around until it does."

"Agreed. At least we have a photo now."

"I already texted a screenshot to Ryan. He's got the tech team on it. With luck, we'll get a hit by tonight. If not, we can call in a favor with Seagrave."

"Good," he said, not at all surprised that she'd already forwarded the image. He may not remember his past with his wife, but he knew her now. And he knew that she was a rock solid agent.

"Back to the office?"

He shook his head. "Let's work from home. I want to get settled." He watched her face as he spoke, both relieved and thrilled when her initial confusion shifted to understanding and, thank God, delight.

"You're moving in." Her bright smile rivaled the California sun.

"It's traditional to live with one's wife." He hesitated, hoping he hadn't assumed too much. "If that's okay?"

"Don't be an ass." Her eyes danced. "I'd kiss you right now, but I don't want to be unprofessional."

He glanced over his shoulder, noting that the two uniformed officers were returning to their car.

"I'll happily take a rain check." He indicated the bike. "I'll drop you off at home, then go leave the bike at Liam's, grab my tiny duffel of personal possessions, and catch a rideshare back to your place."

"Better idea. I'll get a ride with the officers, and you meet me at the house with your stuff. It'll save time. Liam's that way," she said, pointing vaguely toward the coast, then turning and indicating the opposite direction. "And that's us."

"Fair enough." He ran his finger along the line

of her jaw. "I know you're going to want to work when I get there, so I'm telling you right now—I get an hour. Free and clear. And entire hour at my complete discretion."

"Is that right? And what happens in that hour, Mr. Walker?"

"Well, last night I studied your body and learned so many ways to satisfy it. Considering my memory problems, I thought I should see just how well I recall exactly what you like..."

19

As MY TWO cop chauffeurs argue about the thematic similarities in Marvel and Star Wars films, I lose myself in more immediate concerns. Specifically, Cerise and the Face and the mystery of what Mason is supposed to remember. Important enough to attack me on the street, but even such a bold move can't produce results. Not when the information is locked away tight, with no way to get it out.

No way that's safe, anyway.

I frown, thinking about what Seagrave told me. That trying to prime the pump by telling Mason what he's done in the past could permanently injure him. And then my frown deepens as I wonder how in the name of hell I'm supposed to explain getting pregnant.

The patrol car pulls to a stop in front of my house, and I hop out, thanking them for both the ride and the entertaining film discussion. The driver chuckles, and I wave as the car pulls away from the curb.

Instead of going inside, I head to the detached garage that sits at the end of our long driveway. Having lived alone for a while, I've gotten in the habit of eating out or ordering in. Mason was the cook in our family. I was the one who would make a meal of cheese and Ritz crackers if that was the quickest thing to grab.

Tonight, I want to make dinner together. Which is why I get in the car, back out carefully, making sure our neighbor's little girl hasn't left her trike halfway in our driveway, and head down the road to the nearby Ralph's.

Since I'm not a whiz in the kitchen, it takes me a while to navigate the store, which is frustrating as I want to beat Mason back so that I'm there when he arrives. Soon enough, though, I'm clutching two canvas bags with steaks, potatoes, fresh broccoli, and a rather pricey bottle of wine. Plus vanilla ice cream and Chips Ahoy cookies, a sentimental favorite from our early days.

I put the bags on the floorboard, amazed to realize I'm humming. I don't think I've randomly started humming since Mason went away. And this new sense of peace and happiness only drives home how much I missed him. And at the same time, it reminds of how far we still have to go.

With a frown, I silence my tuneless singing. What if he never remembers? What if this is our new beginning and we're really starting all over again, with no history because he doesn't remember and I'm not allowed to tell him?

I have boxes of souvenirs and thousands of digital photos. And I hate thinking that I won't be able to share those with him—or with our child.

I let out a shaky breath, then drive home in a more somber mood. I ignore the garage and park in the driveway, then cross the lawn with my two bags held in my hands.

My mind is on Mason, and my first thought when I see someone moving on the front porch is that Mason beat me home.

But that thought lasts less than a second, and with my next breath, I drop my bags and reach for the weapon I have holstered under my jacket. Because that's not Mason—it's the Face.

The groceries cost me time, though, and he has his weapon out before I do, and this time it's a gun, not a knife. I hear the blast at the same time I feel the sting in my chest, right above my breast.

I gasp, my body reeling, then look down, expecting to see a messy bullet wound. Instead, I see the feathered end of a tiny dart.

A tranquilizer gun?

Oh, dear God. The baby...

Cold panic fills me, and I force it under, determined to rely on my training. I turn toward my car, intending to lock myself inside, get my backup weapon, and signal the SSA. Then I'll defend that small space until Mason or someone on the team arrives to shut this fucker down.

Except I can't manage. My brain is trying to operate my legs, but they're not cooperating. In my mind, I'm sprinting. In reality, I'm collapsing onto the thick turf of my front lawn.

I'm face down, unable to see anything, unable to *do* anything. And then I'm being flipped over, a terrifying and odd sensation, as I can't even feel any hands on me. But I can see, and the afternoon sky comes into view above me, blocked only by the ugly visage of the Face looking down on me. A round face with a bulbous nose and rheumy eyes. There's dirt in the crevices of his skin, and I can smell his breath, like rotten fish and onions. He's the stuff of nightmares, and I don't know what he wants with me. Or, for that matter, what he wants with Mason.

Tell him he needs to remember.

He needs to give back what he took.

That's what the Face had said at the club, and it's what he says again now. I want to scream that I don't understand; that I don't know what he's talking about and neither does Mason. But I can't scream. My throat doesn't work, and even my breathing is slow and laborious.

Am I dying?

"Tell him," the Face whispers before leaning over and doing something on my left. Touching me? I don't know. I can't feel him and I can't move my head to see. "Tell him to look and to see," he adds right before he straightens and stands.

That's when I hear the squeal of brakes, then Mason's voice calling my name as footsteps pound. The Face is standing above me, one foot on either side of my waist.

I can't see Mason, but I know he's there and relief flows through me like wine. He'll catch this bastard. Quince will work his magic with a lie detector, pharmaceuticals, and his other tricks of the trade to get some answers. Everything will be okay.

I just have to hang on long enough.

I have to fight the black that's seeping in around the corners of the world.

"Denny!" Mason shouts again from somewhere off to my left. And then I hear his hard, raw cry of "*No,*" and I watch as the Face jabs a needle into his own neck, then smiles down at me.

But I don't see anything else, because the black has taken me. And the last thing I hear is Mason's anguished cry as he calls my name again and again and again.

20

A TRANQUILIZER*? That's it. You're sure?*

We're still running tests, but so far the lab results are showing only the tranquilizer in her blood stream. And you can see she's already coming to.

Am I? I recognize Mason and Seagrave's voices, but I'm still a little fuzzy on their meaning. Somebody knocked me out. That much seems clear enough. And—

The Face. And the groceries. And—

Why the hell did he knock her out in the first place? So that she couldn't watch when he killed himself? And what the fuck with the phone?

I blink, the world flashing in and out like someone opening and shutting blinds. What do they mean by killed himself? And what phone?

I open my mouth, then whisper, "Mason."

Or maybe I don't say anything at all, because no one seems to hear me.

Mason, please. We're working on it.

I want the SSA working on this, too. They're her team now. They deserve to be in the loop.

I've already talked with Mr. Stark and Mr. Hunter. An SSA team is being fully briefed.

Relief warms me. I don't know what's going on, but I'm glad my friends are working on it, too.

Look.

That's Mason's voice, and he's close. So close.

"Denny? Denny, it's me. Can you wake up?"

I want to tell him that I am awake. Before, it felt like I was dreaming, but I'm awake now. I just feel so heavy. Even my eyelids are so, so heavy.

"Give her a moment," Seagrave says. "It'll take her some time to swim up out of it."

He's right, and it's a good metaphor. It's as if I'm kicking toward the surface, and I actually gasp as I break through into reality, my eyes fluttering open to find Mason's eyes fixed on me, first full of worry and then shifting to relief.

"Thank God," he says, clutching my hand.

"The Face. He hit me with a tranquilizer?"

"He did." Seagrave rolls his chair beside Mason. "Welcome back."

"Just a tranquilizer. Is it safe?" I think of the baby. Please, please, don't let anything hurt the baby.

"Just a tranquilizer," Seagrave says.

I nod, reassured. I know enough about weapons to not be too worried about a tranquilizer dart. "But why? Did he just want to make a clean getaway after he left the message?"

Mason and Seagrave look at each other. "What message?" Mason asks.

"Same as before," I tell them. "That you have to remember. You have to give back what you took."

Again, they share a look.

"Don't keep me in the dark," I say. My strength is flowing back, the grogginess leaving me. I push myself up until I'm sitting in the hospital bed. Then I look around, for the first time noticing that I'm in Mason's old quarters.

Seagrave nods his head. Just a tiny tilt, but it's enough. Mason focuses on me and says, "There are two things you should know. First, the Face is dead."

"What? Was he trying to escape? Because we needed to talk—"

"Suicide," Mason says. "He injected himself with cyanide."

My mouth drops open, and for a moment I'm dumbstruck. "Why would he do that?"

"One of many questions," Seagrave says, and I look between him and Mason, waiting for him to tell me the rest of the questions. And the answers.

After a moment, Mason lifts a shoulder, looking

positively helpless. "He left you a phone. Right in your hand. A smart phone with absolutely nothing on it."

"Oh." I try to process that but it makes no sense. "You tried re-dial? You checked the emails?"

The both just stare at me. Of course they did.

"It's here?" I ask.

Mason points to the side table where what looks like a burner smart phone sits next to a pink plastic jug filled with ice water.

"Can I look?"

He raises a brow, but doesn't protest. I understand I'm being ridiculous; I won't see a thing they didn't. But that knowledge doesn't curtail the urge, and as soon as he puts the phone in my hand, I sigh.

Then I yelp, because the device chirps in my hand.

"What did you do?" Mason says, and I shake my head.

"Nothing. I—look. It's a text message."

They gather close and we read the message together.

The first part is a string of chemical symbols that my poor science can't decipher. I don't need to, though. It's clear enough from the words that follow:

It's in her blood.
72h incubation period.

Give us the encryption key.

We'll make her the antidote.

Reply when you have the key.

My blood.

My blood, my baby. Oh, dear God.

I tell myself it's okay. Maybe this is just a
threat. A scare tactic. The SOC team said there
was only tranquilizer in my blood, after all.

But I know that's not true. Whatever the toxin
is, it's there. The medtechs just weren't looking
for it.

Still, so long as I get the antidote in time, the
baby and I will be fine.

That's what I tell myself, anyway.

But I don't really know if that's true.

And with the location of the encryption key
buried in Mason's head, I don't think I'll ever
find out.

———

"He shouldn't be doing this," I say, looking into the
conference room through the one-way glass
window. Fear burns through me—for myself, for
my baby, for Mason.

"He doesn't have a choice," Quince says, putting
a hand on my shoulder to stop me from pacing.

"There's always a choice."

"And he's made his," Liam says.

I turn, looking at my friends through tear-filled eyes. "What if it breaks him?"

Neither man answers. They don't have too. Mason loves me. And if the only way to pull the location of this encryption key out of his head is by forcing his memories, then that's what he's going to do. Even though the risk is high. Even though he may forget everything. Or worse.

I think about what Mason has told me. About the videos of other agents who'd been forced to face their hidden memories too early. Men who'd snapped completely.

Please, please don't let that happen to Mason.

On the other side of the conference room, Mason sits in one of the rolling chairs. He's wearing a T-shirt, and a variety of monitoring bands surround his chest and head, all hooked to an array of monitors and a computer that sits in front of Dr. Tam.

Mason's arms are strapped down, and he looks like a prisoner. Someone in for interrogation. And that illusion is bolstered by the two IV drips going into his veins. One drip contains a fast-acting sedative so the doctor can knock him out if he starts to tip over into the danger zone. The other contains a serotonin-like compound that is supposed to keep him calm as he moves through the memory stimulation process.

"Happy thoughts," Dr. Tam had said, with an ironic half-smile. "Think of it as forced happy thoughts."

Not exactly a high-level medical explanation, but I understood what she meant. The amnesia had been induced by some sort of horrific trauma. To pull out the buried memories, Mason had to find his way around that trauma. And that meant not sliding back into the mental state that had surrounded the trauma and instead creating a "happy" back door.

All good in theory. In practice, it sounded pretty damn dicey.

"I can't lose him all over again," I say.

Liam moves to stand beside me at the window. "That's why he's doing it. Because he can't live without you, either. And that's going to happen if we don't get the antidote."

I wipe away a tear and nod. Seventy-two hours. That's the window to get me the antidote. After that, there's no cure, and I'll be dead within a week.

That's what the medical team tells me, anyway. All things considered, I don't have any reason to doubt them.

It's more than just me, of course. The toxin in my blood is something never seen before. It's a national security threat. And even if I were completely healthy, I know that Mason would still be sitting in that chair, ready to sacrifice himself to save the world.

Inside the room, Dr. Tam starts to talk to Mason, her voice calm and level. Since she doesn't actually know what he experienced, she's hypnotized him in the hopes of pulling out those hidden memories more easily. I just hope the memories don't turn out to be dangerous.

She's been fully briefed by Colonel Seagrave, and she starts to describe the mission, the details of which I've never known. Nor have Quince or Liam or any of the Stark team, and I'm grateful to Seagrave for giving everyone clearance. I need my friends' support. And their help.

The job was to infiltrate an international mercenary group known as *La Guerre Rouge* in order to relay back information about its various activities, especially arms and drug trafficking. The insertion was a success, and Mason was able to gain the trust of one of the group's high-ranking commanders who eventually tasked Mason with a secret project that was deep in development.

All of that, the SOC knew from Mason's infrequent reports and dead drops. And as Dr. Tam talks Mason through all of that, his vitals stay normal.

I look at Liam and Quince, trying to hold back my optimism. Because surely this means it's going to be okay. Surely it will turn out that we could have done this straightaway, and that Mason had been left in the dark out of an overabundance of caution.

As I watch, Dr. Tam leads him down the path of memory, and Mason describes the day to day of his job. The horrific things he witnessed, even participated in, in order to establish his cover. I understand the work and what it entails, so I'm not shocked. But I also know that too much living in the underworld can taint a man's blood, and I don't want Mason to go back. Not after this.

I look at Quince, wanting to ask him if he thinks Ryan would recruit Mason into the SSA. But I stop myself from asking. Right now, we just need to get through today.

Finally, Dr. Tam leads Mason up to his last communication. He'd discovered something truly horrific in the works, and he'd signaled that he'd be sending more details. But the details never came. Instead, Jack Sawyer woke up in Victorville.

"Let's start with the truck and work backwards. You remember being thrown out of the truck?"

"Yes."

"Do you remember being put in the truck?"

"No."

The electronic lines on the monitors behind Mason begin to spike. I reach for Quince's hand and hold tight.

"Let's talk about that. Let your mind go back. Who were you with?"

The lines spike more. Mason goes pale.

"Did they say anything before putting you in the truck?"

His body starts to shake, and I hold my breath.

Another question, then another and another, but no answers, and with every question his reaction becomes erratic, his body more strained, until finally Dr. Tam asks him to recall the face of the cell leader with whom he'd become close.

A wild, gut-wrenching scream rips from Mason's throat and he stands up, clutching his head, his face screwed up in pain, as wires and IV tubes flail about, until he drops to the floor, curls up in a ball on the tile, and rocks and whimpers and rocks.

His scream, however, continues to echo—or at least I think it does. After a moment, I realize it's me.

"It's no use," Dr. Tam says into the intercom after she's given him more sedative and helped him back into the chair. "Not right now. I see no signs of permanent damage or regression, but he needs time to recover before we try again."

"She can't try again," I tell Seagrave, who's joined us in the viewing area. "You're not going to get anything and it's going to destroy him."

"That period of time is key," Seagrave says,

musing. "Right before they dumped him in Victorville. He learned something. Something dangerous and important. We need to know what that is." He meets my eyes. "And not just because we need to save you. There's more riding on this than the life of one woman, even a woman I trust and admire. And since the toxin in your blood stream is an agent we haven't seen before, we have to assume it's at the heart of a biological weapons attack. We need to know what they're planning, when, and how."

I know all that. Of course I know it.

"We have to try again," Seagrave says flatly. "And we have to keep trying until we get answers. Or we can't try anymore."

21

Mason paced the small suite that the SOC had given to him and Denny for the night, a set of rooms that visiting operatives were permitted to use while on local assignments. Seagrave had smiled when he offered it, calling it a courtesy. After all, the clock was ticking, and both he and Denny needed rest. They didn't need to be driving back to Silver Lake.

That part was true enough. But what Mason also knew was that if they'd said no to the offer, Seagrave would have insisted. The information in Mason's head was too important to let him wander away. Not only that, but while they believed the toxin in Denny's blood was dormant, they still wanted to do regular draws and tests.

Which meant that the suite was more necessity than courtesy.

Even so, it was private, without the monitoring systems set up in the infirmary or the holding cells. And for that courtesy, Mason was grateful. He wanted Denny in his arms. And he wanted their privacy. He wanted them to get lost in each other just in case tonight was the last night they ever could. Or, at least, the last night he'd ever remember.

"I have to tell Dr. Tam to push harder," he said, pausing in front of the table where Denny was reviewing the lab and chemistry reports.

She slammed the laptop shut, obviously frustrated. "I can hack my way into almost any system. I can ferret information out of anything with an electronic brain. But damned if I can figure out the chemistry of whatever they've shoved into my blood."

With a sigh, she dragged her fingers through her hair, then smiled up at him. "Sorry, distracted. What did you say?"

"Dr. Tam. I need to tell her to push harder."

"What? No. We're in this room so we can grab a few hours of rest. So that you can get your strength back. But that doesn't mean she needs to press harder. You started to snap, Mason. Harder, and you will."

"I have to try." He pulled out the chair beside her and sat down. "Seventy-two hour incubation period, and your life is on the line. Do you think I'm going to back off?"

"I think you need to be smart. You push too hard, and you could get lost inside your own head."

"If I don't push, you'll die. Not only that, but they have plans for this toxin. You won't be the only one dead, and we both know it."

She shook her head, but she didn't argue. He knew he was right, and so did she.

"I'm strong," he said gently, standing up and then tugging her into his arms.

She shook her head. "Not strong enough."

He laughed, then wiped away one of her tears. "Thanks for the vote of confidence."

Her lips twitched, but didn't quite turn into a smile. "I can't stand the thought of losing you. Especially not now when—"

She cut herself off with a shake of her head.

"When you've just gotten me back?"

She hesitated, then nodded, and he almost asked her what she wasn't saying. He didn't, though. Instead, he just kissed her. "That's how I feel, too. And I'm willing to do anything to keep you. And, hopefully, come all the way back to you."

"Mason—" She stopped, then slid off his lap and started to pace. "You need to know—"

A hard rap at the door interrupted her, and they both turned that direction.

"Nurse," a deep male voice said, and Denny frowned.

"Come in," she called, then grimaced as she added to Mason, "Time to get stuck again."

A nurse in jeans and a hospital green scrub jacket entered, tossing Denny's chart carelessly onto the table as he prepared the vial. Denny had already taken a seat on the edge of the small sofa in the suite's living area, so he moved to her as Mason hung back at the table.

He'd seen dozens of people have blood drawn, and had himself bled into enough tubes to stock a blood bank. Even so, watching the process ranked low on his list of favorite things, and he looked down instead, his eyes skimming over Denny's chart. He flipped the pages casually, then froze when he reached the doctor's notes.

> Prenatal/Amnio toxin analysis
> @16weeks: negative
> Maternal toxin: positive
> Retest amniotic fluid following 72h
> inc. period

He read the note again, then one more time, first

with ebullient joy, then with a rising sense of dread and betrayal.

She was pregnant.

He was going to be a father.

But even as those thoughts lifted him up, the reality that surrounded them brought him crashing down. And not the reality of the toxin or his memory. The other reality. The darker reality.

The reality in which his wife who purported to love him had sex with another man sixteen weeks ago.

Who?

The question gnawed at him, the thought of his wife with another man bubbling in his blood like some caustic, toxic poison.

He left the report on the desk and started to pace the room, jealousy and doubt coursing through him. He'd fallen in love with Denny—not just before. Hell, he couldn't even remember before. But *now*. Right here, right now. With her cleverness, her humor, her dedication. And, he'd thought, her loyalty.

Was he not seeing the real woman?

Had there been problems in their marriage before?

Had she believed he was dead, and found solace in another man's arms?

For a moment, he let himself believe that, the theory giving him some peace. Then he remembered what she'd confirmed before the first time they'd made love while he was still Jack. She'd told him that she knew Mason was alive.

She'd known that he—that Mason—was out there in the world.

And she'd still fucked another man.

Goddammit all to hell.

"Are you okay?"

He'd been pacing so fast he was practically jogging. Now he looked around the room in a daze. The nurse was gone, and Denny was standing, her face painted in concern, as if she truly cared at all. As if he wasn't the biggest fool in the world.

"Does it matter to you?"

She blinked. "What? Of course." She took a step toward him. "Mason, what's wrong?"

"I have no memory of our time together before I came back," he said slowly. "No memory of what we had or didn't have. How we loved or didn't love."

"Didn't?" she repeated, her brow furrowed.

"You tell me we were in love, but I don't know. What evidence do I have? What evidence other than the fact that I fell in love with you now. Here."

She licked her lips, looking at him as if he were an old jigsaw puzzle with lots of missing pieces. "I love you, too. Then, and now."

"*Don't.*" The word ripped out of him, and he pointed an accusatory finger at her. "Do not stand there and tell me you love me. Don't lie to me and say that you waited for me, that you missed me and mourned me. Not when it's all a lie. Not when you're carrying another man's child."

She'd been walking toward him, but now she stopped, frozen to the spot, and he knew that he'd hit home. That she hadn't expected the secret to be revealed. And although that was a victory for truth, it damn sure felt like defeat.

"I fell in love with you in the here and now. But I guess that was just Jack. You'd already tossed Mason aside."

She shook her head. "No, you don't—"

"What? Understand? Are you going to explain it to me? I think I understand betrayal well enough."

He wasn't pacing, but he was moving around the room. He didn't want this rage, this fury, but at least it was *his*. He'd felt this way only one other time since he'd awakened in Victorville— when they'd made love. Not fury, then, but a fullness. Real, concrete emotions. Everything else was twinged with a sense of hollowness because he was half a person, his past left behind somewhere. But in her arms, he'd been whole. And now he was whole again as he railed against her betrayal.

How ironic that his love for her both saved and destroyed him.

"Who was it? Quince? Before he met Eliza? Liam? Is that why you love that shower so much?"

Her unreadable expression focused into fury. "Those men are your friends and my colleagues. Don't you dare accuse them that way."

She was right, but he swallowed the apology, not willing to give up any ground, his anger eating away at him, but freeing him as well. Had he lost his shit since Victorville? Was this the first time the wounds had opened and he'd let the bile spill out?

Maybe it was—hell, maybe Denny was getting more than she deserved.

Then he remembered that she was four months pregnant and he'd been gone for over two years, and his rage whipped right back up again.

"Was it Peter? Did you sleep with him?"

"Absolutely not," she said, crossing her arms over her chest and tilting her head to the side. "Are you finished? Do I get to talk? Say anything in my defense?"

She spoke so calmly and evenly, that he could feel his fury deflating. He tried to hold onto it, clinging to it like a life raft. "Are you pregnant?"

"Yup."

"Then I don't know what you could possibly say."

"How about this—you're an idiot."

"I'm a—excuse me?"

"An idiot," she repeated. "One who clearly

needed to have the mother of all tantrums because, hello, weight of the world on top of amnesia, so I'm willing to cut you some slack." She screwed up her mouth. "Maybe not for the Liam and Quince comments, though. That pushed the envelope."

"I'm sorry?" The apology came out as a question, not because he wasn't sorry, but because her words and her demeanor were confusing the shit out of him.

"I *am* pregnant, you stupid man. I'm pregnant with your baby."

He just stared at her, because those words didn't—couldn't—make sense.

"I told you," she said. "When you asked if I knew Mason was alive. I told you that he—you—had made contact twice. The second time was now. As Jack, I mean. But the first time—well, that was about four months ago. In February. On—"

"Our anniversary." His voice was barely a whisper. *He remembered his anniversary.* "Valentine's Day."

"You remember? Our wedding? That night?"

He tried to pull it out, but no. All he remembered was February 14. "I remember the date. Like I remember Christmas."

With a sigh, he moved to her, then pulled her into his arms. "I guess that date's important to me. I'm sorry," he added, lifting her hand to his lips and kissing her fingers. "I shouldn't have—"

"No, you shouldn't have." She smiled, then kissed the corner of his mouth. "But under the circumstances I forgive you."

Guilt still clung to him. "I mean it. I'm sorry."

"I know you are. Now shut up, okay? You get a one-time pass. Do something this bone-headed again, and we'll see a different outcome. Okay?"

"Okay." He drew in a breath, the world shiny and new despite all the horror surrounding them. "So we're really having a baby?" Pleasure poured through him. A father—was he really going to be a father?

"We are," she said. "Assuming I survive the next—"

He cut her off with a kiss. "You will," he said firmly. "Don't you dare doubt it."

She met his eyes, the trust he saw there almost enough to melt him. "I don't. But sometimes faith isn't enough. We need a plan. We need information."

"Which is exactly why I need to push harder. Let Dr. Tam go deeper. All these scars on my back. On my neck—I don't know how I got them, but they must be related. They're new. I was tortured. And I stole something. It has to be related."

"Agree."

"Did I have them four months ago?"

She bit her lower lip. "I don't know."

"But I thought—"

"You blindfolded me."

"Did I?"

She smacked him lightly. "Don't look so amused. It was—*Oh!*"

"What?"

"I can't tell you about it. Not now," she added, then grinned at him like a kid with a secret. "But I think telling you with Dr. Tam in the room would be an exceptionally good idea."

22

HE COULD HEAR THEIR WORDS.

Denny's. Dr. Tam's.

They sounded as if they were above, and he was deep in a well, but he could hear them. That was all that mattered.

He was sedated—he knew that.

He knew that he was hypnotized, too.

Most of all, he knew this was dangerous. Something about the path. Something about how it could all fall out from under him and he'd end up someplace else altogether with no map to get back to himself.

He looked out, and he saw the path. Yes. Dangerous. Mines buried everywhere. Barbed wire on the fences. Snipers hiding behind the rocks.

He had to go slow and be careful.

But he had to go. Because he was going to be a

father, and oh, dear God, how incredible was that? He was going to be a daddy, and he had to keep his child safe. Had to protect him from—

From what?

"Was there a meeting?" The voice seemed to come from inside his head. "Do you remember a meeting where you were told what was going on? You were with them a long time. You must have had their confidence."

He glanced over at the rocks where the snipers hid. Had he ever truly had their confidence? Or had they always had their weapons aimed right at him?

"A toxin," he heard himself saying. His body went tense. *Denny.* She'd been given the toxin.

"And the meeting? Was there a meeting? Or perhaps you stumbled across some information?"

His head started to ache and he felt his body rocking. Had to be careful. Couldn't step on a mine.

"Just a meeting." He knew the voice now—Dr. Tam. "No danger to you at the meeting. You're fine now, just fine. It was a meeting, wasn't it?"

"Yes. They trust me. No barbed wire here. But there's a sniper."

"Deep breaths," the doctor said. "Calm down. The sniper won't hurt you."

"No." He drew a breath. Then another. "I don't know about him. Not yet."

"Who—" Denny's voice.

"Shhh. Later. What did you learn, Agent Walker. What did they tell you about the toxin?"

"All about the economics. That's what Jeremy said. They'd think it was a terrorist act when really it was about getting paid."

"Jeremy?"

"The sniper." His body felt cold. "The pumpkin eater. My ally, only he's not. I don't know that—didn't know that?—but he's not an ally."

He was getting close to the ice. To the danger. "So much wrong there. He's not Jeremy, not my partner." The ice was fire, bleeding into his skull. The pain was creeping up on him. Sharp teeth, long claws. "I need—"

"You're doing fine, Agent Walker. I'm monitoring you. Deep breaths. Good. Take another. I'm keeping you safe. And we're over a month before you returned, remember? Nothing's happened to you yet. Don't worry about Jeremy. Right now he trusts you."

"He has a secret."

"But you don't know it yet, do you? Right now, you're on the garden path. Where does their garden path lead?"

"Death," he said flatly. "Unless there's an antidote, it's death."

He heard a sharp intake of breath at the same time the doctor said, "Unless?"

"They contaminate the population. Infiltrate the fast food market. How much wouldn't the government pay for an antidote? The government, corporations, even individuals? Taint the food at the burger barn or taco shack down the street and the big nasty conglomerate will pay to make the population healthy again?"

He remembered. They'd told him. Wanted him to head up the American cell. The first cell with the first batch of toxin. A demonstration for the rest of the world. If the rest of the world ponied up, no need to infect anyone else. The biggest protection racket in the world.

"Was that when you made contact?"

"No." His voice was like a whimper.

"No? Mason, listen to me. Take a deep breath. Loosen your grip—you're going to draw blood if you dig into your thigh that hard. You're still safe. Listen to my voice. If you haven't made contact yet, you're still a long way from when they will torture you. That's it. That's good. You're doing much better. Are you back on the garden path?"

"Yes." But he knew there were still snipers everywhere.

"What did you do?"

"I infected it. The formula."

"The toxin?"

"The antidote. I didn't have time—couldn't erase it. Couldn't destroy. But a virus. A code.

They were afraid—didn't trust their own people. Only one mainframe, one backup. And I was making the trip—coming to investigate supply lines. And I knew I could see her. I could make sure she knew. She'd be my backup in case it all went south."

"Denny? Your wife."

"They didn't know about her. Not then. I went to her. Our anniversary. She couldn't know I was there. Needed deniability."

"You went to her anonymously."

"I—yes." He remembered. Oh, God, he remembered how beautiful she'd looked. How soft her skin had felt. "I had to see her. And I had to give her the code."

"And you did."

"I did."

"And they never knew."

"No. And I went back—I had to go back. There was more to my mission, and I—" His mind filled with red.

"Mason. It's okay. Deep breath."

He sucked in air. Released it. And tried to make his body relax. "Later I learned about Jeremy —that he was the pumkin eater— and when he realized what I knew, he—" His breath was coming in gasps, his lungs like fire. "He didn't kill me. They didn't have the encryption key. Couldn't kill me until they found it."

"You'd hidden it."

"Yes."

"With your wife."

"Yes." An icy calm drifted over him. "They asked me where. They tried to torture it out of me. They came close to getting it. Close to finding it."

"But they didn't. What did you do to keep them from discovering that you'd given it to Denny?"

The cold was peaceful, like fallen snow on a wide open plain.

"I broke."

23

"NONE OF THIS MAKES SENSE," I say as Dr. Tam turns off the music app on her phone, stopping the steady flow of Chopin's *Nocturne*, which she said she'd been using to help make Mason more receptive to hypnosis.

"Why doesn't it make sense?"

I hold Mason's hand as his lids flutter and he comes back to me, opening his eyes as if waking from a nap.

"Because he never gave me anything that night. He barely spoke. And, well, at the time, I didn't even know for certain it was him."

Dr. Tam's brows rise. So do Mason's.

I roll my eyes. "After a point I realized it was you," I say. "Or I convinced myself it was. After all, I didn't think Nikki or Jamie would send me a gigolo. And I was right—it was you," I say. "You just said so."

Dr. Tam still looks about to laugh. I just shake my head, not sure if I should be amused or frustrated. The night had been incredible. A surprise gift of a massage from my friends. A "sensory immersion" experience the attendant had said, then blindfolded me. And then ... well, then there were familiar hands on me and a voice I was certain belonged to my husband. A voice I so desperately wanted to be his...

And it was. *It was.*

"Don't you remember?" I ask now. "Hasn't it all come back? You said you hid the encryption key with me. Can't you remember where?"

But he just shakes his head, looking miserable. "I don't. Dammit, I couldn't find that in my mind. It wasn't there. It just wasn't in my head."

"Probably your subconscious trying to protect Denny. But this is good progress. We can try again tomorrow. Possibly get further."

"And if we don't?" I ask. "I don't have that many tomorrows left."

But Dr. Tam only shakes her head. "He needs rest. I'll be back first thing in the morning."

We both protest some more, but it's no use. Honestly, I'm a little bit relieved. As terrified as I am of this toxin that is threatening me and my child, I still have days left to vanquish it. But one

wrong move—one push that's just a little too hard—
and I could lose Mason forever.

Mason, however, is genuinely frustrated.

"We can still figure this out," I say. "We just
have to try and think like you."

He smirks. "At the moment, you know the old
me a lot better than I do. So tell me. What would I
have done?"

I exhale, then move into the bedroom of our
suite. I climb on the bed and hug a pillow in my lap,
my favorite thinking position. "We know it was an
encryption key, one you used to give an entire
computer system a very bad head cold."

Mason rolls his eyes. "I remember that movie,"
he says, the comment making me giddy. Because
Independence Day was one of our favorite popcorn,
wine, and a movie in bed Friday night rituals. The
kind of flick we both enjoyed ... but also didn't
mind missing if we got distracted.

Right now isn't the time to traipse down that
block of memory lane, though, so I keep the focus
on our conundrum. "It must have been a physical
key, not just a code you memorized."

He nods. "Right. I wouldn't risk something
short. Or something written down."

I think about that, then frown. "I suppose you
could have written it down. Hang on." I pull up my
phone where I keep a photograph of the letter he
left for me after that night. "You left me this. But if

this was supposed to shout, *Hey Denny, I'm a code,* you failed pretty badly."

He takes the phone, and I read over his shoulder:

Lovely Denny,

Thank you for the night. For fueling my heart with new memories. For reminding me that there are things to live for and fight for. Things that burn hotter than a shooting star and last longer than eternity.

We will, I think, see each other again, though I cannot say when or where. But I will hold onto last night and the pleasure we shared.

Don't look for me. Don't try to find me. Don't ask questions to which you don't truly want the answers.

For the time being, last night was enough.

Yours,
The Master

He makes a scoffing sound. "The Master?"

"Hey, don't look at me. You're the one who wrote it."

"Well, you're right. No code there. What we're looking for is a randomly generated encryption code stored on a disk or a flash drive or something of that ilk. Easy to smuggle out, easy to sneak in."

"Agreed," I say. "What kind of op-tech were you issued?"

He tilts his head to the side and gives me a look until I screw my head back on.

"Right," I say. "You don't remember. Hang on. We can figure this out."

I text Seagrave, expecting him to shoot the answer back to me in the same manner. Instead, there's a rap on our door within two minutes. Mason heads out of the bedroom to answer it, and I stay curled up with my pillow.

"There was a drive in the earpiece of your reading glasses." I can hear Seagrave talking to Mason. "Also a Visa with an embedded drive and a fake ID with the same."

He rolls himself into the bedroom, then comes to a halt at the foot of the bed. Mason follows, then sits beside me on the bed. "Dr. Tam just briefed me," Seagrave says to both of us. "I take it you're trying to put the hours between now and the next session to good use?"

"Damn right," I say.

"Good. I can't fault the doctor for wanting to protect a patient. But..."

"Exactly," Mason says, looking at me with such concern and love it makes my heart flutter.

"Any one of those things could have been left behind in the hotel," I point out. "It was the penthouse at the Stark Century. Maybe lost and found?"

"It's a long shot, but worth it," Mason says as Seagrave dials his phone. While Seagrave asks Damien to check with the hotel, Mason makes a good point to me.

"I wouldn't just leave it randomly lying around. We know that I left it with you. That's what I said, right?"

"That you'd hidden it with me. Yes."

"You don't live in the penthouse. It doesn't make sense I'd just stick it in a drawer. Did you have luggage?"

"No." I think back. "I'd been working that day. The SSA uses the sub-basement for recruitment and training. I was putting some agent trainees through their paces."

"And?"

"And I was having a shit day," I say. "It was our anniversary. You were gone. I was lonely. Then Ryan told me about the massage that Nikki and Jamie ordered for me, and he sent me up to the penthouse."

"So you had your backpack or a purse or something?"

"A purse. I remember because I'd gone shopping with the girls the previous Saturday and we'd seen all the Valentine's Day displays." I hug the pillow closer. "I guess it was obvious how sad I was."

"Okay. Good. I would have put the key in your purse."

"Except I didn't find a stray credit card or reading glasses or any other drive."

"No new keys hanging on your ring?" Seagrave asks, rejoining our conversation. "Just because those were our op-tech devices, Mason could have used anything."

I get off the bed and find my backpack, then check my keys. Every one is familiar.

I turn back to the men with a shrug.

"How long did you use the purse?"

"Just a few days, honestly," I confess. "It was a nice bag, but I like my backpack."

"Maybe it's still in an interior pocket. Or hidden in the lining."

I nod slowly. That makes a lot of sense, and I look at Seagrave, who frowns. "So we go, right? We go check my closet right now."

"Or I can send an agent to retrieve your purses."

Mason starts to argue, but I cut him off, something else occurring to me. "Why didn't you send it straight to Seagrave?"

He rubs his temples "I don't know. I don't remember. I might never remember." He paces at the foot of the bed. "Maybe I thought it wouldn't be safe? Intercepted? I don't know. But we need to go look."

Seagrave nods. "As I said, tell me where and I'll send a team."

"No. Denny and me. Together."

Seagrave makes a rough noise in his throat. "Not a good idea. I need to keep you safe—Dr. Tam wants back in your head in the morning."

"My head will be right here on my shoulders in the morning."

"And as for Denise, the toxin—"

"Is safe for now," Mason says firmly.

The colonel aims a commanding glance at both of us in turn. "I can keep you here, you know."

"But you won't," I say. "You know we need to look. And you know we're running out of time."

For a moment, I think he's going to disagree. Then he says, "Go. I'll have an agent drive you. But come back with answers."

We don't hesitate, and as our car races toward Silver Lake, I call Damien to check for news from the hotel.

"Sorry. Nothing in the Lost and Found, or the log for that month. I checked the safe and long term storage, as well, in case Mason left it with someone at the front desk. Nothing."

I bite back then urge to curse, thank him, and fill Mason in.

"That just means the answer's at the house."

We drive the rest of the way in silence. Some idea is bouncing around in my mind, but I can't seem to grasp it. And as we go inside, I can only hope that the encryption key will be shoved down in the bottom of my purse, and whatever thought I can't seem to catch won't be important at all.

But there's no key in my purse. Or my backpack.

Or anywhere in the closet.

"There's something," I say. "Something you said or Damien said—I don't know. But something is bugging me, and I can't figure out what."

"Well, you're doing better than me. I don't have any ideas at all, clear or fuzzy."

He heads out of the closet and back into the main area of the master bath. It's a mess, as we'd started to chip away the old tiles before Mason left, and I haven't wanted to tackle it alone.

He holds out a hand, and I take it, then let him pull me close. "We're going to get through this," he says. "And all of this and the rest of the house? We're going to do it together. And when we're all hot and dusty from working, we'll take long soapy showers, watch old movies in bed, and make love."

"Promise?"

He kisses the top of my head. "At least until the

baby comes. Then it will be all four o'clock feedings and dirty diapers."

I laugh, then tilt my head up as fear dries up my humor. "Do you mind?"

He looks completely blank. "Mind?"

"You hardly remember us at all. Now there's going to be a baby, and—"

He kisses me. Hard and fast and so deliciously deep that I'm gasping when he pulls away. "No," he says with so much intensity that I wouldn't dare doubt him. "I don't mind." He strokes my hair. "But let's make sure we get there."

I nod. As much as I want to pretend it doesn't exist, my own blood is a ticking time bomb.

The trouble, of course, is that we don't know where to look next. So we end up in the kitchen. Mason drinking orange juice and me guzzling milk with Hershey's syrup in it, which I never drink, but sounds amazing at the moment.

"The whole thing makes no sense," he says. "I would have told you something. Given you something."

I manage a thin smile. "You gave me a house. A baby. That note."

"Pretty sure I didn't impregnate you with an encryption key," he says. "As for the house, I didn't even manage to help you fix it up before I disappeared on you. And the note..." He shrugs. "Well, looks like that was just a piece of sentimentality."

I toy with my straw. "I still liked getting it. Having it. Something of you to hold on to."

He nods. "I'm sure I knew you'd hold on to it. Which is why it makes sense that I would have used that to communicate. So why didn't I?" He slams back the last of his orange juice. "The least I could have done was told you what color I wanted all the rooms."

I laugh, which is what he intended, of course. But then I freeze, that niggling sense that I know something returning.

"Denny?"

"I think I've got it," I say. "Not exactly, but maybe sort of."

His brow furrows. "I'm listening."

"Earlier, you said the answer's at the house."

"Which is why we're here, and there's no answer."

I push my chair back. "I think there is. Come on."

The house has four bedrooms, and we were using one as command central for the renovations. That's where I take him now. "You wouldn't know that I was going to stop the work," I tell him. "That I couldn't face doing it alone. So you left the key in here. You came while I was at work, and hid it. Then you left me the clue at the hotel."

He looks around at the cans of paint samples and full gallons. At the books of carpet remnants that we were still debating. The boxes of hardwood flooring that still needs to be installed. The tiles, the fixtures, and all the other things that we'd collected but not yet installed or cleared out.

He shakes his head, looking overwhelmed. "I don't know, babe. The odds of us finding it in here. It's small, remember? And that's assuming it's here at all."

"It is," I say, feeling positively giddy. "You told me."

24

"I TOLD YOU?" Mason stared at his wife, wanting to tell her that she was an optimistic crazy person. He knew better, though. For one, he wouldn't have married a crazy woman who latched onto unsupported optimism. For another, in the short time he'd come to re-know Denny, he'd learned all over again how smart and capable she was.

If she said that he told her, he must have told her. And under the circumstances, the fact that he couldn't remember didn't mean a whole hell of a lot.

"So when exactly did I tell you? And what exactly did I say?"

She reached out and took his hand, then eased close to him for a kiss. "You told me in that brilliant note of yours." Her delighted laugh caught him off guard, washing away the building worry. Maybe they really would get the antidote in time. "Want me to explain how brilliant you were?"

"Yeah," he said. "I really do."

"First of all, calling yourself The Master. Innocuous, right? But it's a clue. Only not the kind you'd see until you saw the other clue. They go together."

He narrowed his eyes. "Now you're just toying with me."

She shook her head and pulled out her phone, then passed it to him, the screen showing an image of the note.

"*Burn hotter than a shooting star,*" she read, looking at the screen with him. "That's another clue. And *last longer than eternity*. Taken together, they lead right over there." She pointed to a shelf in the corner with at least two dozen cans of paint.

He headed over to the shelf and started reading off the paint names. "Moonrise. Nightfall. Shooting Star." He shook his head, still clueless. "They all deal with night?"

"Good guess, but no. *Longer than eternity* is the clue that tells me you're talking about paint." She grinned. "You don't remember, but before you left on assignment, I bitched about how we should have waited to buy the paint until you got back—remember, we never expected you'd be gone so long."

"And I told you that paint's not like eggs." *He remembered.* It was fuzzy, but he remembered.

Her eyes widened, and she nodded slowly. "Yes. You said—"

"—there were so many chemicals in paint that an unopened can would probably last longer than eternity." He pressed his fingertips to his temple and started to idly rub. "Denny, oh my God."

"I know, right? You did this. You sent me a message, and I was too dense to even think about looking for one."

"And when you said that The Master was a clue, it meant that we were talking about colors we picked out for our bedroom?" He said it as a question because he didn't remember, but that seemed to make sense.

She nodded. "And as for *shooting star*..." She pointed to the shelf, where three quart-size cans of off-white trim paint sat in a row. "The walls are going to be a pale, pale blue. You said this would be a perfect complement."

"I don't believe it." His words were barely a whisper. "Whatever we're looking for is in one of those cans."

"Is that a memory or a guess?"

He squeezed her hand. "A guess. But I think it's a good one."

"Me, too."

They looked at the cans together for a moment, then she shrugged and grabbed a flat head screwdriver from a box of tools. "So now we open and dump?"

"That one," he said, pointing to the one closest to him. "See? Looks like one of us cracked the lid."

She nodded, grabbed it off the shelf, then used the screwdriver to pop the lid off. "It's just paint," she said, peering into the can.

He passed her a bucket. "Let's waste some paint, shall we?"

"With pleasure." She upended it, the paint dripped out, and there, in the stream, a small plastic baggie slid out, too, then landed in the bucket with a plop.

He used two fingers to pull it out, and then laid it on a sheet of plastic set up beneath a sawhorse.

"There's another bag inside it," she said, after returning with a damp sponge and wiping off the goo.

Careful not to get paint inside the bag, they opened the seal, then pulled out five nested bags.

"You weren't taking any chances," she said, and he silently agreed.

Finally, they were down to the end, and he held up the small device. "A flash drive."

"Do we need to check it?"

He shook his head, wincing as the low-thud of a headache started to beat behind his eyes. "It's the encryption key. I remember."

———

Mason stared at the map on the burner phone the Face had left with Denny. A pin marked a set of coordinates in East Los Angeles. Then he read aloud the message that made his gut twist. The message that he and Denny had privately discussed for five full minutes before calling the information in to the SOC:

> Send the woman and the key to this
>   location.
> Alone.
> Surveil her, she dies.
> Follow, she dies.
> Disobey, she dies.
> Cooperate, she will be treated and
>   returned.

When he was finished reading, silence hung in the room. Then a voice came over the speaker of Mason's phone.

"And there's no way to reverse-engineer the antidote's formula from that key?" The question was posed by General Montero, a member of the oversight committee responsible for policing the

SOC. Mason hadn't been thrilled when Seagrave put him on the line. In Mason's experience, bringing in retired officers tagged with oversight to spec out missions was a universally bad idea.

"No sir," Mason said, hating wasting time going over information again. "I sabotaged their mainframe. I didn't steal the formula. Once they have the key, they can decrypt the formula, manufacture the antidote and vaccine, and sell them to the government and consumers."

"Why haven't they already released the toxin into the food supply?"

"Their plan requires the antidote," he said. As the only SOC agent in the room, he was doing the talking. As far as the General was concerned, Denny was simply a civilian.

"They don't think of themselves as terrorists," he continued. "They're entrepreneurs. They want to create a threat and profit off of providing the solution. And sir, I remember now what the toxin does." He drew in a breath, hating the thought of the toxin biding its time in Denny's blood, a horrific threat hanging over her and their child.

"It destroys tissue, sir," he said, trying to keep his voice even. "Breaks it down completely. Basically, it makes Ebola look like a bad case of the flu."

"Good God." That curse came from Seagrave.

Beside Mason, Denny went pale. He took her hand, and he watched as she drew a breath and straightened her shoulders. She wanted to break down—he was certain of it. And he was equally certain she wasn't going to. The woman was amazing. More than that, she was his.

And he wasn't about to lose her again.

"This organization can't give in to terrorist tactics." Montero's deep voice boomed across the line, firm and authoritative. "As I understand, Agent Marshall has not yet entered the final twenty-four hours prior to infection. That means we have time."

"Begging your pardon, sir, but that means we're lucky. I beg you not to squander this opportunity."

"We won't," he said. "Reply that you accept their demand. Then forward us the coordinates. We'll send a team to intercept their transport. I assure you, we'll obtain the antidote."

"And if you don't? They're going to start shipping out their tainted preservative. It's going to go into commerce. They'll offer the antidote for sale right away, but folks tainted early won't believe. They'll get the antidote too late or not at all. And these bastards are counting on that. They need to make the news. They need a huge scare and bloody, gooey deaths. Because that will drive up the price of the antidote and the vaccine."

"I think you're aware of the skill level of this organization. And for a threat like this, we'll take extraordinary measures to stop the toxin from leaving their facilities."

"And get Denise Marshall killed in the process?" Rage underscored Mason's words.

"Agent Marshall understands that this office must focus on the big picture. If we utilize this opportunity to send in a full team, we can shut them down. This toxin cannot be permitted to enter the chain of commerce. Not with an antidote. Not without an antidote. Not at all."

"Denise Marshall is no longer with the SOC. You're destroying her chance of getting the antidote in time. You're putting a civilian's life at risk and—"

"You have your orders, Agent Walker. Forward the coordinates."

He looked at Denny, and she looked back evenly, her expression flat and emotionless. A agent calling on all her training so as to not give a single thing away.

But they'd talked about this. The risks. The possible outcomes.

They'd talked, and he knew what he had to say now. As much as he hated what was going to happen, he knew what he had to do.

"I'm sorry, General," Mason said. "We're going to handle this my way."

25

THIS, I think, is a prime example of why I prefer tech work to fieldwork.

Because I would much rather be holed up in windowless room with a computer and some computer-based riddle I had to solve. Or someone whose identity I had to track down. Or even some dumbass game I wanted to code in my spare time.

But, no. Instead I'm standing on a corner in East LA waiting to either get picked up and hauled off to some secret facility or to get shot between the eyes, after which someone will rip the encryption key out of my cold dead hands.

Neither Mason nor I really like this plan, but I'm out of time and the general is an idiot. Seagrave isn't, but his hands are tied. Which means we're going rogue.

Which means I'm following instructions.

Which means I'm a sitting duck.

"We don't have a choice," Mason had said. "We have to get you that antidote and we have to find the facility. But God, it worries me sending you in like this." He'd brushed his hand over my hair, then cupped my cheek. Then he'd shaken his head. "No. We need to rethink. There has to be another way. I can't risk—"

I'd pressed my hand over his. "If we don't risk it, I'm already dead. And so is our child." I'd drawn a breath, gathered my courage, and told him the one fact that I was certain of. "They won't kill me on the street. We both know that. They have to use the encryption key at the facility to make sure it's real. If they kill me early, they know you'll never give them the real thing."

"And once they know it's real?"

I'd shuddered, then I'd met his eyes. "I'm banking on them using me as a test case. Inject the antidote, then test my blood. But they might just kill me. That's why you—"

"I'm tracking you," he'd said. "I'm tracking you, I'm making sure you get inoculated, and I'm getting you out of that place before we destroy the computer, the toxin, the files, and anything else that could ever let them recreate this threat again."

Mason had remembered enough to know that the toxin was only on the one mainframe because of a lack of trust between cells. So the computer that housed both the toxin's formula and the vaccination were standalone machines not connected to the internet. Great for keeping the threat contained, but unfortunately it also meant we couldn't hack in and wipe the thing out.

"I'm not scared," I'd told him right before I'd gotten in my Highlander, the burner phone's map open to guide me. "I know you've got my back."

"I do," he'd promised before kissing me.

I can still taste that kiss on my lips, as well as the lie. Because of course I'm scared.

It's late, almost midnight, and this is not exactly Beverly Hills. There's not much traffic, but what there is notices me. A number of cars have slowed, and I've been asked several times how much I charge for a blowjob. Apparently I'm camped out on a very entrepreneurial corner.

Ten more minutes pass, and then a van I've seen three times already draws to a stop. The passenger side window rolls down, and I look up— and then gasp when I see Peter looking back at me.

"Oh, good," he says when he sees the expression on my face. "I was afraid you were expecting me, which means that I didn't keep my secret nearly as well as I thought I had."

"I don't—you. Why?"

"We're blocking traffic. Hop on in. We have an antidote to prepare. Wouldn't want you to get all oozy, would we?"

I get in—I don't exactly have a choice—and he pulls back into traffic.

"Here," he says, passing me a blindfold. "Put it on. Can't release you if you know where the facility is, can I?"

I hesitate, but I put it on.

I try to pay attention to the cars twists and turns. Try to make a map in my head. But that's a skill better suited to movies than real life, especially when your captor is chatting with you and making it impossible to focus.

"Give me the burner," he says. "And your phone, too."

I hesitate—Mason can track me through my phone—but I also know I don't have a choice. I pass them over, hear the window roll down, and then back up. The phones, I know, are now smashed somewhere on the side of the road.

I twist my wedding ring nervously, thinking about Mason. Imagining him coming for me.

"A pretty ring," Peter says. "Plain, though. Can't say I think much of Mason's taste."

"I love it."

"Do you? It's shit. Hand it over and we'll give it a toss. Just like it deserves."

I clutch my right hand tighter over my left.

"Really? You're going to risk your life over white gold?"

"Platinum."

"All the better. Hand it over."

"I just got him back," I say. "You don't get the ring."

There's silence, and then my head is thrown back by the violent smack of a palm against my cheek. "You little bitch. We worked together and I never realized what a little bitch you are. Give. Me. The. Ring."

I try to pull it off, but of course I can't. So I lift my finger to my mouth, suck, and swallow the ring. *Fuck. Him.*

"Oops."

I can practically feel him glaring at me. But I know that he can't kill me. Not until he tests the encryption key.

Doesn't mean he can't hit me again, and I wait for the blow. It doesn't come, though. Instead, he just laughs.

"That's my Denise," he says. "Ballsy as hell."

"I'm not your Denise."

"No, you're Mason's."

I cross my arms over my chest. "I am."

"I told him I fucked you, you know. I told him much you liked it. How you begged for it."

"We *never*—"

"And I told him I killed you. That part was a lie, too. But we might be making it the truth soon enough."

A cold chill settles over me. "You know what

happened to him." I remember Mason's headache at Westerfield's. I'd thought it was the lights. Now I'm thinking it was a memory. A memory of Peter.

"You know why he lost his memory."

Peter laughs. "You sweet, naive little girl. Of course I know. He lost it because of me."

26

MASON PACED THE KITCHEN, his phone in hand, his head feeling like it was about to explode. Not because memories were threatening to rip him up. But because he'd lost her.

They'd known that her captor would most likely toss the phone. Unfortunate, but inevitable. Useful, though, because surely he wouldn't look for another tracking device.

And it turned out that his Denny had another device. A brilliant, amazing device. A gizmo so clever it only reinforced his belief that she was one of the best op-tech wizards in the business.

Because she'd installed a tracker in her wedding band.

"It's been my pet project at the SSA for a while now," she'd told him." Watch enough Bond movies, and you want to make the fantasy real."

"And you did?"

She'd nodded, obviously pleased with herself. "I had to hollow out a tiny bit underneath, but the band's wide enough and deep enough, and we've been working on micro-tech. The power supply's the problem, which is why mine is rarely on. You have to constantly recharge for a mission. It only lasts about twelve hours. But it charges fast, so..."

She'd trailed off with a grin, and he'd kiss her again. Just because he had to.

They'd thought the twelve-hour window would be enough, but apparently she'd been wrong about battery duration. Because the phone was offline and the ring was offline ... and that meant his wife was offline.

Goddammit.

He had to find her. They'd agreed that she'd go into the lion's den because she didn't have a choice. Go, and the outcome might be horrible.

Don't go, and the outcome would definitely be dire.

But the plan all along was that he would find her. He would track her. He would save her.

And now he was about to fail her.

The woman he loved. Not just once in his life, but twice over. He couldn't lose her. Lose her, and he might as well let himself get lost inside his own head, in the mishmash of nonsensical memories.

Lose her now, and that might be the only place he could find her again.

With a violent motion, he grabbed his Perrier bottle off the counter and hurled it across the room. It hit a window leading to the sunporch and broke through with a crash, showering glass everywhere.

The sound and destruction should have been satisfying. They weren't. Instead, he just collapsed onto the ground, his back sliding down the cabinetry, his arms encircling his legs. He put his forehead on his knees and waited for the tears. Waited for the darkness, longing for inspiration, but knowing that it wasn't going to come.

He didn't know how long he sat there, praying for either a plan or oblivion. All he knew was that when he heard the crunch of glass under a shoe, he was on his feet in seconds, a knife from the block in his hand.

"What the fuck happened here?" *Liam.*

"It's a bloody mess, that's what," Quince added. "The situation and the kitchen."

Mason put the knife back on the counter, his pulse returning to normal.

"What are you—"

"We tracked her as far as Ontario." Liam said. "Damn chopper lost her."

Mason looked between the two men, trying to make sense of their words.

"Seagrave called Ryan," Quince explained. "Unofficially, of course."

Mason couldn't help his grin. He knew his friend wouldn't screw them over. Not even when a general was looking over his shoulder.

"Denise rigged a tracker in her wedding ring," Quince continued. "Bloody brilliant, actually, and—"

"I know."

"You remembered?"

"She told me. I was tracking it and her phone. They both went offline."

"On our end, too. Fortunately, we were able to get a chopper in the air before the ring died on us, but the pilot lost them in traffic. Ended up tailing the wrong damn van."

"So she really is lost," Mason said, the hope that had been building in him fading. "All we know is that she's somewhere in the Inland Empire, or she was. Who knows where she'll end up?"

"Hopefully we will," Quince said. "It's a bit of a long shot, especially with your rather dicey memory, but we might get lucky."

The hope that had died started to flutter. "What are you saying?"

Quince pulled out a chair and sat at the breakfast table. "According to Seagrave, one of the gadgets she was trying to make work back when she was at the SOC was a flash drive that sent out a tracking signal when it was plugged into a power source."

"Like a computer," Liam put in.

"You said *trying*," Mason said.

"She never got it to work. And the tech stayed at the SOC when she moved over to Stark. Probably why she started fiddling with her ring," Quince added. "Anyway, Seagrave says that his team managed to make it work after about a year of trial and error."

"I would have been deep undercover by then."

"You were," Liam said. "But that's why God invented dead drops. The SOC got you one after you relayed that something major was going down."

"Which leaves us with one question," Quince said.

"What's the code?" Mason filled in. "And the answer is, I haven't got a clue. Little bit shallow in the memory department, remember? And even if I did know, how would we log into the tracking system?"

"We know how to do that," Liam said as he pulled open the fridge. "Seagrave sent over the app."

At the table, Quince pulled the app up on his phone and showed Mason. "Alphanumeric. Three letters—the same letters. And then an eight digit number string."

"And you think I set up a code that matched those parameters?"

"Well, we're hoping," Quince said.

"I didn't."

He pulled up the photo app on his phone and slid the image of the letter across the table to Quince. "This led us to the drive. The first paragraph references a specific paint can—seriously. But nothing in there matches the code you're describing. And if there was some other communication, then I don't know—"

He froze, then grabbed the phone back again, using his finger to tap as he counted out letter.

Eight digits later he looked between the two men, grinning broadly. "For a man with no memory, I'm a fucking genius. Gentlemen, let's go save my wife."

27

I'VE TRIED ALL my life to keep my faith. That Pollyanna belief that things will work out, even though so much in my life turned to shit. My father. My mother.

Despite all that, I'd kept a good thought. And the first time I truly broke was when Mason's mission turned from days to years. But even then...

Even then there was some tiny bit of hope inside of me. A small spark of faith that burned in the dark places of my soul.

I'd fed it, nurtured it. And when he returned, I knew that I'd been rewarded for keeping faith alive.

Now though...

Well, now I'm looking at the world through more pragmatic eyes.

I'm locked in a room inside a building inside a city. But I don't know what city, and even if I did, it's not as if I could do anything about it, as I'm cuffed to a metal chair.

My husband is undoubtedly trying to find me, but the tracking device in my phone is useless now, and I'm beginning to fear that the tracking signal emitted by my ring wasn't as strong as I'd hoped. Even if it did make it out of my body, it wasn't intended as a location device inside a concrete building.

And though I've only seen this one room, if it's any indication, this building is one big concrete slab.

In other words, there's really no way for Mason to find me. Which means no one is coming to rescue me.

Maybe if he had all the time in the world to pull traffic camera footage and contact the government to review satellite imagery from the relevant time frames.

But I don't have that kind of time. I'm ticking down toward oblivion.

Because as much as I'd hoped that Peter would give me that antidote, he's made it quite clear that's not going to happen.

So, yeah, my faith is on shaky ground now.

On the other hand, I no longer have anything left to lose. A philosophically freeing thought that does me absolutely no good.

The door on the far side of the room creaks

open, and Peter comes in. The room I'm in is cold and windowless, with only the computer, my chair, and its mate. When he steps inside, I feel even colder.

"Hello, Sugarplum," he says cheerfully. "You'll be happy to know the first batch of the antidote has been synthesized, is currently going through the Q&A process, and soon we'll know if we can get this party started."

"You mean taint the food supply," I say.

"And then fix it. For a price."

"And me? When do I get the antidote? Or aren't you a man of your word?"

His eyes widen. "What show have you been watching? Of course I'm not a man of my word. You think I want you running around out in the world? Trust me, we'll all be better off with you dead."

I want to whimper in response to his words. To curl up inside myself. But I don't. I'm too well-trained for that. And that training is all I have to cling to now that faith has fled.

"What happened to you?" I ask as I try to surreptitiously tug on my wrists, cuffed behind me to the chair. But I'm not going anywhere. Maybe if I could do some sort of martial arts flip and break off the back of the chair, but that's really not going to happen. "We were friends once, weren't we? You were sane once."

"I'm sane. More sane than you. Scrimping by on a government salary with the kind of skills you have? How is that sanity?"

I stay silent.

"But you had your virtues. Of course, if you'd slept with me I might be inclined now to treat you better."

"No, you wouldn't."

He grins. "No. I wouldn't."

"And Cerise? You dragged her into this. Why?"

"Even without his memory, I banked on lover boy finding his way back to you. I needed to be close. I watched, learned she was a new friend, saw she could use a security system. Nice girl. Doubt she'll get sick. She's not the type who eats fast food. And as for you..."

He crosses to me, and I shrink back, wanting distance. He crouches in front of me and grins. "You did your part well. After all, you two managed to find the encryption key, didn't you?"

"Who was the man at the club? The one who attacked me and killed himself?"

"Oh, just one of my hired hands."

"Mason recognized him."

"Yes, he used to work in our group. Transport. Errands. That kind of thing. Homeless until we gave him a better life."

I frown, confused. "He stuck himself with cyanide. Why?"

"I gave it to him, of course. Told him he could die the way you're going to, or he could end his suffering before it began. And I told him that I'd provide for his ex-wife and children if he took care of a few teensy tasks before he popped that syringe into his neck." He shrugs. "Everyone has their uses."

I stare at him, horror-struck.

"Oh, don't look at me like that. He was grateful for that syringe. He's seen what that toxin does. And once you're past the incubation period, there's no antidote." He glances at his bare wrist as if he were wearing a watch. "You have a bit of time. But still, tick tock. Tick tock."

"You're despicable."

"Me? Do you know what your husband did? He used a time delayed virus on our computer. So when he went out into the world on his little fucking spree with you, he'd already loaded the virus. But we didn't know. So when he came back, it took a while until we understood what happened. We were all very annoyed. I was very annoyed."

"Good for Mason."

He puts his hands on the arm of my chair and gets right in my face. "You have a choice to make, girlie. You can be polite, and I'll put a bullet in your brain. Or you can be a bitch, and I'll let you and your precious fetus melt away like so much bloody tissue. I'm kind of hoping you'll be a bitch. I do like you—don't get me wrong. But you never should have ended up with a guy like him."

My body goes cold with fear and dread. "I was your partner."

He shrugs. "And I was your husband's good friend Jeremy. Another agent in deep cover—his alias was Jack then, too. Jack Sloane. The man does like his television references."

Alias. Another show Mason and I used to binge.

"He found out you were a double agent," I said. "And he fried your computer. He beat you and you couldn't stand it."

"I don't think you can call it *beating* since I won. He's a mental basket case and his wife is soon to be goo. Kind of a Pyrrhic victory, don't you think?"

"You're a monster."

"Maybe. I did tell him a few lies. And beat the shit out of him. Remember that mission in Aruba? You wore that tiny bikini. So I was able to tell him all about a rather intimate birthmark at the same time I was whipping him. His back's splitting open, and there I was, telling him how I fucked his wife. Then put a bullet in her brain. A lie, but he didn't know. All he knew was that it was his punishment for what he did. For going to you. For telling our secrets to you. And do you know what he did?"

My throat is dry. My body hollow. I don't want to hear any of this.

"He snapped. He's weak and pathetic and he snapped." He grins at me. "It wasn't me. It was you. You were the straw that broke the camel's mind. How does that make you feel?"

I can't get much saliva, but I still manage to spit in his face.

He wipes it away impassively. "And on that note, I'm going to go check on the antidote. Maybe we can work out an arrangement for you to earn it. I wonder as the clock winds down if you'll get down on your knees to save your life. Not to pray, but to suck my cock."

"Bastard."

"Why, thank you."

He leaves, and my shoulders sag as tears start to flow. I can't stop them and I can't wipe my eyes, and I really don't want to give him the satisfaction of seeing me like this.

I close my eyes, breathe, and try to will the tears to stop.

Too late, though. I hear footsteps and realize that he's back already. Probably forgot some scathing, parting insult.

But then he stops, and something in the air shifts. I open my eyes and swallow a cry of joy as Mason hurries to me. He falls to his knees and kisses me even as he curses the handcuffs.

"Dammit, I don't have a key. Quinn's right behind me, though."

"He's here?"

"And Liam and an entire SOC team."

"Oh, thank God. The tracker in the ring worked."

"Actually, no. But the one in the SOC flash drive did. And Seagrave worked some magic and got the general on board. They're securing the lab and—"

"Well, look who the cat dragged in."

The words echo in the room at the same time as a shot rings out. I see Mason's body shake, then realize that the bullet's entered just below his collar bone. He stumbles, then falls, his hand reaching for his weapon. He doesn't make it.

Peter stands in the doorway looking smug. And me? I'm fucking useless. And it's taking all of my effort not to scream and scream and scream.

"She's going to die, you know. But she's got a while before she starts to fall apart. I plan on getting good use out of her before then. I'll let you watch if you're a good boy. And after she's goo, I'll keep you for a pet. Those marks on your backs? That's just the beginning. We're going to have some fun, you and I. Do you remember what we did before? The burns? The whips? Of course you do. I can see it in your face that you remember every lash. Every burn. I'm going to fuck you up even better this time."

He takes another step forward, and on the floor Mason's eyes squint and he grabs his head as he mutters something unintelligible. I cry out, calling his name, but his face contorts with pain, and I think about Dr. Tam's horrible videos of strong agents just like Mason who got lost inside themselves.

"No!" I scream. "Focus. Mason, please, please focus."

But he just rocks and moans to himself as Peter walks closer. Close enough to thrust out a foot and kick Mason's leg. I can see Peter grin. A sick, horrible grin, and I wish to hell I could thrust my leg out and kick him in the balls.

And then—for one horrible, wonderful moment —I think I've done just that. Because there's an explosion and a scream and his crotch is covered with blood. He cries out, falling to the ground, grasping his bloody, mangled balls.

And that's when I realize that Mason was faking it. And now he's on his back, his body braced, and his recently-fired gun still aimed at Peter.

Grimacing, Mason struggles to his feet. "I should kill you right now," he says, "but I think I'd rather see you writhing in pain. I can't inject you with the toxin, but maybe this is the next best thing."

"Fucker." Peter's voice is hollow, but filled with hate.

"I beat you, you bastard," Mason says, swaying slightly. "I don't even have a memory, but I know I beat you."

"The hell you did." He's still on the ground, and he cries out in pain as he lunges for his fallen weapon. He gets it, lifts it, and I hear a blast—two blasts. And then a scream.

I realize the scream is my own, and that Mason is on the ground. I think at first he's been shot, but then I realize that it was only the recoil of his own gun that knocked him over, weak as he is from his own injury.

This time, the bullet hit Peter in the chest.

And the second shot wasn't from Peter's gun either. That shot came from Liam, who stands now in the doorway, his gun still raised.

Liam's shot went through Peter's throat, and now the man is sprawled on the ground, his position reminding me of the Face, the man to whom he gave a horrible choice.

And as Peter gasps, I can't help but think that he had a choice, too. He made the wrong one, and now he's gasping like a fish and dying as his blood spills from him.

Honestly, I think Peter is getting off easy.

I turn my head, my eyes finding Mason's. He lifts his head and grins weakly, then his eyes roll back and he collapses as I scream for someone to help him.

A second later, Quince races into the room. He crouches beside Mason and puts pressure on the wound. He looks my husband over, then meets my eyes and nods. "He'll be okay."

I sag with relief. "You're late," I say.

"I have the antidote."

"In that case, you're forgiven."

He grins, but doesn't leave Mason until Liam sets me free. Then I fall on the ground beside my husband, whose eyes flutter open.

"It's over," I tell him.

A soft smile touches his lips. "No. It's a new beginning."

28

"How is Mason doing?" Cerise asks me as I navigate Damien's back patio with two wine glasses full of Diet Coke. One for me because I'm on the nine-month no drinking program. One for Mason because he's still on antibiotics from the bullet wound. Which, thank goodness, is healing up just fine. At least that's what the surgeon confirmed when he removed the stitches today.

"He's doing really great," I tell her, and it's true. I don't add that he almost convinced me that we should both bail on this party in our honor. But I reminded him that we could spend the entire rest of our month off in bed if we wanted to.

Today, however, is about celebrating with our friends.

"So long as I get you tonight," he'd said. "And every night after."

It had seemed like a fair trade to me.

Cerise hugs herself. "I can't believe Peter turned out to be..."

"Evil?" I suggest, when she can't find the word.

She lifts a shoulder. "Pretty much."

"Surprised me, too," I tell her. "But look at it this way—any guy you date next will be a step up."

She laughs. "I like the way you think," she says, then waves to Jamie and Ryan before leaving me to go talk with them.

Quince and Eliza are chatting with Emma, who's already back from Europe. Cass is standing with them, and I can't help but notice the way she's looking at Emma. What I can't tell is if Emma is interested, and I hope that Cass isn't setting herself up for more heartbreak.

When I make my way back to Mason, he's surrounded by Liam, Seagrave, Dr. Tam, and Damien.

"It was what you said about happy thoughts," Mason is telling Dr. Tam. "Or however you put it. Point is, when Peter was trying to get me to fall back into the memories of the torture, I stayed tethered by thinking about Denny. And the baby."

"And I'm very glad you did," Dr. Tam says, smiling over at me.

"Which explains why you didn't regress," Damien says. "But I still haven't heard how you figured out the tracking code for the flash drive."

Mason looks just a little too pleased with himself, but before he can answer, Liam steps in. "Bloody brilliant, as Quince would say. A paragraph with sentences all beginning with the letter D—so that was the triple-letter part. And then right after those three was a paragraph with only with eight words. The number of letters in each of those eight words made up one digit in the eight digit code."

"I was inspired," Mason says, smiling at me.

"An incredible job," Damien says. "And damn good timing."

"Is it true that you've confiscated the toxin?" I ask Seagrave.

"Now, Denise, you know that since you're no longer with the SOC, I can't confirm to you what I just told your husband about how we've ripped the legs out from under that entire cell, shut down the manufacture of the toxin, and taken the leaders into custody."

"Right. I forgot I'm out of the loop now." He and I share a grin as I settle onto the chaise next to Mason, on the side without the injury.

"With luck, Mason will be out of the loop soon, too," Damien says. "When I see an asset, I go after it."

"Do you?" Seagrave asks, but he's looking at Mason.

Mason looks between them. "For the next four

weeks, I'm not available to anybody but my wife. So both of you just hold your thoughts."

"Fair enough," Damien says, shifting his attention to Seagrave. "Mason isn't the only new recruit I'm interested in negotiating with."

I watch the colonel's face, wondering. A few weeks ago, I'd have said he'd never leave the SOC. But with the way the general and the oversight committee have been meddling...

Well, who knows?

I catch Mason's eye and we share a knowing look, only to be interrupted by Liam's phone.

He frowns, then steps away to take it. When he comes back a few minutes later, he looks shell-shocked. "That was Ella Love," he says, referring to the pop star he'd been assigned to protect recently. "I need to go."

"What's wrong?" I ask, but he doesn't answer, and I look to Damien, who stands. "I'm going to go check in with Ryan," he says. "He may have spoken with Love's people. In the meantime, Mason, I'm thrilled your shoulder is healing so well. How's your memory?"

Mason shakes his head. "Still Swiss cheese. Honestly, we don't know how much of my past I'll get back."

"I'm so sorry," Damien says. "That must be horribly frustrating."

"It is," Mason agrees. "But it has a few unexpected upsides." He takes my hand, and smiles at me with so much love it almost melts me. "The best is that I get to fall in love with my wife all over again. And how many men get to say that?"

EPILOGUE

Five months later

"Oh God, oh God, oh God!"

Mason grimaced as Denny squeezed his hand so hard it was a wonder every one of his bones hadn't shattered. As far as he could tell, giving birth was an endless cycle of pain coming in regularly timed intervals, the purpose of which seemed to be to torment his wife without ever actually producing a baby.

He hated seeing her like this. Hated knowing that he couldn't do anything except be there for her to squeeze and rail against.

"You did this," she said as the contraction passed. "I totally blame you."

"I willingly shoulder the burden," he said, wiping

down her forehead as the nurse checked her vitals and cervix. He didn't mention that she could have opted for the drugs, which would have at least lessened the pain he was now shouldering the blame for. Really not the time. Besides, he understood her reasoning. After being injected with both a deadly toxin and its untested antidote, she hadn't wanted any more pharmaceutical products near their unborn child.

He understood. He did.

But he still hated seeing her in pain.

"Oh, Christ, it's starting again."

"The doctor will be here any second," the nurse said. "It's time."

Mason's heart pounded, the sound of his pulse filling his head. *It was time.*

The next half hour was a blur of holding Denny's hand, reminding her to breathe, and swallowing his own awe as he saw his child's head crowning.

"You have a little boy," the nurse said moments later, and Mason felt tears prick his eyes as he looked from the tiny, shiny baby to Denny's beautiful, exhausted, elated face.

"Would you like to cut the cord?"

He almost said no, afraid his hands would shake too much, but he did, amazed that he was there in that room with this new life that he helped create.

"You're incredible," he said to Denny, stroking her damp hair.

"Men always think that. And women have been doing this forever."

"Incredible," he repeated, then teared up all over again when the nurse brought his now-clean and swaddled son to his side.

"Would you like to hold him?"

He nodded, feeling like a bumbling caveman. But then the little boy was in his arms, his tiny little face scrunched up and his little fingers grasping. Denny was beside him and his son was in his arms, and Mason knew that his lost memories didn't matter any more. Get them back or not, he didn't care.

He had this memory now.

And it was a perfect one.

———

Want to find out what happens to Liam? Be sure to grab your copy of Ruined With You!

SHADOWS OF YOU

BONUS CONTENT - CHAPTER 1

I gape at the closed circuit image on my terminal, completely flabbergasted by the extent of my assigned agent-candidate's idiocy. "Left! I said *left*."

I stare at the screen, then I throw up my hands in surrender as Agent Idiot turns to the right. "*Left*," I repeat into the microphone. "Your *other* left."

He immediately corrects, which is more than I can say for some of the applicants I've tested, and continues through the course. When he gets to the ordnance area, I pull off my headset and lean back in my chair, glad to be passing him off to another unfortunate operations manager.

"A little frustrated?"

The male voice is smooth and deep, and I turn in my chair to find myself staring at my immediate boss, Ryan Hunter, the Security Chief for Stark

International. He's tall and lean with chestnut hair and patient blue eyes. More patient than my green ones, I fear. Especially today.

"Sometimes I wonder where you find these candidates."

"That's why we call it an evaluation." I hear the humor in his voice, and I sigh loudly as he pulls out the chair at the empty station beside mine. He sits, his elbows on his knees as he looks earnestly at me.

"What are you doing, Denise?"

I've worked for Ryan for years, and we've become good friends. I adore his wife, and I know that they're both genuine, caring, talented people. Honestly, I couldn't have found a better place to work.

But that doesn't mean I want to be coddled. Especially not today when I'm feeling particularly raw.

"I'm just doing my job, Mr. Hunter."

One of his brows rises almost imperceptibly. He's no fool. He knows he's treading on dangerous ground. But Ryan doesn't pull his punches where his friends are concerned. And as much as I want to just go home and sleep straight through this horrible night, I know he's not letting me out of here until he says his piece.

"You should be in the field," he says. "Not operating a desk. Not putting agent candidates through their paces." Stark International has a private security force, the highest level being the newly formed Stark Security, which is where I'm currently assigned. At all levels of the organization, though, the security officers are called agents. And with Ryan at the helm and Damien Stark overseeing the entire organization, the team is at least as well-trained as any government operative.

I should know. I used to be one of those government operatives before I signed on for field work at Stark International. But that feels like a lifetime ago.

"I like what I'm doing," I say, unable to silence the defensive note in my voice. "We both know how burnt out on field work I became. And this way I can—"

"What?"

I shake my head. "Nothing. Have a life. A normal schedule."

"Review confidential files? Tap into international resources? Monitor communications channels?"

I swallow, but say nothing. Just hold my body stiff. I didn't realize he knew how much I've been using—and abusing—corporate resources.

He watches me, then sighs. "Dammit, Denny," he says, calling me by the same nickname that Mason used to use. "Why didn't you just come talk to me?"

I lift a shoulder. How can I tell him that I'm

drowning. It's been two years. Two long, lonely years since my husband went on a deep cover assignment. I haven't heard a word since the day he walked away. Not a postcard. Not a phone call. Not a single rose on my birthday. Just days upon days of empty, lonely hours. And today is one of the hardest days of the year. Not only Valentine's Day, but also our anniversary.

"I don't even know if he's dead or alive."

My voice is so low that I'm not even sure Ryan hears me. But he takes my hands in his, then leans forward earnestly, looking me in the eye. "We tried to find him."

"What? Who?"

"Damien and I. We used all our resources. Put out feelers to every government agency we could contact. Reached out to mercenary organizations, anyone and everyone. I'd hoped he'd get wind. Figure out a way to reach out to you. I'm sorry, but we didn't hear a word back." He exhales, and I hear genuine regret in his voice. "We all know you're hurting, Denise. And we're all your friends."

I lick my lips, fighting back tears. I'm not going to cry in front of my boss. That is just not happening.

"You know you're not happy in this work. He wouldn't want you stuck at a desk. It's not you."

I lift a shoulder. "Honestly, I don't know.

Maybe it's the me I've become. But I can't think about it now. Not today of all days."

"I'm sorry."

I nod, knowing he means it. I try to conjure a smile, but it's just not in me. "Thank you," I say. "Tell Jamie I said hi. Do you guys have big plans for Valentine's Day?"

"We're using a company limo to go down to La Jolla for dinner. But I'll be back at work tomorrow. I better not see you. You need to take a day off."

I make a face, but I also nod. I can see he's serious.

He passes me an envelope. "And here. From Damien and me."

I frown, confused. "What is it?"

He just cocks his head.

"Sorry. Stupid question." I rip open the envelope and find a hotel card key with a room number scrawled across it with a Sharpie.

"The penthouse," he says, looking up. The agent monitoring station is deep in a sub-basement of the Stark Century Hotel, forty-six floors above us.

"I don't understand."

"We thought you needed to be pampered. Actually, it was Jamie and Nikki's idea," he adds, referring to his and Damien's respective wives. He glances at his watch. "You should get up there if

you want some time to yourself before the
appointment."

"Appointment?"

"At seven. According to the girls, a massage is
just the thing to help you relax. I hope they're
right."

Despite myself, I smile. If I can't have Mason, I
can at least lose myself in a good, hard, relaxing
massage. And then I can fall asleep watching a
sappy movie on the big screen knowing that, at the
very least, I'm blessed enough to have some truly
incredible friends.

SHADOWS OF YOU

BONUS CONTENT - CHAPTER 2

Despite working in the basement for years, I've never actually been in the penthouse, and when I step through the double doors, I gasp. I'm facing a wall of floor to ceiling windows, the lights of the city stretching out toward the dark, moon-dappled Pacific beyond.

It's as if I'm floating in a calm, dark world, and already I feel more at peace. I want Mason desperately. I miss the man who was—*is*—husband, lover, and friend. But he has uncommon skills, and I know that he's doing important work. That doesn't make it better, not really. But maybe it makes it easier to bear. And the fact that I have friends holding me up when times get tough ...

Well, that definitely helps. As do the roses that fill the room, their beauty and their scent making me smile. They are everywhere. Vases on the table tops, and petals on the bed and floating on the surface of the already drawn bath.

There are even petals on a silver tray on which sits a chilled bottle of Pinot Grigio, my favorite.

I'm definitely feeling pampered.

The only thing that would make it better would be Mason beside me. And since that's not happening, I may as well enjoy myself.

I pour a glass of wine, then glance at my watch as I explore the suite. It's almost seven, so I don't have much time before my massage. But as I wander through the spacious, well-appointed rooms, I consider my options for the rest of the night. There's a television over the deep tub as well as one mounted opposite the bed. So the question is, do I watch in a bubble bath or snuggled up in the soft cotton sheets?

And, of course, the bigger question of sweet romance or soft-core porn. Because if I let my mind wander to Mason while I'm getting my massage, I just might be in the mood for the latter.

A girl gets lonely after two years, and I'm not the type to stray. Not as long as I believe he's out there and that he's coming back to me.

I take a sip and sigh.

Maybe I'll mix it up. A bath and an orgasm. Then bed and a sweet movie as I fall into my dreams.

I'm thinking that actually sounds pretty good

when the doorbell chimes. I hurry that direction, and open the door to a fifty-something woman in a severe white uniform. "I'm Melisse," she says. "I'm here to get you prepped."

My brows rise. *Prepped?* It sounds like a surgical procedure. And when she rolls in a high-tech looking massage table, I wonder if maybe I've misunderstood what Ryan and the gang planned. "Trust me. The Master is the best. You will be very relaxed."

"The Master? I'm not sure this is—"

"Trust me," she says firmly. "There is no pressure. You can terminate the session at any time." She finishes setting up the table, then spreads the sheet over the top.

"Should I go change?"

"In a minute," she says, passing me a spa robe from a duffel she brought with her. "The massage package that was selected for you is the sensory immersion experience. So when you return, we'll put on your aromatherapy blindfold."

"Blindfold?" I've spent too many years in intelligence. I'm not sure that I like the idea of being naked under a sheet and blindfolded. Even if it is for an incredible massage experience.

"Please. Mrs. Stark and Mrs. Hunter selected this package. I assure you, it is a favorite."

I take a deep breath, then nod. I trust Nikki and

Jamie completely. If they say this is the way to
experience a massage, then who am I to argue?

Melisse hands me the robe, then nods toward
the bathroom. Dutifully, I head in that direction. I
strip, slide on the fluffy robe, take a deep breath,
and return. The last time I had a really good
massage was from Mason, who has the best hands
of anyone I know. We'll see if this Master can
top him.

Melissa turns to give me privacy, and I climb
onto the table and cover myself with a sheet. She
adjusts it, then ties the blindfold over my eyes. I
can't say I like the sensation of being so vulnerable,
but I take calming breaths and remind myself that
this encounter was orchestrated by my friends.

I hear a tap on the door, followed by Melisse's
footsteps heading that direction. The soft exchange
of a conversation, and then the heavier tread of a
man's footsteps.

"Melisse?"

I feel the pressure of a large hand on my back
through the sheet, and then the brush of air as it's
pulled down, exposing my back and shoulders.
"Shh," a man says. "Melisse is gone."

My breath freezes in my throat. I know that
voice. Oh, God, I *know* that voice.

"Mason?" His name is barely more than breath.
I must be wrong. Surely I'm wrong. But he doesn't
correct me. And when his large hands spread out

on my shoulders, a rush of memories overwhelms me, so palpable I'm surprised I don't pass out.

I lift an arm, determined to rip off the blindfold, but he holds it down. "No."

"Please. Please," I beg. "I have to see you. It is you. Isn't it?"

"Relax. Just relax." He takes my arm and moves it to the edge of the wide massage table. Before I realize what's happening, he's cuffed my wrist to the bed. I struggle, but he's too quick, and soon my other wrist is bound as well.

"I'm sorry," he says. "The blindfold is important, and I can't risk you removing it. But if you don't like it, I can unstrap you and leave. It's up to you."

"Is it really you? Your voice. Please tell me. Mason, is it you?" I hear the desperation in my voice. The growing need. I want to know, and yet I also understand. If it is him, he must have learned of Ryan and Damien's efforts to locate him. He couldn't come officially, and so he came surreptitiously. I've worked in intelligence long enough to know that he could have learned of the massage gift and twisted the appointment around to his advantage. It wouldn't be hard at all

If it is him, he's breaking all sorts of rules to be here.

And if it's not him ... well, maybe just for tonight, I need to believe the fantasy.

I draw in a breath. "I don't want you to go."

"Good," he says, and then focuses those miraculous fingers on the tight muscles of my back, working and kneading. Warming me. Exciting me.

Lower and lower his hands go, until he's so close that I'm certain he's going to trail his fingertip down the crack of my ass. He doesn't, though. Instead, he comes just close enough to tease, then moves down the table to my ankles.

I gasp when he ties them to the table as well. "What are you doing? I can't take off the blindfold with my toes."

He slides his hands up my body, then brushes his mouth against my ear. "You're beautiful," he says. "I want you open for me. I want to see you when I touch you. I want to watch your cunt. I want to see your arousal. I want you wet for me, and I want to know that you want me, too. That you crave me. Crave *this*."

I swallow, telling myself again that this must be Mason. But damn me, part of me doesn't care. I'm too aroused by his touch and his raw, evocative words. And too lost in the fantasy. Even if he's only a shadow of my memory, a manifestation of my desire, I want the touch he's offering.

I feel a tear trickle down my cheek. Sweet and melancholy. I miss being touched like this. I want Mason, yes. But I *need* this.

Slowly, he strokes me. Warm hands moving

over my calves. Fingertips teasing my inner thighs. My body responds. My sex throbbing. I know I'm wet. Desperate. And when his fingers gently part my folds, I gasp with both surprise and pleasure.

He slips a finger inside me, then another and another. He fills me with slow, sensual thrusts, then teases my clit with one hand as he traces a path from my pussy to my ass, making me writhe with desire, longing for a rough touch along with the sweet caresses.

"Please," I beg. I shouldn't want it. I don't even really know that it's him. But I do. I want him inside me. I want to feel the weight of him above me and his cock filling me. I want his mouth on my breast, his teeth scraping my nipple. I want the man, the fantasy, the sensation. I want to lose myself in pleasure. And so help me, I'm not too proud to beg.

"I shouldn't," he says. "It's too risky."

"What is?"

"You. Seeing me. It's not safe."

I bite my lip, trying to make sense of those words. Is he in disguise? Has he changed his appearance? Is he no longer dark-haired with deep-set brown eyes accenting a face highlighted with a cleft chin? It would make sense. How else could he get so close without anyone recognizing him? And how better to stay deep undercover for two years, getting lost from even the likes of Damien Stark's exhaustive resources.

"Plastic surgery?" I ask, and am not surprised when he stays silent.

"I need your word," he says. "The blindfold stays on."

"Yes." *It is him. It must be him.*

He moves quickly to release my wrists and ankles, and I think that he must be as eager as I am. I'm true to my word, and I don't touch the blindfold as he gently lifts me, then carries me to the bedroom. I'm not expecting it, but he ties my wrists to the headboard, and when I murmur a protest, he says only, "It's for your protection as well as mine. If you see me—if they find out—then you're a liability."

I want to ask what he means. I want details of what he's doing. But the questions don't come. They leave my head like so much fluff as his mouth closes over mine, and we kiss, hot and wild and with such familiar abandon that my doubts fade almost entirely away. *This must be Mason. It must. It must.*

"Dear God, you taste like Heaven," he says. "Like sweet memories and warm chocolate."

I laugh, because isn't that just the kind of thing Mason would say?

But the laugher dies in my throat as his mouth closes over my breast. His teeth scraping my nipple, making me arch up toward him. "That's it, baby. Tell me what you want."

"Fuck me," I say boldly. "Please, I want you inside me."

His fingers cup my sex, thrusting slowly in and out. "Like this?"

I shake my head. "I want your cock. Please, Mason. I want to feel you explode in me."

Thank God I don't have to beg. I hear the rustle of material as he strips, then the weight of him above me. His cock rubs against my belly and I writhe against him, anxious. "Please. Now. Hard." I haven't been fucked in years, and I want it wild. I want to be taken. I want the full fantasy that this night is giving me.

He understands—when hasn't Mason understood me?—and I feel the pressure of his cock against my entrance, then the sharp sweet pain as he thrusts inside, forcing my body to yield to him.

I cry out, and as he moves rhythmically inside me, he muffles my cries with his mouth.

I wrap my legs around him, using my muscles to push him in harder, deeper, until I don't know where he ends and I begin. All I know is that right now, in this moment at least, he *is* Mason. He has to be. Because no one but my husband could make me feel this good.

I'm unprepared for the force of the orgasm when it finally takes me. I arch up, my muscles squeezing him tight so that he explodes inside me. Finally, my body goes slack, the tension easing out of me as every muscles turns soft and heavy.

"That was perfect," I say, as he spoons against me.

"*You're* perfect," he replies, and I smile sleepily as I snuggle my back against his chest. Gently, he strokes my arm. "Sleep now."

I don't want to, but I can't fight the heaviness in my eyes. "Will you be here when I wake up?"

He kisses my shoulder, but he doesn't answer, and I know that means he'll be gone.

I want to beg him to stay. I want to tell him we can run away. Hide somewhere. Be together.

I want to ask him if this fantasy was real. If *he* is real.

But I don't. I'm too tired. Fading too fast.

And maybe, just maybe, I'm afraid of the answer.

SHADOWS OF YOU

As I'd both feared and expected, I wake alone.

I explore the penthouse, but he's not there, and the massage table is gone, along with the robe and other paraphernalia.

There's nothing left but my memory. That, and a single rose on the dining table, laying across a sheet of white paper.

The note is written in block printing, and I can't tell if it's Mason's handwriting or not.

But I smile as I read the note:

Lovely Denny,

Thank you for the night. For fueling my heart with new memories. For reminding me that there are things to live for and fight

for. Things that burn hotter than a shooting
star and last longer than eternity.

We will, I think, see each other again,
though I cannot say when or where. But I
will hold onto last night and the pleasure
we shared.

Don't look for me. Don't try to find me.
Don't ask questions to which you don't
truly want the answers.

For the time being, last night was enough.

Yours,

The Master

I pick up the note and press it against my heart,
holding the memories close. I think he was Mason,
the man who always spoke to me of stars and eternity. I hope he was. But in the end, it doesn't
matter. The man—The Master—gave me back
hope, along with a fresh taste of joy.

And for now, I think, that is enough.

———

RUINED WITH YOU

When her high maintenance boss is assaulted, manager Xena Morgan contacts the only person who can help—the sexy, arrogant, incredibly capable Stark Security agent Liam Foster. The former vigilante takes every case personally, and he's determined to find answers—particularly since he thought he'd cleared this threat already.

Xena had been thrilled when Liam completed his assignment, because he affected her in ways she didn't want to contemplate, awakening yearnings that threatened her deepest secrets.

But now she needs him, and her body won't let her forget it.

As their attraction heats to a feverish degree, the

web of lies, danger, and passion they find themselves in tangles further. Liam will stop at nothing
to protect his client, even if it means sacrificing
everything he holds dear.... and exposing the
secrets that may destroy him—and Xena—forever.

TAME ME

CHAPTER ONE

Please enjoy this excerpt from Tame Me, the first book featuring Jamie Archer and Ryan Hunter!

That, I think, *was one hell of a party.*

I am standing with my back to the Pacific as I watch the efficient crew break down the lovely white tents. The leftover food has already been packed away. The trash has been discarded. The band left hours ago, and the last of the guests have already departed.

Even the paparazzi who had camped out on the beach hoping to snag a few choice pictures of my best friend Nikki Fairchild's wedding to multi-bazillionaire and former tennis star Damien Stark are long gone.

I sigh and tell myself that this vague emptiness I'm feeling isn't melancholy. Instead, it's an aftereffect of staying up all night drinking and partying. I am, of course, lying. I'm melancholy as shit, but I figure that's normal. After all, I've just watched my best friend get married to the one man in the entire universe who is absolutely, positively perfect for her. Great news, and I'm really and truly happy for her, but she found him without trolling through the entire male population of Los Angeles.

Compare that to me, who's fucked approximately eighty percent of that population and still hasn't found a guy like Damien, and I think it's safe to say that Nikki got the last decent man.

Okay, maybe not the last one, I amend as I catch sight of Ryan Hunter coming down the walking path that winds from Damien's Malibu house all the way to the beach where I'm now standing. Ryan is the Chief of Security for Stark International, and he and I have been the *de facto* host and hostess for this post-wedding soiree ever since the bride and groom took off in a helicopter bound for marital bliss.

Ryan is not among the eighty-percent, and that is truly a shame. The man is seriously hot, with piercing blue eyes and chestnut hair worn in a short, almost military style that accents the hard lines and angles of his face. He's tall and lean, but strong and sexy. I've seen him now in both jeans and a tux, and the curve of his ass alone is enough to make a woman drool.

We've gotten to know each other over the last few months, and I consider him a friend. Frankly, I'd like to consider him more, and I think he feels the same, even though he has yet to make a move.

I've seen the way he watches me, the heat that flares in his eyes when he thinks I'm not looking.

Maybe he's shy—but I doubt it. He's got a dangerous edge that perfectly suits his job as the head security dude for a guy like Damien and an enterprise like Stark International.

Nikki once told me that there was nothing Ryan liked better than chasing monsters. I believe it, and as I watch him stride down the walking path, his movements a combination of grace and power, I can imagine him in battle and am certain that he would do whatever it takes to win.

No, I don't believe that Ryan Hunter is shy. All I know is that he's never made a move on me, and that's a damn shame.

And now, of course, it's too late. Because I'm heading back home to Texas tomorrow as part of my newly implemented life goal of getting my shit together. And, as part of the whole Repair My Life plan, I've put the kibosh on sleeping around. I'm focusing on Jamie Archer. On figuring out who she is and what she wants, and step one of The Plan is to not do the nasty with every hot guy who crosses my path.

Honestly, men are so five minutes ago.

So far, The Plan is going pretty good. I found a tenant for my Studio City condo a few months ago, then went home to live with my parents in Dallas. It's hard being a twenty-five-year-old actress in Los Angeles, especially one who has yet to land a decent gig. There are too many guys who are prettier than me—and who know it. And way too many opportunities for a fast fuck.

Texas is slower. Easier. And even though it's hardly the acting capital of the universe, I've already had a few auditions, and I think I may even have a decent shot for a job as an on-air reporter at a local affiliate. I'd auditioned right before flying out here for the wedding, and I'm hoping to hear back from the programming director any day now.

And, yes, true, I'd also auditioned for a commercial here in SoCal, but I didn't get the job. I tell myself that's a good thing because I would have taken it and stayed in Los Angeles, because I love Los Angeles and my friends are here. But that would have put me right back on that hamster wheel of auditioning and fucking, and then starting the whole destructive process right over again.

The Plan is good, I tell myself as I watch the crew finish the job. The Plan is wise.

As a dozen workmen haul the last of the tent poles to a nearby truck, the supervisor approaches me with a clipboard and a pen. He takes me through the list, and I duly check off all the various items, confirming that the final details have been attended to.

Then I sign the form, thank him, and watch as he climbs into the truck and drives away.

"So that's it," Ryan says as he approaches me. He's still in tuxedo pants and the starched white shirt, but the cummerbund is gone, as is the jacket. He really does look sexy as hell, but it's his bare feet that have done me in. There's something so damn devil-may-care about a guy in a tux barefoot on the beach, and I can't help but wonder if there really is a bit of the devil in Ryan Hunter.

And if there is, will I ever get to peek at the wickedness?

"No more cars in the driveway," he continues, as I try to yank my thoughts back to reality. "And I just signed the invoice for the car park company. I think we can safely call this thing a wrap. And a success." His smile is slow and easy and undeniably sexy. "It really was one hell of a party."

I laugh. "I was just thinking the same thing." My stomach does a little twisting number, and I tell myself it's hunger. After all, champagne isn't that filling, and I'm sure all the dancing I did during the night burned off the three slices of wedding cake I'd devoured.

I'm lying again, of course. It's not hunger that's making my stomach flutter. It's Ryan. And as I stand there silently wishing he'd just touch me already, I'm also getting more and more irritated.

Because why the hell *hasn't* he touched me already? We've spent time together. We've even danced together during various club outings with friends. Not touching, maybe, but close enough that the air between us was thick with promise.

And once, when Damien had a security scare, he sent Ryan to check on me. I'd been wearing a tiny bikini with a sheer cover-up, and I looked damn hot. But he hadn't made a move. We'd ended up talking for hours, which was great, and I even made him eggs, which is about as domesticated as I get.

I'm certain I haven't been imagining that sizzle between us—and yet never once has he made a move. I can't fathom why, and the whole situation grates on me.

Except I'm not supposed to care—Ryan is not part of The Plan.

He starts to walk toward the surf, and I fall in step beside him. I'd kicked off my own shoes once the workmen hauled away the dance floor because beaches and two-inch heels really don't go well together, and the sand beneath my feet feels amazing.

I love strolling the beach in the morning. There's so much to look at—the seagulls that scavenge for their breakfast, the waves that pour like latte foam onto the sand, the tanned hard bodies of twenty-something surfer dudes out to catch a morning swell. It's like a little slice of heaven.

This morning, Ryan adds value to the view. His sleeves are rolled up, revealing well-muscled fore-arms, and when he bends down to pick up a lovely purple seashell, I find myself fascinated by his hands. They're large and strong, but as they hold the shell, I can't help but think that his touch would be surprisingly gentle.

I start to pick up my pace because, hello, mind really not supposed to be going there, but he reaches for me, holding the shell in his outstretched hand. "A souvenir," he says, and though his smile is casual, there's nothing easy about the heat in his eyes. His gaze is hot enough to cut right through me. The hair at the back of my neck prickles, and for a moment, I'm not certain I remember how to breathe. "I'd hate for you to get back to Texas and forget everything you've left behind."

"Oh." My voice sounds breathy, and I take the shell, my fingers brushing his palm as I do. I feel the shock of contact all the way down to my toes, and I expect him to pull me close. To touch me. To do some damn thing so that I'm not just standing there feeling all hot and horny.

He does nothing—and the sharp prick of irrita-tion breaks through the wall of lust. I close my hand around the shell and force myself to aim an equally casual smile back at him. "Thanks."

I'm grateful my voice sounds normal despite the fact that I am both genuinely moved and undeniably irritated. Moved because it's a lovely shell and the gesture is very sweet. Irritated because now I'm getting mixed signals from a hot guy who still hasn't touched me and who I have absolutely no business being interested in.

My libido, however, still hasn't gotten the message because there's some serious sizzle and pop going on. To be honest, there's been sizzle and pop since the first time I met Ryan.

Down girl.

I take a deep breath and mentally recite what has now become a mantra: *Plan. Texas. New leaf.*

New Jamie.

I start walking again because he's made me too antsy to just stand still. "Are you flying back today?" he asks, falling easily into step with me.

"Not flying. Driving." I see the confusion on his face—Nikki had been stuck in a meeting and had asked Ryan to pick me up at the airport just over a week ago. Yet another encounter where I felt both sizzle and pop—but he didn't touch me once.

Honestly, I need to stop this mental tally; I'm going to give myself a complex.

"Planning on doing a little recreational car shopping today?"

"Nikki and Damien gave me a car for my birthday," I mumble, because I'm still a bit embarrassed by such an extravagant gift. Not that it's extravagant to a guy like Damien. I'm pretty sure that to him, Australia wouldn't be too much.

"Happy birthday," Ryan says in the kind of voice that makes me think that he would make a damn good present. Especially with a big red bow in just the right place.

I clear my throat, banishing the thought. "Right. Yeah, well, it's not really my birthday. They were planning on just giving it to me because, you know, my Corolla has seen better days. And I said I couldn't accept it, and Nikki said..." I trail off, shrugging.

"She's a good friend." He's walking in the surf now, the waves breaking around his feet.

"Cold." I say, nodding toward his feet.

"A little." He tilts his head up, his gaze taking me in before he finally meets my eyes. "But I'm willing to put up with all sorts of things if it gets me something I want."

Wow. "Right." I swallow, then curl my hands into fists so that I don't lean in, grab his collar, and kiss him. "Um. So. What is it you want?"

"To walk on the beach with you, of course."

And there it is. That *pow*, that *snap*. He takes my hand, the gesture light and casual. Seemingly friendly, but really it's so much more.

He's intense, I think. *Strong. Silent. Steady.* The kind of guy who knows what he wants and goes after it methodically and relentlessly.

Is he going after me? I shiver a little as I slide into a nice little *From Here to Eternity* fantasy. Not that I've ever actually watched the movie, but I've seen that famous sex in the surf scene, and I'm more than happy to let my imagination fill in the blanks.

"You're not driving back to Texas today, are you?" He is watching me closely, his eyes as deep and intense as the Pacific behind us. "You were up all night. You shouldn't risk it."

"I'm not," I say, imagining the surf crashing over me and Ryan's body hot above me. "I'm staying the night and heading out first thing tomorrow."

"I'm very glad to hear it." His voice is as smooth as whiskey, and I wonder if I'm getting a little bit drunk on it. "I'd worry about you."

I stand there, feeling nine kinds of itchy, and wait for him to make a move. But the move doesn't come.

I tell myself that's a good thing.

Then I tell myself I'm a goddamn liar.

Then I remind myself about The Plan.

But you know what? Screw The Plan. The Plan is for Texas, after all. I mean, I've pretty much already established that when in California, Jamie

Archer is a hot mess. So why not be a mess one last time with this incredibly sexy guy who is making me tingle?

Except that doesn't seem to be an option.

Because Ryan isn't making a move. I consider making a pass myself. After all, I've never once been shy about going after a guy I wanted in my bed. With Ryan, though, I can't seem to take that first step, and it's weird. I'm feeling shy and awkward, and I am never shy or awkward.

Maybe it's the lingering effect of The Plan. Residual guilt. Pre-justification. My subconscious telling me that if he pursues me, then a California fuck is okay. But me going after him is totally against the rules.

All of which is a load of twisted and convoluted bullshit, but I never said my subconscious was a linear thinker.

Just go for it.

Holy crap, this shouldn't be that difficult. I mean, honestly. When I decided to bang Kevin in 2H, I cornered him in the laundry room, put my hand on his crotch, and asked him if he wanted to fuck. So why the hell am I all sixth-grade girl with a crush where Ryan Hunter is concerned?

Right. Okay. Diving in now...

I clear my throat. "So here's the thing," I say, and I don't get any further. Maybe, I think, he'll pick up the thread.

He doesn't. He just looks at me, all innocent interest and calm curiosity. His expression is bland, and yet I have the distinct impression that he's amused.

"It's just that I can't figure you out," I blurt.

"Can't you?"

"We've had some good times, right? And I've seen you look at me." I lick my lips, hating how nervous I feel. "And I know I've looked at you. So what's the deal?"

"The deal?"

I tilt my head a little and give him my best seductive smile. "You've never made a pass at me," I say in the kind of voice that makes clear I would be very receptive to one right now.

"No," he says, "I haven't."

"Oh." I mentally backpedal. That wasn't the response I was expecting. "Okay. So, why not? You're just not interested?"

"On the contrary. Maybe I assumed you weren't interested."

"Seriously?"

"I've had my eye on you for a while, Ms. Archer. And as far as I've seen, you're not the least bit shy about making a move on a man you want."

I hear the raw heat in his voice, but I can't tell if he is serious or if he's playing me. All I know is that the more he looks at me with those fathomless blue eyes and the more he speaks to me in that musically sexy voice, the more I melt, until I fear that I'll dissolve right there and be washed away when the tide comes in.

"Oh," I say stupidly. Dear god I want him to touch me. I've slept with a lot of guys, but right now, I don't think I've ever been more desperate for a man's touch.

I think about The Plan. I think about my loophole.

I think about the fact that the loophole calls for him to make a move on me.

And then I think, *what the hell. Just go for it.*

"All right," I say as I quash those damn nerves, then fist my hand in his shirt and move in close.

He smells like musk and desire and I breathe deep, letting the scent of him fill me, warm me. We're not even inches apart, and the air between us seems to shimmer, thick with passion.

I press my other hand to his thigh and stroke slowly up, up, up, until I brush against the hard length of his erection. My thighs quiver, and my sex tightens with need. I'm aware of every inch of my body, as if I'm a live wire, sparking and popping.

We're well-matched in height, and I only have to rise up a little on my toes in order to claim his mouth with mine. I close my hand over the steel of his cock and feel it twitch under my touch. I hear his moan, and it only makes me wetter.

His hands twine in my hair, pulling me closer

as he deepens the kiss, fucking me with his mouth, going deep, making me wet, so incredibly wet, so that all I want is to slide my hand into his trousers and free him, then fall onto the sand, yank my dress up, and scream as he fucks me harder than I've ever been fucked in my life.

I am gasping when he breaks the kiss. I'm alive with need, my breasts aching for his touch, my cunt throbbing with demand. I'm wild, desperate, and when I see the matching wildness in his eyes, I know that this is going to be one hell of an amazing morning.

"All right," I say again, my voice breathless and heavy with longing. "That was me, making a move."

"And this," he says gently as he takes a single step away from me, "is me, saying no."

ABOUT THE AUTHOR

J. Kenner (aka Julie Kenner) is the *New York Times*, *USA Today*, *Publishers Weekly*, *Wall Street Journal* and #1 International bestselling author of over one hundred novels, novellas and short stories in a variety of genres.

JK has been praised by *Publishers Weekly* as an author with a "flair for dialogue and eccentric characterizations" and by *RT Bookclub* for having "cornered the market on sinfully attractive, dominant antiheroes and the women who swoon for them." A five-time finalist for Romance Writers of America's prestigious RITA award, JK took home the first RITA trophy awarded in the category of erotic romance in 2014 for her novel, *Claim Me* (book 2 of her Stark Trilogy) and the RITA trophy for *Wicked Dirty* in the same category in 2017.

In her previous career as an attorney, JK worked as a lawyer in Southern California and Texas. She currently lives in Central Texas, with her husband, two daughters, and two rather spastic cats.

Visit her website at www.juliekenner.com to learn more and to connect with JK through social media!